# THE DEAD
# WHISPER ON

# Books by T. L. Hines

*Waking Lazarus*

*The Dead Whisper On*

# T.L. HINES

# THE DEAD WHISPER ON

BETHANY HOUSE PUBLISHERS
Minneapolis, Minnesota

*The Dead Whisper On*
Copyright © 2007
T. L. Hines

Cover design by studiogearbox.com and Paul Higdon

Published by Bethany House Publishers
11400 Hampshire Avenue South
Bloomington, Minnesota 55438

Bethany House Publishers is a division of
Baker Publishing Group, Grand Rapids, Michigan.

Printed in the United States of America

ISBN 978-0-7642-0519-4

---

**The Library of Congress has cataloged the hardcover edition as follows:**

Hines, T.L.
    The dead whisper on / T.L. Hines.
      p.  cm.
    ISBN-13: 978-0-7642-0205-6 (hardcover : alk. paper)
    ISBN-10: 0-7642-0205-7 (hardcover : alk. paper)
    1. Refuse collectors—Fiction. I. Title.

PS3608.I5726D43    2007
813'.6—dc22                                 2007011980

---

To my parents,

John and Ruth Hines,

for sharing the dream.

# THE DEAD
# WHISPER ON

A DEAD MAN SPOKE TO HER from the shadows. "Seven o'clock," the voice rasped, barely audible over the wind tumbling through the dry heat of late summer. "The Mint." Even as the wind carried away the whisper, she began telling herself it was an illusion, a ghost speaking to her from the shadows of her own mind rather than the shadows of this pothole-laden street.

Still.

She put down the garbage can and glanced at Steve on the other side of the garbage truck. He was bending down to pick up a couple of clipped branches; if he'd heard the voice, it hadn't stopped him.

"Hold up," she said as she opened her ears, opened her eyes, opened all her senses.

Steve pitched the branches into the gaping maw of the truck, oblivious to her words. She'd forgotten he liked to wear headphones while he worked, listening to the Monsters of Rock on KXKX as he toted the trash. A real conversationalist, Steve.

She was turning toward Steve, getting ready to walk over and stop him, when a sudden movement caught her eye. It was the shadow of the garbage can she'd just put down: as it intersected with the shadow of the giant truck, something inside it *shifted*. Part of the shadow—a darker shade, she could tell, even though she only saw it for an instant—moved from the can's shadow to the truck's shadow.

Like a fish, flashing silver just beneath the surface of a brook as it darted away.

She drew in her breath and held it, waiting. Would she see the shift again? Would she hear the voice again?

No.

Nothing happened, and after a few moments she was startled by a tap on her shoulder.

Steve. He lifted the headphones away from the side of his head. "Hey, Canada. Whatchas waitin' for, Christmas?"

She shook her head, the spell broken. "Sorry, Steve. Just thought I saw something."

"Like what?"

"Like something. Let's get going." She lifted the lid back on the silver garbage can at the curb, her eyes still searching the shadows, then pounded the side of the truck with her gloved fist two times: the signal to move to the next set of cans.

Even as the truck growled forward, she watched and listened, hoping for another glimpsed shadow, another whispered secret.

In the bright, crisp morning, Candace MacHugh listened for another word from her dead father.

Late that afternoon, she drove her car onto the patch of bare ground next to her trailer—her version of a driveway—and turned off the '72 Dodge Charger. She sat, listening to the engine ticking as it cooled.

Yes, it had been her dad's voice. She knew his voice well even though it had been eleven years since she'd last heard it. His today had been mostly *sotto voce*, but she recognized it immediately. So many wonderful memories entwined in its throaty rasp. Memories of bedtime stories, tales of Butte's earlier years filled with ash-filled smoke and noodle parlors and underground bars and Al Capone's hideouts and fresh pasties with gravy. Memories of Dad's taut, cabled frame in the wooden bleachers, yelling at her as she stepped up to bat: *"Lookin' for a dinger, Canada! Let's have a dinger!"*

She smiled. Yes, even her name reminded her of the dearly departed Bud MacHugh, copper miner. She was born Candace MacHugh, a name her mother had lovingly picked, but her father had soon twisted the name, dubbing her Canada, and it had stuck since.

Canada gave her head a quick shake and pulled the keys out of the ignition. Time to get out of these clothes.

From her mailbox she retrieved another day of boring mail, then walked to the trailer and unlocked it. The trailer, together with the '72 Charger, were the two remaining threads that still connected her to the memories of her long-dead father. Heaps of junk, yes. But they were her father's heaps of junk. And now hers.

She turned the key in the front door's lock, replaying the whisper in her mind. *Seven o'clock. The Mint.* Made sense. Her father had always loved that bar, had knocked back many a stale beer there after a long swing shift in the copper mines.

A deep, elemental part of her was terrified by the voice. But another part of her was relieved, because as of about eight o'clock this morning Bud MacHugh had kept his last promise to her.

He had said he would come back.

He'd told her, if there were a way to contact her, let her know everything was okay, he'd reach back across that gulf between life and death and let her know.

Unfortunately, it had taken eleven years for him to do that. And in that time she'd given up any hope of it ever happening. Had never really had much hope of it happening in the first place, to be honest. But now, with the whisper, with the moving shadow . . . the old wound caused by his death, once healed over, had opened once again. And if she did nothing about it, it would become infected.

The front door opened wide, an entry to the darkness of her

trailer. Just inside, a stack of newspapers, nearly eight feet tall, threatened to topple. Next to that, a stack of magazines. Behind those, more stacks of periodicals, mailers, and inserts. Just on the other side of the door sat a beat-up washing machine, with clothes heaped on top.

Canada walked through the narrow path between piles, making her way to her bedroom. Along the way, she passed more stacks: boxes, boards, three old televisions, cases of boxed and canned foods. No one but she had been inside this trailer—no one—for several years. How many? Five, at least.

Not that anyone else would be able to fit.

On the way to the bedroom, she pulled off her denim overalls. She hadn't received her father's physique; he'd always been thin and hard, as if he were wrought from lengths of cable. Her own body was rounder, softer. She had his height, his freckled complexion, his red hair, but her body carried a bit of extra padding. None of her father's hard, sinewy physicality.

Her mother always described her form as "feminine," which was really her way of saying "chubby." By that definition, she was quite a bit more feminine than her mother, as well.

Canada shook her head, banishing thoughts of her mother. No need to go there.

She hung the overalls on the back of the bathroom door. She had three sets, one still clean, so she didn't need to wash yet. But maybe she'd do it, anyway. It felt like a night to wash her clothes; something about the day had been extra gritty.

She raked the dirty clothes from the top of the washing machine, stuffed them inside with two sets of overalls, and started the water. It cascaded on top of the clothing as she poured in detergent.

Even as she did this, she knew the extra grit she was feeling wasn't on her clothes or her skin. It was in her mind. The voice.

*Seven o'clock. The Mint.*

That hadn't been her dad. Not really. Couldn't have been her dad. Even in a city like Butte, America, clogged with all the wonders and oddities of P. T. Barnum's most famous sideshows, the dead stayed dead. Sure, the city was filled with ghost stories, tales of miners coming back to haunt the tunnels where they'd met their bitter ends. But that's all they were: stories.

Weren't they?

After her father died, when she was still working on the blast crew in the pits, she'd picked up a biography of Harry Houdini. The book said Houdini had promised, if at all possible, to communicate with his wife after he died.

His wife died several years later, never having heard from her husband—they had picked a secret code word, if she remembered correctly. So if Houdini hadn't been able to contact his wife, why would Bud MacHugh be able to contact his daughter?

And what about those shadows? Her eyes had to be playing tricks on her, seeing things that weren't there or warping what was. Maybe she was getting cataracts, although she couldn't recall a history of them on either side of her family.

*Seven o'clock. The Mint.*

She shut the lid of the washing machine, took a deep breath, and looked at her watch. She had just over an hour to make up her mind.

At a few minutes past seven, Canada walked into The Mint. Regulars joked it was a hole in the wall, because it was, in fact, just that. In the early 1900s, when prohibition tried to dry out America, the movement had only one notable effect in Butte: it forced the city's drinking establishments underground. Literally. More than a hundred lounges and speakeasy pubs flourished beneath the streets of Butte in cavernous rooms carved from rock. The Mint was a last vestige of that, and the only surviving lounge still operating underground.

It had no windows, of course. Just an unassuming door at street level, cut into the side of a vacant brick building, and a flight of concrete stairs leading down to the bar's true entrance. But windows were never much use in a place where drinking was the main order of business. Neon signs adorned the walls, and sawdust scoured the hardwood floors. Canada hadn't been inside The Mint for years, but it still smelled exactly the same: a little bit like musty dirt, a little bit like peanuts, a little bit like stale beer. A lot of people loved the M&M—perhaps, all told, Butte's best-loved bar—and Canada did wander there occasionally for a bite to eat.

But she never came here to The Mint. Not to her father's favorite haunt.

"Well, well. If it ain't our old friend Canada Mac." Joe, the barkeep who had worked at The Mint roughly since the Confederacy had surrendered in the War of Northern Aggression.

"If it ain't, then what?" she asked, trying to hide a smile.

"Just if it ain't."

"How ya been, Joe?"

"Been here, mostly. You?"

"Well, I haven't been here," she answered. "Mostly."

"How long?" Joe asked.

"I don't know. About a decade." Actually, she knew very well. It had been eleven years since she'd visited The Mint. Eleven years since her father's death.

"What'll yas have?" Joe asked, the folds of his jowled face moving as he spoke. Joe had mined once long ago, Canada had heard, but she'd always known him as a barkeep.

"I suppose a cranberry juice would do me fine," she said.

"Do me fine, too, if we had any."

"How about a bourbon and Diet Pepsi, then? Hold the bourbon."

"Still one a them teetotalers, eh?"

"Wouldn't you be?"

"I should wash yer mouth for such blasphemy."

Canada smiled, shook her head. "No, I mean, if you were me? You wouldn't drink, would you?"

"I know whatcher sayin', Canada, and I ain't goin' anywhere near the subject of yer mudder."

"I usually try to avoid it myself."

He held up his hands, tilted his head and shrugged. "An abomination, havin' yerself a mouth and refusin' to ever let a drop a Kentucky bourbon touch it. Why, it's a good thing Our Lady of the Rockies can't see you down here or—"

"Okay, I haven't missed the lectures, Joe. Just get me that Diet Pepsi."

"Diet, even." He spat the words, looked ready to say something else, then shook his head and wandered to the other end of the dark wood bar. Canada turned to look for the window, thinking she might get a glimpse of Our Lady of the Rockies, the statue Joe had referred to.

Wait. She'd already forgotten. She was underground, in a bar without any windows. A long time since she'd been here, indeed.

Joe brought her drink. She pulled out the straw. "I don't like straws, Joe. Thought you'd remember that."

"I did." He was rubbing the bar down with a rag, wiping up a spill. She saw a smile creasing his face.

Canada set the straw on the hardwood bar. Same old Joe. She picked up the glass, took a long draw, listened to the clinking of the ice cubes shifting inside the glass, then set it back down on the counter and tapped her finger on the rim. "Make this a double," she said.

Joe took the glass, squirted more Diet Pepsi in it from the tap's nozzle, slid the glass back in front of her. "That diet stuff'll make yas sterile," he said. "Ain't yas never read that anywhere?"

"I've indeed read such things," she said, putting the glass down after another sip and wiping her hand across her face. She wagged her finger. "But ya shouldn't believe everything yas read." She smiled to herself; it was amazing, really, how quickly she could slip into and out of Butte-speak without thinking about it. It was like a second language, in many ways. But for anyone born in the Copper City, it was really a first language.

"Amen to that," he said as he started dipping beer glasses in soapy water, then rinsing them in hot water and putting them on a towel.

"A lot of the guys still come in here?" she asked.

"Sure. Disco, Lucia, Binkowicz, Hambone—"

She chuckled. "Haven't seen any of 'em for, I dunno, forever. Lucia and Binkowicz still have their secret stash?" Those two were rumored to have "acquired" quite a collection of mining equipment before the mines finally closed. Rumor was they could keep on digging for two years on their own.

"Oh, yeah, they still got the stash. Talked a bit about packing up Montana Power's headquarters with some ANFO, sending 'em into bankruptcy in style."

Canada wasn't sure if Joe was serious or joking about blowing up the building. Perhaps he wasn't sure himself.

She let her eyes wander over the bar's interior. Still the same dark wood. Still the same beer signs. Still the same smoke stains on the ceiling.

"Love what you've done with the place since I've been here."

"Change. That's what we're all about," he said without looking up. "So, yas gonna tell me?"

"Tell you what?"

"Whatcher doin' back in here after ten years."

"Actually, it's been eleven," she corrected.

"I know. I just didn't want ya to feel bad because ya just said it's been a decade."

"I said 'about a decade.'"

He finished dipping and rinsing the glasses, snapped off the towel draped over his shoulder, started drying his hands. His eyebrows arched again.

She wondered if she should even mention anything. But of course, if you couldn't say anything to Joe, you were in serious trouble. Over the years, Joe had counseled more people on their problems than any psychologist or therapist in Butte. Maybe more than all of them put together.

"When's the last time you saw my dad?" she finally asked.

"Well, I s'pose the last time I saw yer pop was maybe a week before he died. And that, as ya just said, was eleven years ago."

She nodded, sipped her drink, listened to a fresh sizzle from the direction of the kitchen in the back. Immediately, the distinct smell of grilling onions wafted by. Maybe she'd head over to Muzz & Stan's Freeway Tavern for a wop chop, a pork cutlet (*beat 'n battered*, the sign above the Formica bar said) served on a burger bun; Canada took hers with onion, mustard, and pickles. She loved to sit at the Freeway and look at the old posters of Evel Knievel at the end of the room.

The famous daredevil still visited his hometown every year for a weeklong celebration called Evel Knievel Days. Daddy had known Knievel, even worked with him in the mines briefly. Not close, but they'd grown up around each other, known each other in the way any two young men from a rough-and-tumble town would know each other.

Joe's big paw was on her hand now. Gentle. "I still miss him sometimes, too."

Canada forced a smile. "Thanks, Joe."

"But you ain't answered my question."

"Your question?"

"What's bringing yas back here?"

"Ah. Well. I'm not so sure I like the answer to that myself."

Joe smiled, leaned over the bar. "Who said we have to like the right answers?"

Canada shrugged. No harm, really, and well, it *was* Joe. She hadn't seen him, hadn't talked to him for years, and already all that lapse had disappeared. It was as if she'd been in here just yesterday, surrounded by the smell of cooking onions and spilled beer, the sounds of shouting voices and sliding chairs. The place even tasted the same; that ever-present sawdust, for whatever reason, always felt like it was in your mouth. Probably why people always ended up drinking more than they should here—trying to get rid of that taste.

She sighed, looked down at the dark veneer of the bar. "Well, I know Daddy's dead." She swallowed, looked back at Joe. "But I heard him today. He talked to me." She chanced a look at Joe's face, searching for a reaction. Nothing.

"What'd he have to say?" Joe asked in much the same way he might ask her what the weather was doing outside.

"To meet him here at seven o'clock."

Joe nodded, glanced at the clock as if this was the answer he expected. "Yer old man never was too good with time."

TWO DIET PEPSIS LATER, Canada walked up the stairs and out onto the street above The Mint.

"Tap 'er light," Joe said as she walked out the door and started climbing the steps.

"You too," she said, smiling. Tap 'er light. Something miners used to say to each other when they were setting explosives: tap 'er light, meaning go easy with the charge so you don't blow yourself up. Since then, it had transformed itself, becoming the traditional way to say good-bye in Butte.

Sitting there for a couple hours gave her plenty of time to think about just how utterly stupid she'd been. Wasn't particularly hot—mid-eighties, maybe—but she could have been suffering from a bit of heat exhaustion or something earlier in the day. Yeah, she'd been dehydrated, and that made her mind go a little woozy. Those were much more logical explanations than her dead father speaking to her from a slithering shadow.

She realized part of her had never given up hope. Not totally. He'd indeed promised her he would contact her, and she had always believed that part of it: she knew he would reach across that gulf between life and death if it was possible.

But that was exactly where this whole thing fell apart: she never thought it was possible.

Until today.

She shook her head and huffed to herself as she walked to the Charger, keys in her hand. It had to be bits of her subconscious mind—long-buried memories of her dad, bubbling to the surface. Probably not so surprising her mind would play tricks on her like that. She looked at her watch. Almost nine-thirty. Time to go home and catch the local news at ten.

Darkness was spreading as the sun had long since disappeared behind the mountains west of Butte, and the streetlights around her suddenly blinked on. When they did, a fluid movement caught her eye. Across the street. The harsh, orange-tinged glow of the streetlights made it hard to see details, but Canada held her breath as she detected a rippling movement.

Shadows. Moving.

She immediately thought of snakes, hundreds of black, coiling bodies in the darkness at the harsh edge of the streetlights. She shuddered at the thought, especially as she saw the movement rippling through the surrounding blackness, spreading in a gelatinous wave. Soon, the inky blackness around her was swimming in ever-shifting patterns. She wanted to run, wanted to jump in her Charger and turn the key, but he was out there somewhere, wasn't he? Daddy. She could feel him.

"Hello, Princess." Bud MacHugh's voice, a bass drum with a bit of gravel in it.

Canada was afraid, still afraid of the shadows around her. But one of them was her father. "Daddy?"

"I'm a little late. But you know me and time."

She smiled a bit, relaxing. "Yeah, Joe said something about that inside."

"I bet."

Canada took a few deep breaths, trying to hold back her tears.

"How you been, Princess?"

"Been better, Daddy."

"Haven't we all?"

The shadows continued to roil and slither, and Canada felt tears trickling down her face. She was on the verge of sobbing. "I've . . . I've . . ." She stopped, wiped at the tears on her face with the back of her hand, tried again. "I've wanted to talk to you every single day."

"So have I, Princess. So have I."

"You've been here all this time, and—" She spun around, suddenly overwhelmed by all the moving shadows. "Where are you, anyway? It's hard to talk like this."

"I know. I'm sorry; I'm in . . . all of the shadows, if that makes sense. Have been for . . . how long now?"

"Eleven years."

"Eleven years. But I'm back now. Maybe you can't see me, but there's really nothing of me to see. But you can hear me."

She smiled, relaxing again. So she couldn't see him. That was fine. It was still an indescribable feeling, hearing his voice again after so long. "So you really are . . . dead?"

"Yes. But it's not what you think."

She shifted her weight to her other foot, looked up and down the street. No one. Odd for this street to be so dead. Ha ha. "And what, exactly, do I think?"

"Pretty much whatever you want, from what I remember."

She smiled, letting herself be drawn back in by Daddy's soothing voice. "Pretty much."

"It doesn't end when you die, you know."

Canada stayed silent, unsure how to respond to such a statement.

"There's so much over here," her father's voice continued. "So many wonderful things none of you know."

"None of us?"

"None of the living."

"Like what?"

"So much, so soon. But right now, I have a question for you. A proposition."

"Okay."

"Join us. Join *me*. There are people, like you, who work with us in the shadows. You can be one of them, and we can work together. We never really had much of a chance to do that, did we?"

"No, we didn't." She could hear her voice now, far off and dreamy. She'd gone into mining, putting college and other plans on hold after her dad had been too sick to work. Kept at it a couple years after he died. She reveled in the memory for a moment, then realized something was changing in the shadows.

"We'll talk more later," her father's voice said. "We can talk about so much more."

Abruptly, the shadows began to recede. Within seconds, they were gone; the ripples smoothed, the shimmering calmed, and the darkness surrounding her flattened.

"Wait—" she sputtered, but already she could tell it was too late, and she was alone on the street. She looked up at the streetlight, then shifted her gaze to Our Lady of the Rockies, the statue on the mountains above Butte. It was a ninety-foot Virgin Mary a local group had decided to put up in the '80s. Just another "only in Butte" landmark, but Canada had always taken solace in the statue's pose of blessing. God knows Butte needed it.

Our Lady was bathed in a bleach-white glow, her arms outstretched toward the city.

"What do you think?" she asked the statue. "Been talkin' to you since I was a kid, and now shadows are talking to *me*. Should I just punch it in now, head over to Warm Springs and tell them I'm hearing voices?"

The statue remained silent.

After a few moments of silence, Canada moved down the street, doing her best not to think about what had just happened.

Fifteen minutes later, Canada jiggled her key in the rusty lock of her trailer and opened the door. She walked in, banged the door shut behind her—hitting it a few times with her hip to get it to latch— then turned to survey the interior. The trailer had been Daddy's, but most of his stuff was gone. She hadn't been able to save that. He really didn't have many possessions, especially after her mother, Diane, had kicked him out of his own house. True, Diane had let him back into the house at the end—at the very end—but it didn't make up for the pain her mother had inflicted on him. Nor for the pain her mother had inflicted on *her*.

Why had she kicked him out, anyway? Sure, Bud MacHugh had been something of a drinker, but that couldn't be it. Diane had probably tipped twice as many tumblers as her father, so pot-kettle-black and all that.

Okay, no time to start thinking about her mother. The night had been rough enough.

She moved to the couch, cleared off some old stacks of newspaper, sat down and took a deep breath. She stared at the old wooden coffee table in front of her, its dark cherry stain, its four spindly legs. Along with the Charger and the trailer, it was the one item she still had from Daddy. He'd left a will, much to the surprise of everyone, and stated Canada should get this table. In fact, it was the only thing he had specifically left to her; the trailer and the Charger she'd had to buy at an estate auction. Hadn't cost much, really, but she'd only paid off the loan a few years ago.

Why on earth did he want her to have the table? She'd asked her mother—an act that, itself, said how curious the table made her— but Diane had just shrugged. Classic Diane MacHugh response to any situation, as long as it was followed by a swig of sugared gin.

Canada leaned forward, jiggled the table. The legs were a bit wobbly, but still not too bad. The table was holding up okay, although it did look as if there were a bit of dust on top. She stood and went toward the kitchen, negotiating her way past boxes filled with newspapers and magazines, a pile of somewhat-folded clothing, and a stack of ten cases of diet store-brand soda she'd inexplicably found herself buying a few years ago. Under the sink, she found the can of Endust and a dust rag—one of about ten she had stuffed into every available space—then went back to the table. She sprayed the polish on the table's surface and rubbed, taking off the offending layer of dust. Her mind wandered to thoughts of her father as she stared at her muddied reflection in the table's wood-grained surface. Yes, he'd given her a table, odd as that seemed. But he'd given her so much more: fond memories she could sift through even now. Columbia Gardens was her favorite place. That ticklish feeling in her stomach as she rode the "go round," her dad's term for the car- ousel. The cotton candy melting hot and sticky on her tongue. Scents of sugar and almond mixing together with the delicate smell of pansies and daisies.

Many Butte residents remembered Columbia Gardens fondly; anyone her age who had grown up in the city could recall free bus rides to the park every Thursday all summer long, or the annual Children's Day, when any kid—no matter what age—was invited to pick a free bouquet of pansies in the Children's Flower Garden.

Canada shared those memories with her peers, but for her the smell of those fresh pansy bouquets was inextricably linked with her dad. She loved the "go round," even when she was ten or eleven years old. She closed her eyes, felt her dad's strong arm around her shoulders, smelled the tang of his Aqua Velva aftershave mixing with the fresh flowers, saw the glint of the giant garden pavilion whizzing by with each revolution of the ride.

Abruptly, she put down the can and dust rag on the floor and worked her way toward the bathroom at the back of the trailer.

Inside, she opened one of the cupboards above the washing machine and dryer, and pulled out a small box. She set the box down on top of the dryer, then unfolded the taped flaps.

Inside, a stack of photographs—some Kodak snapshots, some fading Polaroids—lay in a jumble. She picked up a stack of the photos and began looking through them. Daddy in his grungy overalls, just back from the pits. Daddy holding her on his lap, the both of them in that grungy old orange lounge chair. The sight of the chair made her heart wince a bit; she wished she'd been able to get that at the auction, too, but she didn't recall seeing it. Sometime, she realized just now, it had disappeared. Still, she got the trailer and the Charger. Those were the most important. And the table, of course.

Her eyes settled on a different photo, one she didn't realize she had. It was a photo of her and her mother at Yellowstone National Park. She was maybe six or seven, standing on the boardwalk. Her mother, in a pretty red and white checked top and jeans, was leaning down to embrace her. Behind them, the giant plume of Old Faithful spewed into the air. She studied the photo, her mother's smiling face, her own grin. That meant her father had snapped the photo.

They had been a happy family, a *real* family, once. Before her mother had pushed her father out the door unceremoniously. Maybe she'd kept this photo, without remembering, as a memory of the good times.

Or, maybe she hadn't realized the photo was in the mix.

She stared at the image a few more moments, sighed, and dropped it in the white garbage can beside the washer. The picture still stared back at her, the only item in the can, so she shut off the bathroom light and made her way back to the bedroom.

She straightened a stack of boxes that had worked themselves off-kilter, peeled off her clothes, slipped on a T-shirt and slid into bed.

That night she dreamed of Yellowstone. She was at Old Faithful, in the parking lot, with her mother only, and they were rushing. Old Faithful was about to erupt at any minute, but they were late. If they didn't hurry, they would miss the eruption, and their trip would be wasted. A tall but chubby eight-year-old, she pulled on her mother's arm, begging her to pick up the pace as they walked across the planked walkway surrounding the world's most famous geyser.

And then, it was sputtering a bit; the steam increased, and beneath her, in the vast tunnels and caverns, she could feel and hear the water moving. Beginning its boil to the surface.

Tourists with cameras crowded the walkway, but Canada let go of her mother's hand, knowing what she had to do.

She had to go to the geyser's opening.

She pushed away her mother and stepped off the walkway, beginning to walk across the sparse grass and trenched mud. Cameras turned toward her; people began whispering and murmuring, and a few even called out to her. But no one stepped off the walkway, and no one ran to stop her.

She felt the water shifting beneath her again, now more insistent, and she began to run. Her red hair flew in the wind behind her as she ran, and soon she was standing over the gaping maw of Old Faithful. Belches of fetid steam poured from its opening, and deep down she saw a pool of turquoise with her face reflected in it a moment—just a moment—before the water came rushing toward her.

And still, she knew what she must do. She dropped to her hands and knees over the opening, watching the bubbling water surge toward her like a lost love, and just before Old Faithful erupted, she closed her eyes and opened her mouth.

And she opened her mouth impossibly wide, taking in the whole plume, gulping and feeling the lava-heated steam scald and slough away the skin of her mouth and throat, the skin of her face, the skin of her whole body. She wasn't eight now; she was an adult. She knew this even though her eyes were closed, and she knew this even though she felt her body being ripped away by the scalding steam, but still she kept swallowing because she knew it was what she had to do.

This was her pain, and she swallowed it as fast as she could, welcoming the bitter, overwhelming taste.

## 3

HE OPENED HIS DUSTY EYES, but saw only darkness.

The expected screams, however, hovered in the distance, dimly filtering through the labyrinth of underground tunnels.

The first contact—the first *whisper*—had come several hours ago. That whisper, a continent away, had sparked a tiny glimmer deep inside him, which then bloomed into a steady light, which had started his rise to the surface of consciousness. And now . . . now his eyes were open again. Unseeing for now, yes.

But open.

He felt a faint series of pinpricks in his hands and feet; soon, the tingling sensation would radiate through his limbs and, eventually, his whole body. He would be free to escape the confines of this granite tomb, to step into the bright light of the world above ground again.

To hunt the woman.

The new contact, he could tell, was a woman. He heard it in the murmurs and the screams filtering through the tunnels. But more than that, he felt it deep inside; that whispered spark, breathed into life inside his chest, carried an image of her. He latched onto that image, turning it over and over in his mind. He had no name yet, but that would come in time. For now, the image would do.

An image of the woman he had to stop.

Yes, others would certainly die. Others always died. But he

would stop her. He would find his way to the nearby town of Cal-ama and begin his long journey to North America. A couple of days, perhaps, if he were willing to fly.

And he thought, in this case, he *was* willing to fly.

The screams and murmurs continued above him; he caught snatches of their whispered secrets, their whispered pains. If they knew he was entombed here, in their midst, in the tunnels of their beloved Chilean Chuquicamata copper mine, they would be silent. They would give nothing away. They would try, at least.

They would be fleeing these underground tunnels, seeking other mines, perhaps the nearby Escondida. They would want to hold on to their secrets as long as possible.

It would all be futile, of course. He knew this. They knew this. When he was fully awake, fully mobile, he would force their secrets from them. Ultimately, they were powerless to resist him, and their network of chatter—even a continent away—would give him some-thing of her scent.

Feeling came to his arms and legs as his body continued waking from its slumber. By his side, his index finger raised the slightest bit, which made him want to smile. And he was pleased to discover the edges of his mouth moved, forming that smile.

Yes, he would have her scent very soon.

———

The next morning, Canada shifted the Charger into park, shut off the engine, and sat for a few moments, debating.

She looked at her mother's tiny clapboard house. Its front yard hadn't been mowed or watered in the last several weeks, obviously: tall blades of yellow brittle grass surrounded the home like a sick moat. The white picket fence, for its part, could only be seen as *white* by the most eternal optimist: nearly all the paint had flaked off long ago.

It had been a couple of years since she'd been to her mother's house. Make that her father's house—the one her mother had taken from him.

She looked in the rearview mirror, ran her hands through her hair, wiped at her cheeks, and opened the Charger's door. Might as well do what she'd come to do.

She shuffled up the walk, started to ring the doorbell, thought better of it, and knocked instead.

After a few moments, she heard a crash inside the home, followed by a steady creaking sound. The door opened, and an old woman stared at her. Her mother, Diane MacHugh. Streaks of gray clouded once-auburn hair that had now tarnished to a dull brown. Wrinkles pinched her face, and she looked as if she had two black eyes.

"Hi, Mom."

Diane lifted a glass of clear liquid on ice Canada's direction in a toast, then raised it to her lips for a good draw. Sugared gin. Canada recognized the smell. And here it was about ten in the morning.

"Well." Diane said nothing else, but simply stepped back and ushered Canada inside with a broad, sweeping gesture.

Canada obliged and stepped into the dark cocoon of the old home, memories and smells immediately assaulting her. She could still sense her dad in here, even though it had been years since he'd been in the house.

Canada moved to the small living room and chose the brown love seat. Her mother followed, sat down on the couch adjacent. She took another swig, tilted the glass Canada's direction. "Get you something, Candace?" she said. Everyone in the world called her Canada, but her mother hated the nickname. To her, she had always been Candace.

Canada shook her head. "No, I'm fine. I'm here about Dad."

Diane drank again, smacked her lips loudly, stared into the bottom of the glass. Then she sighed loudly and looked back at Canada. "So what is it about your dear father you'd like to discuss?" She took another drink, draining the glass, then ran her finger inside the rim to remove a layer of the sugar sediment. She stuck her finger in her mouth and sucked off the sugar crystals.

"Well, I'm not sure. How he died, kind of."

Diane stopped, her index finger still in her mouth. She arched an eyebrow, pulled her finger out of her mouth, tipped the glass toward Canada again.

"The best way to start that subject, I'd say, is with another refill. Sure I can't get you something?"

"Maybe some ice water."

"Tch. Water by itself? Good waste of a mixer."

"You sound like Joe."

"Joe?"

"Your old buddy Joe. At The Mint."

"Smart man." Her mother turned to go to the kitchen. "Be right back."

Canada sat quietly, looking around while she waited for her mother to return. She hadn't been in the house for so very long, and she was surprised to discover Diane still had photos of her and her father around: framed ones on the end table, a family shot hanging in the hallway. Odd, considering Diane had thrown out her father. She sighed deeply, trying to will away the sick, sinking feeling in her stomach. It made her uncomfortable to be here. Especially because she was skipping out on work right now.

Diane returned with a fresh sugared gin and a glass of ice water. She put the glass of water on the coffee table in front of Canada, then retreated to her chair. "Now, where were we?"

"How Dad died."

"Oh, yes. There."

"Why haven't we ever talked about it?"

"You mean like all those other things we've chatted about these last several years? Our Sunday evening dinner conversations and all?"

"Okay."

"Anyway, you know the story. Cancer. You were here; I don't know why you think there's some grand secret or scheme in the whole thing. Just cancer, you know? Hazards of being a miner." Drink. Diane's gaze became distant, glassy. "Just cancer," she said softly.

Canada pressed forward. "This is going to sound odd, but . . . are you certain he was dead? I mean, absolutely certain?"

Diane didn't seem to think it an odd question. "You ask me, I woulda thought your father was too stubborn to ever die. Wouldn't fit into his plans, you know. But then, no one asked me. They went to the county coroner, instead. 'Cording to him, your father died."

Canada nodded. "But since then, have you . . . I don't know . . . had any strange experiences? Heard him? Seen him?" Canada cleared her throat, uncomfortable with the question as soon as it was out.

Diane leaned forward, took another drink, swigged it around in her mouth like mouthwash while she studied Canada's expression, swallowed. "Am I haunted by your father? Is that what you're asking?" She leaned back in her seat again, exhaling loudly. "Every day. That make you feel better?"

"No, no. I'm not here to lay some guilt trip on you. I'm serious about this. Have you ever . . . um, felt like his . . . presence . . . around?"

"I'd like him to be. I'm sure you don't buy that, but it's true." Diane tipped back her drink—she'd worked her way through this one in about two minutes—and took an ice cube in her mouth. "All right, Candace. Tell me what you're up to."

"Okay, I'll just say it. I think I've been seeing his ghost." Pause. "No, that's not really it. Haven't really seen him—just his shadow.

Actually, it's almost like he's a shadow himself. But I've talked to him. More than once. He asked me to work with him. And, uh, I don't think I ever told you, but he said to me, before he died . . . he said he'd come back, if he could."

Diane continued to chew on her ice cube a few moments while staring at the floor before she nodded solemnly, then focused her gaze on Canada and spoke again. "Butte has more than a few ghosts, doesn't it? It surely does. To think of your father as one of them." She shook her head.

This was a bad idea, and it was only getting worse, listening to her mother dissolve into her drink. In fact, the whole idea was stupid: the idea that she could talk to her dead father. The idea of *working* with her dead shadow father. Almost as stupid as coming to visit with her mother about it. She rose from the couch. "I know it sounds crazy. Especially when I say it out loud. Don't even know what I was thinking."

"Don't worry about it. I certainly know how it feels."

"How what feels?"

"Crazy thoughts—things you feel like you shouldn't say out loud. But you can't just keep 'em inside, or they eat away at you. Acid. Like this." She held up her glass, now empty except for a few ice cubes.

Canada stopped and looked at her mother, actually held her mother's gaze. Some new feeling had stirred in her. Pity? Remorse? What was it?

She shook her head, watching Diane tilt her head back and throw the last two ice cubes in her mouth. Nah. Wasn't really her mother talking. It was just the gin.

"Okay, Mom. I'm gonna go now." She rose from the couch, moved to the door, stopped just before reaching it and turned around. Her mother stared back from the middle of the room, munching on ice. Awkwardly, Canada moved back to her mother and hugged her. Arms stiff, but still, at least it was a hug. And why did she need to feel bad about the hug, anyway? This was further than she'd stepped in years; her mother should be thankful she was here at all, considering their past history. "Sorry I haven't been here for a while," she said, feeling as if she needed to explain something. "I'm not sure where all of this is going, and I just . . . I don't know." So much for an explanation.

Diane patted Canada's arm, looked out the window as if watching a movie on a screen there. "Yeah, well. I don't know either. Knowing is so overrated, when you think about it. So many things I wish I didn't know."

4

"SO WHAT DID YOU TELL your wife this time?" From the small table in the corner, Rob Brandt watched Francine close the door behind her and walk into his motel room. He made no move to get up.

"Hello to you, too," he said. He ran his hands through his salt-and-pepper hair as he watched her sit down on the bed. "Are you really here to talk about my wife?"

"No, I suppose you're not much interested in talking."

Rob tried to hold down the temper he felt flaring. His life hadn't scaled quite the heights it should have; he'd been stuck in Butte with a nowhere sales job, saddled with debt and a family he hadn't planned. He deserved an outlet from his everyday life. Francine was supposed to be the cure, not part of the problem.

He squinted to see her, but the bed where she sat seemed . . . darker. No, she herself seemed dark. He could see her clothes quite clearly, he realized. But her skin was gray, a bit fuzzy, as if she were being broadcast through a poor signal on an old black-and-white television.

He moved across the room to join her, figuring his eyes must be playing tricks on him. This was just why he needed these kinds of interludes; he'd been working too much, sitting in front of his computer hours at a time, and now his mind, his eyes, his nerves, were always off-kilter.

Francine, however, would take care of that. He sat next to her on the bed and leaned in to kiss her, closing his eyes. She responded, and her lips were yielding, willing, parting to—

Rob's eyes flew open in surprise, and he lurched. She had fainted, or passed out or something.

No, that wasn't it. Francine was melting. Her fair skin, usually white and creamy, really was gray; his eyes weren't deceiving him at all. It was the color of ash, like the remnants left in a cigarette tray, like—

No, that wasn't right either. Her skin *was* ash. He saw lazy tendrils of smoke arcing lazily from her body—most notably from the top of her head—and he actually felt her skin crumpling, turning to soot before the heat made him pull back in alarm. He stood, backed up a few steps, stared in shock at the woman's body smoldering on the hotel bed in front of him. No orange flames; instead, more and more of her body simply smoked and smoldered, first turning gray and then collapsing into brittle flakes.

He had to do something. Put out the fire, call for help. He threw the bedspread over her smoking body, reached for the phone. He even started to hit the button to call the front desk before his better sense returned.

How was he going to explain this? All of it? To the front desk, sure, but also to the police, to his wife Betty? He was in a room at the Copper Camp Inn in the middle of a weekday, and he had a burning woman's body wrapped in the comforter. Even a fast-talking insurance salesman such as Rob wasn't going to just explain that one away.

He took a deep breath and coughed, realizing now that smoke was thick in the room. It was like being in a bar, surrounded by idiots puffing on Camels and Marlboros. He unwrapped the comforter and looked inside; Francine's body was gone. Totally gone in less than a minute, nothing left behind but a pile of gray soot and her clothing. He put his finger in the soot and pulled back; the gritty substance was still hot.

He backed away, wiping his hand on the front of his pants, not liking the sandpaper sensation of it on his fingers. Nothing he could do for her now, was there? He'd tried. Sure, he'd tried. He'd picked up the phone and started to dial. He'd thrown that comforter over her to smother the burning. But there was nothing he could do. Now the important thing was to get out.

He turned and started for the door again, desperate to be out of the room, but stumbled and went down on the carpet. It was hot, so very hot in the room. A wonder the fire alarm hadn't been set off with all the smoke and heat. He pulled himself up onto his elbows and tried to stand, but his legs didn't seem to be working.

He rolled to his side and looked down at his legs to see what the problem was, but it was too smoky in the room. Ashy clouds encircled his legs, obstructing his view. Maybe when Francine caught on fire, she'd ignited the carpet.

Rob's mind finally registered what his eyes were seeing, and he closed his eyes and opened them again. Smoke was obscuring his legs, yes, but that was because the smoke was coming *from* his legs. Or where his legs used to be; as Rob watched, his lower half turned to a fine gray grit and fell to the floor.

Rob's hands flashed hot, and he closed his eyes again, not wanting to look. But his eyes overruled his mind and he opened them in time to see his hands crumbling beneath him. His body collapsed, and Rob felt the heat—the numbing, sickening heat—devouring him like a mindless beast. He opened his mouth to scream for help, but as he did, he felt his tongue and lips boiling, then numbing, then . . . disappearing. A weak, whimpering sound escaped his throat before it, too, flaked away.

As his mind dissolved, Rob Brandt thought this was a vivid

dream, a very vivid dream indeed, and he knew he'd be waking up at any moment in his bed, shivering at how realistic the nightmare was.

And then, Rob Brandt thought nothing at all.

# 5

CANADA THREW OPEN THE front door of her trailer, walked in, made her way back to her bed, and collapsed. It had been a rough day at work, physically exhausting even though this wasn't her day to be on the streets slinging trash. She only did that two days a week; the other three she was in the office or at the warehouse, shuffling papers. In Butte, trash collectors these days didn't truly exist; people were "sanitation workers" who, by virtue of having an office environment a couple days a week, could avoid having to think of themselves as trash collectors.

Canada, on the other hand, preferred the collection days. She liked the physicality of it, as opposed to the mind-numbing time in the office or shop. True, she'd rather still be mining than slinging trash, but Butte's glory days as a mining city were behind her. Behind all of them.

She'd insisted on the blast crew because her father had been there himself when he started. It was dangerous, sure, blasting in the open pits; you were, after all, the person who spent the day hauling death. But there was a certain power in that, as well. When you hit the Charge button on the transceiver to build the electrical current, then flipped the switch to detonate, you held power in your hands. The blast, the ground shaking as you stood on it, were physical reminders of that power. Being part of the blast crew, you were in control.

Many miners were afraid to handle the explosives at all, and anyone who was on the blast crew had a certain otherworldly mystique. After all, why would anyone want to spend their life carting around oblivion, dropping it into holes, twisting and wrapping wires around it?

She couldn't say. Those were better questions for Freud. She told herself, if given another choice, Murdock, Ten-spot, and Comet would have taken themselves off the blast crew. They would have wanted to avoid the mistimed explosion that killed them. They would have chosen, instead, to be something calm and normal. Factory workers or delivery drivers.

Maybe even trash collectors.

But deep in her heart, even though she tried to convince herself otherwise, she knew that was wrong. She knew Murdock, Ten-spot, and Comet would have picked the blast crew all over again, even knowing such a decision would cut their lives short.

She knew this because she knew the miners who worked blasts weren't just prepared for the possibility of an eventual accident.

Deep inside, they hoped for one.

Call it a death wish, call it a morbid fascination, call it a compulsion in need of counseling at a hundred twenty-five dollars an hour. Whatever it was, Canada knew that she herself had it. Maybe it was something in the genetics from her father, maybe it was something learned. But it was there, inside her. Barely hidden.

She put her face in her pillow and breathed deep, as if breathing in the memories of her days in the pits.

A sound from out in the living room.

Canada lifted her head, trying to listen, but heard nothing else. Yes, she was sure she'd heard something. She sat up and let her feet drop to the floor. On the wall in front of her, a shadow began to shimmer and melt. Canada narrowed her eyes. Maybe she hadn't heard anything, as such. Maybe she'd *felt* it. And now, she knew what she had felt.

Or more appropriately, *who* she had felt.

She stood and walked slowly out into the living room, careful to avoid the piles and stacks. When she cleared a stack of newspapers, she saw a shadow moving over the surface of her couch. It didn't have a form, really; it wasn't a shadow in the shape of a man. Instead, it looked more like an undulating wave, moving back and forth across the surface of the couch like surf on a beach. Canada stared a few seconds before she softly cleared her throat and spoke.

"Daddy?"

"Hello, Princess."

Canada had no idea how the shadow was speaking to her. There was no mouth to be seen, no features to study. Was it really talking, or was she just imagining the voice in her head? They had a name for that, didn't they?

She shook off the thought. This *was* her father, dead so many years, coming back to speak to her. She'd prayed for this very thing to happen so many times—so many times, since his death had torn something deep inside her.

Now, after all these years, just hearing his voice had helped ease her pain. Was that so bad, to have her pain relieved for a bit?

"Where you been, Daddy?"

"I've been hanging around. Watching you. Making sure you're okay."

"I don't mean just since last night."

"I don't, either."

Canada smiled at the thought of her dead father watching over her. "Can I . . . um . . . sit by you?"

"Looks like it might be the only place you can sit in here."

"I know, Daddy. I just . . . hate to throw it out." She moved to the couch and sat. The shadow shortened its undulations, confining itself to one half of the sofa; still, at the end of each wave, Canada could feel the shadow brushing the bare skin of her arm. It felt hot and cold at the same time, a bit wet. Strange, but not entirely unpleasant.

"You realize, of course," her father's voice said, "the irony of that situation."

"What situation?"

"The trash collector who can't throw away anything."

She shook her head. "You know that's not what I am. I'm a powder monkey, just like you were."

"*Were* is the key word there, Princess."

Canada pulled her feet up under her on the sofa, drawing her body into a tight ball. She felt as if she had to do this, or she would unravel and fall to the floor like so much string. "Okay, Daddy. You got me. So what am I now?"

"That depends on you."

"On what, specifically?"

"On what you want to do. I asked you a question earlier."

"You asked me to join you."

"Yes."

"To join you as . . . um, what exactly? A shadow of some kind?"

"Think of me as one of the undead. No better way of putting it."

"A vampire?"

Canada's father/shadow laughed, an odd, deep sound that seemed to come from everywhere in the room. "Vampires are imaginary, Princess. This is real. Undead, meaning only dead to this world. One of the people caught between the simple living of this world, and the glorious living of the next."

The wave of the shadow brushed her bare skin once more, and now Canada shivered. She shifted a bit away from the shadow, hoping it wouldn't come into contact with her again. It was her father, yes. But it was still . . . unnatural, to say the least. Old Bud

MacHugh sounded positively excited about this whole afterworld business, and he wasn't usually an excitable personality.

"I'm sorry," she said. "I . . . I'm not sure I can. I'm not sure you, any of this, is real, if you want the truth."

"I understand. But I know you can. You have the heart for it—you're the kind of person who always wants to help others. That's all this is about. You'd be like . . . think of it as working for the Red Cross."

She smiled. "The only difference being that the Red Cross, in this case, is a bunch of living shadows."

"Minor detail."

"And what about you? You . . . well, you were a miner. I mean, that's not exactly training for saving the world, or whatever you're trying to tell me you're doing."

"No one is exactly what you think they are, Princess. You, for instance. As you just said, you're not really a trash collector."

Canada put her finger in her hair and twirled her red locks, thinking for a few moments. Okay, maybe the polluted groundwater of Butte had leached some mercury into her home's water supply, and she was having some very active hallucinations.

Or, maybe her dead father was sitting on her couch—in a way—and speaking to her.

She took a deep breath and exhaled. "I don't know. It's so much all at once. I can't just say yes."

"But you can't just say no, either."

She bit at her lip. "No, I guess I can't."

"I thought you might feel that way. So how about a dry run?"

"A dry run?"

"Tag along on an operation. A try-it-before-you-buy-it kind of thing. Meet a few of the other operatives. See what they do, how they work. Decide then."

Her heart was telling her to jump at the chance to work with her father. After eleven years he had returned, and this was an opportunity to spend time with him. Time she'd lost so long ago. Her mind told her she knew nothing about any of this; none of it even seemed real.

On the other hand, what would she be giving up, really, to leave all this? A few stacks of newspapers, an old trailer and a thirty-something-year-old car? Her job as a trash collector? These weren't exactly huge sacrifices.

She could play it by ear, see where it went. Saying yes to the dry run, as her father called it, wasn't saying yes to all of it. She could back out at any time. She was still young, smart, able to think on her feet; if things were going a direction she didn't like, she could walk.

And as he'd said, she was a person who tended to follow her heart; she wanted to help others. If this was a chance to help people, how could she pass it up just to keep tossing trash?

Canada put her feet back down on the floor, stared across the room at a stack of old magazines and nodded her head a few times.

"You got one day," she said.

## 6

THE NEXT MORNING, CANADA STEPPED into the humid air outside the Des Moines airport.

Nearby, standing by the taxi queue, she saw a man holding a handwritten sign: MACHUGH. She stopped walking and took a deep breath—the first breath, it felt to her, since the previous night. Yes, she'd agreed to this try-it-before-you-buy-it scheme of her father's, but was she really ready to follow through? She could still turn around and walk back into the airport, schedule the flight back to Butte on her return ticket.

Yes, she could still do that.

She ran her hands through her red hair, wiped at her forehead, and started walking toward the man with the sign again. His eyebrows rose as she approached, asking the question.

"Yes, that's me," she said.

He let his left hand, still holding the sign, drop to his side. His right hand he held out until she took it. "You can call me Blake," he said, giving her hand a firm grip. Even with the humidity and heat of late summer building, his hands were cool and dry. Almost powdery.

"You can call me—"

He interrupted. "Don't need to call you anything, ma'am. Might be better if I don't know your name." He turned and started to walk past the line of taxis parked at the curb.

"You have a sign with my name on it," she said. "And I know your name."

"I have a sign with a last name on it—a sign you responded to. And as for my name," he called out over his shoulder, "I told you to call me Blake. I didn't tell you that was my real name."

He was moving fast, almost running, and Canada had to adjust her gait to catch up with him. "Okay, then," she said, a little put out. "I'm not big on the 'ma'am' thing, so just call me Annie."

He came to a black Lincoln Town Car with smoked windows and went to the other side, opened the door, then looked at her across the roof of the car as she finally caught up to him. "Annie?" he said.

She ran a hand through her red hair and smiled. "As in 'Little Orphan.' Hair's a little longer, I realize."

His mouth became a thin line, and Canada guessed that might be as close as Blake would get to a smile. "Well, Annie," he said, "it's tomorrow, the sun has come out, and we have a tour to take." He crawled into the car and shut the door.

She opened the passenger door and slid in beside him, barely getting her belt fastened before he wheeled the big Lincoln out into traffic. "You had this car parked at the curb," she said.

"Yes."

"How do you get away with a thing like that? TSA won't even let your average Joe on a plane with hair spray in a carry-on."

"First, I'm not your average Joe," he said, keeping his eyes on the road. Or so she thought—she couldn't really see his eyes behind his sunglasses. "Second, I get away with a lot of things."

They sat in silence for several minutes, until Canada saw the city beginning to give way to a more rural area. She was beginning to get a bit uncomfortable, riding in a car with a man she didn't know, going to a place she knew nothing about to see . . . something she hadn't been told.

And, oh yeah, she was here because her dead father, who was now a living shadow of some sort, told her she should.

Surprisingly, Blake broke the silence. "Almost there," he said, turning onto a secondary highway.

"Almost where?"

"Ground zero. Yesterday's big tornado."

"Tornado?"

He turned to look at her. "Not a news watcher, are you?"

She returned the stare. "Usually. But yesterday I was a bit busy."

He nodded, looked back at the road again. "Okay. Well, we had a big tornado touch down just outside Des Moines yesterday. Took out several homes. Killed a few dozen. We're going there now."

"Why?"

"To help. You'll see."

She stared at Blake for a few more moments, then returned her gaze to the plains rolling by outside the window; even with the air-conditioned car interior, she could smell fresh earth seeping in. The scent of fresh rain. Still watching the landscape, she spoke. "So you're . . . an operative, I guess? Is that what you call yourself?"

Blake shrugged. "Good a term as any. Works for me."

"And you work with the . . . um . . . shadows."

"I work with a lot of partners. The shadows, as you call them, among them."

"So what do you call them?"

Blake smiled. "The Dead Heads."

"Cute."

"Works for me. Anyway, whatever you want to call them, it's important work. More important than anything I ever did before."

"Which was?"

He ignored her question. "One of the big Dead Heads must like you; I've only given a couple VIP tag-alongs. Don't know anything about you or your background, but I can remember what I was thinking before I made the leap. But once you do a couple assign-ments, it gets into your blood."

"What gets into your blood?"

He lifted a hand from the steering wheel and waved to the countryside outside. "All of it. This."

Canada looked outside again, and was surprised to see the dev-astation; they'd obviously entered the tornado's zone of destruction. Wooden remnants of crumpled homes surrounded them like the bleached bones of skeletons. Shredded trees and branches blanketed the open wounds of dirt. And Canada realized the sweet, pleasant smell of fresh rain had been replaced with something darker, mustier.

"Wow," was all she could say as Blake parked the car.

"I'm not saying this stuff, specifically, is what gets to you. Not the destruction, you understand." He paused, as if considering, then switched off the car's engine and turned to her. "You remember how you felt after 9/11? Or Hurricane Katrina? I think it was the same for a lot of us. You looked at the aftermath, and you felt, I don't know . . ."

"Powerless," she said.

"Yeah," he agreed. "Powerless. Hopeless. Like you wanted so much to do something, to make it better. But you couldn't. It's all about communication. All about letting people know what to do in a disaster or an attack. It's power." He sat, looking out the wind-shield for a moment, then abruptly opened the door and got out. Canada did the same, following Blake through the destruction. Other workers swarmed around them, digging through piles, look-ing for survivors: paramedics, Red Cross volunteers, family mem-bers. She'd always thought a scene like this would be filled with noise and activity, but it was eerily quiet and solemn.

They walked together for a while, picking their way through piles of wreckage: twisted metal and two-by-fours, parts blown off cars, shredded clothing, even a stuffed teddy bear lying forlornly in the mud, the bottom half of its body missing and the stuffing leaking out in a billowy cloud.

And paper. Paper everywhere. Flyers, newspapers, bills, tax records—some of it tattered and torn, some amazingly intact, but all of it like a blanket of snow, covering the landscape in a thin layer of white.

Blake suddenly stopped and pointed ahead of them. Canada looked at what he was indicating: a television crew, capturing footage of cleanup efforts. "For us," Blake said, "for *you*, if you join us, this is what it's all about. Getting out the word. Showing people how to prepare. Showing people how to recover. Giving them hope."

Abruptly, in the distance, Canada heard a thin, plaintive wail. A child, crying. Evidently Blake heard it, too, because he stopped talking and surveyed the wreckage around them.

The crying was close. Very close. Canada looked at a giant section of roof beside her, shingles and boards still attached to a few partial trusses. She moved to the other side of it and saw a little girl huddled underneath, shivering in the mud. Her eyes were shut tight, her hair matted. A smudge of dull crimson started under her nose and spread to her cheek, the remnants of a bloody nose.

"Hi," Canada said softly.

The girl continued sobbing. Maybe she hadn't heard.

Canada ducked and crawled in between the trusses until she was directly in front of the girl. She put out her hand and touched a dirty knee. The girl recoiled in shock, her eyes suddenly opening in wide saucers. Still, she shivered uncontrollably. Even though her eyes were now open, no recognition registered there.

Canada reached out and took the girl's hand (*cold, so very cold*) and tried a reassuring smile. "My name's Canada. What's yours?"

The girl's grip suddenly tightened. Her mouth moved, a bit of spittle forming at the edges, but no sound came.

Without any conscious thought, Canada leaned forward, swept the girl into her arms, stood and turned around, clutching the girl to her chest. She felt the child shivering, and continuing to utter soft whimpers, and now Canada felt tears streaming down her own face. "Shhh," she whispered into the child's ear. She wanted to say something comforting, but couldn't imagine what would erase the terrible images that might be floating through the girl's mind. So she hummed. A soft, wordless tune her father had always hummed to her while she struggled to fall asleep. A melody with no name.

She looked at Blake, who was standing behind her, and nodded. He returned the nod and moved away, out of sight.

Canada closed her eyes and let herself be absorbed by the hummed tune, losing herself in the sweet memories of early child-hood, being picked up and held by her father. And after a few moments, she felt his arms around her, smelled the faint musty smell of his skin covered by a thin coat of cheap aftershave, heard the distant beat of his heart inside the vast oceanic wonder of his chest, and she was the one being held, the one being comforted, the one being told all was right with the world.

"Hey." A hand on her arm. She opened her eyes, saw the waste-land of destruction around her once more, felt numb and hollow as she was sucked back across decades of pain and loss to the present. She wanted to close her eyes again and make it go away.

Again: "Hey." She focused, saw the man who had brought her to this devastation. What was his name? Her mind was still fuzzy, still unwilling to let go of her father's warm embrace.

(*Blake.*)

"Walk over here a minute," Blake said, motioning with his arm and backing away from the giant section of roof she had crouched in with the child.

She took one numb step, then another, and another; each one

was a step away from those pleasant memories of Daddy, and a step toward . . . this.

Blake was ahead of her by several steps, but she followed him obediently. And now he bent down and tapped a man on the back. A man slathered in mud, huddling defeated on a car tire. Canada could see this, even before Blake gently tapped the man on the back. Even before the man turned to look, his eyes pink and bleary and unfocused, then wide with surprise and recognition. "Zari!" he said, and he stood to rush toward them. After a few steps, he slipped in the mud, but Blake was there to right him again, and he continued his short sprint toward Canada and the miracle in her arms. Canada heard a soft, whispered "Daddy?" and she looked down at the child, who was now straining toward the approaching man. But even so, Canada wasn't sure if it had been her or the child who whispered the single word, because the man approaching looked so much like Bud MacHugh—that wiry frame, that patch of red hair.

But of course it wasn't him, and now that he was there to take his daughter from her arms, tears tracing clean lines on his dirt-caked face, she could see it looked nothing like her own daddy. He whispered into his daughter's ear, and he swayed from side to side, and he rubbed at her hair, and Zari put her head on her father's chest to find that deep, hidden heartbeat, and Canada smiled.

(*Yes.*)

She turned to Blake as he made his way through the mud. She nodded at him, and he returned the gesture.

"Well?" he asked.

"Well," she answered, "I think this Little Orphan Annie may have just found a new home."

## 7

CARL BENTON HATED HAULING cattle because, simply put, they stank. They produced a steady stream of urine and feces in the trailer, and any time he stopped—to take a break, to grab a bite, to pull over for a couple hours of shut eye—the smell overpowered him.

Each time he delivered a load, he promised himself it would be the last. Lots of trucking firms were looking for OTR drivers, paying a good rate for each mile. He could do fine hauling reefer loads of butter and cheese.

But then, after unloading each trailer, he'd convince himself cattle weren't *that* bad, and the routes weren't as long, and that meant he could spend less time on the road itself.

He sighed, rubbed at his eyes, listened to the throaty rumble of the Mack's diesel engine pulling the whole load through the darkness at eighty miles per hour. Legally, he wasn't supposed to go over seventy-five on this stretch of Interstate north of Salt Lake, especially at night, but then he was probably one of the slowest tractor-trailers at a comfy eighty.

To take his mind off the load of cattle behind him, he let his thoughts wander to other things. One thing in particular: that fine, fine waitress—the one with hair the color of midnight—at the Husky Diner just outside Idaho Falls. He looked at his watch, decided he just might be able to get there for an early morning breakfast—say, four o'clock—and inched his way up to eighty-four miles per hour.

Maybe she'd be working. Maybe she'd be wearing one of those skirts, the ones that slid up high on her thighs any time she went around the counter to a table and poured coffee or collected dishes. He closed his eyes briefly, savoring the thought of being there and—

He saw it too late. An animal of some kind, crouching in the road. Not walking or hopping or running, specifically. It was just suddenly *there*, appearing like a ghost in his headlights.

He braked, hard but not too hard—no use jackknifing and spilling a load of cattle all over the Utah desert. But it was a feeble gesture; even as his foot went for the brake, the front grille of his truck hit the animal with a wet *thunk*. In an instant, the creature was under him, sliding first under the front tires, then thumping through the rest of the rig before being spit out the back in what had to have been a mangled mass.

He kept braking, bringing the hurtling mass of steel and rubber to a final stop as he pulled to the side of the Interstate, then flipped on his flashers. He looked in his side mirror while the air brakes hissed and the diesel's exhaust clattered. Too dark. He couldn't see if the thing—whatever it might be—was still in the road or not. Probably flat after five tons had rolled over it, but he couldn't very well leave it in the middle of the road for some idiot in his twenty-cent Hyundai to hit at full speed.

Carl sighed, rubbed his face again, grabbed a flashlight from the cubby under his seat, then kicked the door open. Immediately, the Utah breeze brushed against his face, bringing the smell of fresh dung to his nostrils and the aggravating sound of mooing to his ears.

He really needed to look into hauling refrigerated loads. Reefer loads were perfect, reefer loads were easy. At least hard goods or something.

Carl slid down the steps, hitched up his pants, wiped at his face again and started to walk down the road. No lights approaching from behind him yet, so that was good. He turned, surveyed the other direction. Looked like maybe some lights in the distance, but it was hard to be sure; might be a small town ahead of him.

He turned back around, still walking, and noticed something unusual about the animal as the flashlight beam rolled across it.

It had arms.

For an instant, his face tightened, and he felt the last cup of coffee in his stomach start to churn. *That's not an animal; that's a man.*

He quickened his pace, not quite wanting to run, but not quite wanting to walk either. There was really nothing he could do for the guy, of course, he'd be oatmeal by now. You don't do the funky chicken under a tractor-trailer combo and then jump up to take the wife and kids out to Denny's for a Grand Slam breakfast. This guy, wherever he'd come from, whatever he was doing out in the middle of the Interstate in the dead of night, was long gone.

But one of the arms was moving.

It was at an odd angle, almost seemed like it was bending the wrong way at the elbow, but it was definitely moving.

Carl decided he maybe could work himself into a run after all, and broke into a jog, heading the last twenty yards or so to the body. As his flashlight illuminated more of the scene, he noticed the body looked much better than he thought it would. It wasn't flat, by any means.

He glanced back down the I-state again, checking both directions for oncoming cars. Just this guy and some salty sand. And the stupid cows, clattering and falling into each other in the trailer.

The guy's body was . . . well, it was glowing, wasn't it? Not a megawatt glow, not the glow of a sign on the Vegas strip, but the steady bright-white glow of a child's nightlight. In the glow and the beam of his own flashlight, Carl could see the guy was dark-complected, maybe Pakistani or something. But his hair was white. Long and white, a marked contrast to his complexion. The man's face pointed away, and Carl began convincing himself that bit about the arm moving was just an illusion in the darkness. Heck, you could see just about anything in the dark, convince yourself monsters were hiding in the folds of night.

Until the man's face turned toward him and opened its eyes.

At the same time, the man's arm—the one Carl had seen moving—snaked out to grab his pant leg.

Carl yelped, sounding like a terrified three-year-old girl who has just wet her pants, but not caring about it a bit. He tried to step back, but the dark man's hand still clutched his jeans, and he windmilled his arms for a few seconds to catch his balance before toppling backward. The flashlight rolled lazily for a few feet before coming to a stop pointed directly at the stranger who was holding his leg.

Now Carl had some images in his mind, some very bad images of flesh-eating zombies in those Friday Night Creature Feature flicks he always watched at his grandmother's on her tiny black-and-white television as a kid. The guy couldn't be alive, no way on earth he could be alive. Which meant he was dead. And if he was dead, but moving, that had to mean he was *undead*. Yeah, like those zombies. Or maybe vampires.

He kicked his leg, trying to scramble to his feet again, but the man's grip was an iron claw; he could feel the denim of his jeans beginning to tear slightly as he struggled to pull away.

Carl was looking at the guy's face, and he could see the face was . . . well, it was *healing*, wasn't it? A garish split in the man's scalp was closing, and blood on the Interstate was now flowing back toward the body. Almost as if the body itself were a sponge, soaking up the red liquid.

Carl gave a mighty pull, felt the denim of his pants give way, and pulled his leg free. Just as quickly, the zombie guy had a hold on his other pant leg.

Abruptly, the dark man's form sat up and stared at him, actually tried to smile. The teeth were all broken and knocked loose, but Carl saw them regrowing, mending, as the smile stayed.

"Carl Benton," the man said, sitting up. "Do not be afraid." The man's leg, which had been twisted the opposite way at the knee, suddenly spun into form and the thigh muscle reattached itself; the man was wearing some kind of khaki pants or something, but Carl could see the muscles moving, reassembling below the fabric. And the man-thing's insistence that Carl should not be afraid had the opposite effect. It even knew his *name*. Carl was afraid. Very afraid.

He swiveled his head jerkily, looking up and down the road, hoping to see another car coming. No such luck. A few hundred yards away, a moo from one of the cattle went up a couple octaves as the stupid beasts beat themselves against the walls of the trailer. Suddenly, the cows didn't seem so bad after all; hauling them down the road would be decidedly better than having his brains sucked out by this zombie guy. That's what zombies did, after all.

He tried to flop over onto his stomach and crawl away, but the zombie guy was too strong, too quick. Within moments, he flipped Carl to his back again, and pinned his arms to his sides.

Zombie Guy was close to him now, close enough to feel zombie sweat dripping onto his own body, close enough to smell the faint whiff of chalk or dust emanating from his pores.

"I—" The single syllable was pinched in Carl's throat, so he tried again. "I . . . I have some money—"

Abruptly, the Zombie Guy released him and stood, looking physically perfect in every way. His clothes were road torn and tattered—a dirty denim shirt, khaki pants with smudges and holes—but his physical features were perfect. No visible signs that he'd been ground to hamburger under five tons of metal.

"I believe you're headed through Butte, aren't you?" the stranger asked him as he stared down. It was dark, but Carl realized, somehow, the man was still glowing—he could see the features perfectly. Carl wanted desperately to scramble away, but he was frozen. His muscles refused to do the work his mind asked. The breeze kicked up a notch to a wind, blowing through the man's flowing white hair.

Carl lied. "Um . . . no. Kind of headed the opposite—" No way Carl wanted to go anywhere near Butte with this guy.

"You're a poor liar," the white-haired Creepy Guy said, extending his hand and offering to help Carl to his feet. "We can be in Butte in about eight hours, so I'm afraid we won't be stopping at that diner you've been thinking about. Her name's Laura, by the way; she does work the graveyard shift, but she's not there tonight. Another time perhaps."

He smiled, but it reminded Carl of a grinning skull. "Graveyard shift," he repeated. "When all the most interesting characters come out of the shadows." Carl didn't want to take the man's hand, didn't—

But the stranger obviously grew tired of waiting; he grabbed Carl by the front of his shirt and lifted effortlessly. All 220 pounds of him.

"Your name, of course, is Carl. As for mine," the man said, looking deep into his eyes and curling up the edges of his mouth, "I have none. I have many. But you can call me Keros."

## 8

CANADA STUMBLED OFF THE PLANE, back in Butte again. In the short span of the flight—a couple of hours—she'd been able to replay the events of the day a thousand times in her mind. The devastation surrounding her. Blake, talking about power in the midst of the helplessness. Most of all, the face of the little girl as she recognized her daddy.

She had been a part of it. And she wanted to be a part of more.

Throughout the flight, she kept watching the shadows shifting across the jet's interior. Looking for a ripple or shift. Looking for Daddy, just like the little girl in Iowa.

Yes, she would become part of this all. She didn't understand all of it yet, but she understood a fair amount. She would be working with her father, and she would be helping people. That was enough; she would do whatever she was asked.

Her father didn't appear in the shadows during the flight, of course; she hadn't truly expected it to happen with all the other people around. But she still had to study each shadow, waiting expectantly. The truth was, she couldn't wait to talk to him, tell him her decision. She was looking forward to it.

Whatever *it* might be.

Now, on the ground, she felt frazzled; the adrenaline that had fueled her energy in Iowa had settled into her muscles, making them achy and lethargic. More than anything, as she walked past the baggage claim, she needed some fresh air.

Outside, the heat of the day had dissipated with the darkness. Canada looked at the canopy of stars overhead, breathed deep, and nodded to Our Lady illuminated on the mountain above her. She was only mildly surprised to hear a voice speaking to her from the darkness nearby.

"Hey, Princess."

"Wondering when you'd show up."

The shadow coiled. "Head to your car," her father's voice said. "We'll talk on the way. Time's kinda short."

"Short for what?"

"For you."

"I'm not getting you."

"You're going to have to make your decision tonight. Now, I'm afraid. But someone else may be making that decision for you. He's on his way—news travels fast through our network. He'll be here sometime tomorrow morning, we think."

Canada moved toward the Charger, opened the door, and slid behind the wheel. As she did, she noticed the shadow sliding into the darkness of the car's interior. Canada felt a shiver, like the old wives' tale of someone walking over your grave. Father or not, this shadow business was a bit creepy. A bit too . . . otherworldly.

She turned the ignition, revved the Dodge's 318 a few times, then threw it into drive and wheeled toward the airport exit. "Okay," she said. "We're leaving the Flats now. Where we headed?"

"Back uptown," the shadow voice replied. "Sorry to be pushy, but as I said, he will be here soon—very soon—looking for you. He's alive again specifically to stop you."

"Alive *again*?"

"In a sense. He's never truly been alive. He's a machine, more than anything. But we can talk more about that later."

"You said he's coming to stop me. Define 'stop' for me."

"He's coming to kill you. But with any luck, by the time he gets here, you'll already be dead."

Like most Butte residents, Canada had a love/hate fascination with the Berkeley Pit. The Pit, as everyone called it. The best of times, the worst of times, and all that. Between 1955 and 1982, the Pit had become a giant mile-wide gorge as miners drilled holes, packed explosives, and literally blew apart the mountain above the city of Butte. When mining had stopped at the Berkeley Pit in 1982, it began filling with polluted groundwater. Now it held forty billion gallons of water—along with assorted heavy metals and other contaminants—making it the world's largest Superfund disaster site.

The Berkeley Pit was, in many ways, a microcosm of Butte. For years, it had sustained mining, the lifeblood of Butte and, by extension, America itself. Without the massive amounts of copper ore pulled from the mountains above and tunnels below Butte, the country's great electrification would never have happened. But in the end, the veins of copper also carried the heavy metals and contaminants that would poison the Pit, and the city itself.

Now, as she stood overlooking the contaminated lake glowing in the darkness, Canada thought it seemed to be, all in all, a pretty good place to die. She turned her back to the Pit and faced the moving shadow confined in her own. "Here, then?" she asked the shadow.

"Well, not here, exactly. Where Shields Avenue turns and becomes Continental—nice long stretch to build up speed. Have to be going pretty fast to hit the water. I'm guessing a hundred would do it."

"And you think that will work? They'll just leave it alone?"

"This is Butte, Princess. Many, many secrets are buried in that pit."

"I don't know." She glanced back at the water, shuddered. Maybe this was a bad idea.

"You crash your car into the Pit, nobody's going after it. Once it sinks a hundred, a hundred-fifty feet, it gets into the really heavy contamination. Arsenic, lead, all kinds of bad stuff. We'll make sure the accident is seen—well-documented by witnesses—so they'll know it was you."

"You mean they'll *think* it was me."

"Of course that's what I meant."

Canada breathed deep, closing her eyes. Water this full of heavy contaminants seemed like it should smell fetid, carry the odor of death. Instead, it smelled fresh, inviting, especially mixed with the late summer blossoms of fruit trees from nearby neighborhoods. She opened her eyes again, studied the city lights reflecting off the ripples of water several hundred feet below her. "Doesn't look that bad, really. I mean, it's just water."

"You know the story. The geese."

Canada did indeed know the story. Anyone who lived in Butte knew it. In 1995, 300 geese had landed on the surface of the Berkeley Pit while migrating south. All 300 of the geese died, poisoned by the toxic water. Since then, officials at the Berkeley Pit had played loud music to keep birds from landing on the water's surface. She sighed. "Yeah, everybody knows the story."

The shadow made no reply; it simply modulated, wavering in the darkness beside her.

She turned back to the Charger, parked several hundred feet from them on the side of the road with its headlights still on. Below them, red lights blinked on one of Butte's famous head frames. "Hey," she said, "whaddya think of the lights on the head frames?"

"The what?"

"The lights? You know, the red lights they string up on the head frames, light 'em up at night." She pointed at a large wooden structure resembling the Eiffel Tower. These head frames—the dozen or so that still stood—were reminders of Old Butte; in the nineteenth and early twentieth centuries, head frames functioned as crude elevators, lowering miners into the underground tunnels and bringing carts of ore back to the surface.

In the last few years, the city of Butte had outfitted all the remaining head frames with strings of red lights, turning them into crimson beacons at nightfall.

"Haven't given 'em much thought."

"They're just about done putting giant spotlights on all the head frames now. Shine 'em into the night sky. Most cities, they want to hide their ghosts. Butte, they put big old red lights on 'em and turn 'em into tourist attractions."

"Play the hand you're dealt."

"And now I'll be one of those ghosts, too, huh?"

"Join the club, Princess."


The next morning, Canada stood on the platform of the observation deck and looked out over the water, adjusted her sunglasses, worried about whether her blond wig had shifted and exposed a few of her red locks underneath.

At first, visitors could come look at the Pit for free, see the dark underbelly of mining exposed to all. Recently, the city had begun charging an admission fee. Some had snickered, making jokes about entrance charges to see what was essentially the world's largest toxic cleanup site. But for Canada, it was simply an illustration of the uncrushable Butte spirit and that old saw about lemons and lemonade.

Much to the surprise of naysayers, attendance at the observation deck hadn't dropped at all. In fact, the fee had brought new publicity for the Pit and the town of Butte.

Lemonade, indeed.

She stood on the deck, overlooking the water a few hundred feet below, and tried to appear as if she was scanning the size of the Pit. In reality, behind her sunglasses, she was straining to search for the car she knew would be approaching.

On some level, she knew this was stupid, stupid, stupid. She was about to officially end her existence so she could join some secret network she knew nothing about. All because her dead father, now a shadow, had told her to do so.

But on another level, that was all the reason she needed. It was her father, come back to her after all these years. The sharp, stabbing pain of her grief had never left her; it had dulled and blunted itself, to be sure, but that dullness had only cut more painful wounds. Surely, after eleven years of that, she deserved a chance to be with him.

She turned her head and looked at the other people sharing space on the observation deck. Two couples, it looked like—one middle-aged couple passing a video camera back and forth, the other a twenty-something couple chattering about Yellowstone National Park.

That brought back her dream of gulping the scalding water of Old Faithful. She closed her eyes, pushed the image away, swallowed hard and tried to ignore the feeling that her throat had been burned.

She turned her attention back to the others. One teenaged girl, maybe there with the middle-aged couple, but not really interacting with them, so it was difficult to say. A dark-haired woman wearing giant sunglasses and carrying a garish orange purse. Some heavyset guy in jeans and a T-shirt with a message proclaiming STOP LOOKING AT MY SHIRT.

"Hey, Clint, get that car!" It was the middle-aged video-camera woman, although she didn't currently have the camera. Her partner did, and she obviously wanted him to capture footage of a speeding car leaving the road and heading straight for the Pit.

A '72 Dodge Charger Canada recognized immediately.

Gasps went up from a few of the people on the deck as the car jounced over the baked dirt and went to the Pit's edge, then jetted, Evel Knievel-like, into the open air of the Pit before arcing downward a few hundred feet and hitting the water's surface with a wet smack they could hear from the deck.

At first, they all stood silent, motionless.

But then, Canada heard the woman in the big sunglasses speaking. "I need to report an accident." She turned to see who the woman was talking to, then noticed the cell phone pressed to her ear. Obviously, she'd retrieved it from her hunter-orange purse. "There's a car—it crashed into the Berkeley Pit." Pause. "Yes, the Pit. *The* Pit. The giant hole at the top of the city." Another pause. "Okay, sorry, I'm just . . . um, I'm at the observation deck, and it's maybe a quarter of a mile to the left off of . . . off of . . . I'm not sure—"

"Shields Avenue," the man running the video camera said without turning.

"Off of Shields Avenue," she continued.

Canada turned back to the water. The car was nose down in the water; only the trunk and the rear of the vehicle were visible, and it was sinking fast. Abruptly, a woman's arms and face broke the surface of the water. She had red hair, the same shade as Canada's, and she struggled for a few moments on the surface of the water, trying to swim. Now there were murmurs and a few more gasps, Canada's among them. She didn't know someone was actually going to *be* in the car. She thought they'd just run it off the edge, like in the movies. This . . . this was a woman, a real woman, drowning in the Berkeley Pit.

The young man in the twenty-something couple moved toward the side of the observation deck and hopped over the railing, starting toward the car even though it was several hundred yards away.

"No, Trent!" his partner cried out. She was blond and tan, very pretty. "The water, it's poison. Didn't you read any of this stuff?" She pointed to the interpretive signage on the observation deck.

Trent turned around and looked at his pretty companion for a few seconds. "I can't just . . . do nothing." With that, he began scaling the fence surrounding the observation deck.

Canada looked back to the surface of the water. The car was gone from sight, and the woman hadn't surfaced for several seconds. Trent wouldn't be there in time to help; he was probably too late already. He should have listened to his girlfriend, wife, whatever she was.

"Please tell me you got that on tape." Canada turned and saw the video-camera wife speaking to her husband.

Video-camera husband closed the viewfinder of his cam and looked at his wife. "Got all of it."

The woman who had called 911 spoke. "I bet the police will want to see that."

"I bet," the man with the camera answered.

Suddenly, as if on cue, everyone began chattering about the accident, comparing their observations, wondering if Trent would make it down to the water to help the woman. Amid the chatter, Canada turned to the man with the video camera, tilting her head and peering over the top of her sunglasses to get a better look. At first, his attention was focused on the chattering crowd around him. But within moments, he swiveled his head and locked eyes with Canada. After a few seconds, he gave a slow, purposeful nod.

Canada pulled back in shock as all the pieces fell into place. Her father had said the crash would be documented.

This guy was part of that.

Her father hadn't said anything, though, about killing another woman in the crash. And *she* was part of that. She felt the acid rising in her stomach, and the heat of the day pressing in around her, and Canada suddenly needed to be out of there. She stumbled toward the tunnel that connected the observation deck to the parking lot and her rental car, her whole body feeling oversized, numb, alien.

In the distance, a thin wail of sirens began to approach.

# 9

JUST A FEW HOURS AWAY from Butte, Canada flipped on the television to catch the late news. The lead story, unsurprisingly, was the crash. *Her* crash. Except it really wasn't hers, was it? Someone else had died in her place. She shuddered, watching the newscaster deliver the story.

The anchor looked at the camera and read. "Witnesses say the car accelerated off Shields Avenue before reaching the Pit, as captured in this dramatic footage from a home camera. A witness and local firefighter, Trent Gibson of Butte, went into the Pit in an attempt to help the driver, and is now being treated at St. James Hospital for chemical burns."

"It was a nice thought, Trent," Canada whispered. "Stupid, but nice."

The newscast continued. "Authorities are still investigating the accident, and withholding the victim's identity until family members have been notified. In other news—"

Canada flipped off the TV and sat, silently, trying to collect herself. She'd just made a big mistake.

A shadow slid beneath the door of her room, then settled into the corner by the TV.

"And with that, Princess, you are officially dead."

"Along with whoever that woman in the car was."

The shadow shifted, undulated, for a few seconds. "Don't always believe what you see."

She paused, felt a tear trickling down her cheek. "What's that supposed to mean?"

"No one died in that accident, Princess. At least, no one who wasn't already dead."

"Already dead?"

"The spirits of the dead occupy the shadows. That much you know, as I'm sitting here now. But you also know—everyone knows—about apparitions, phantasms, ghosts."

"The woman in the car was a ghost?"

"It takes a great deal of energy to manifest a physical presence, and we can only do it for a few brief seconds at a time."

Canada stared at the floor, shaking her head. What had she walked into? She'd heard her dead father speaking to her, and almost instantly she'd let herself be transformed into a five-year-old again, blindly trusting everything her dad's voice said. And why had she done that?

Because in her heart, she had wanted to.

"This was stupid," Canada said, starting as a whisper. "I made a big mistake. All of this: listening to your stories, agreeing to be part of your woo woo network . . . I didn't do anything with the trailer, with my job. I didn't even say anything to Mom. And now I'm dead to the world, because I was too stupid to . . . to . . . I don't know." She gave a pained chuckle, wiped at her eyes with the sleeve of her shirt.

"Some things about this world aren't rational. Some things about the next world aren't rational, either. There are always things we discover, things we learn, that don't make sense."

Canada closed her eyes, pursed her lips for a few seconds, and spoke. "I have to ask you a question."

"Yes?"

"When I was young, you and I always went someplace special. What was it?"

The shadow didn't hesitate. "Columbia Gardens, Princess. It's me. Believe it."

Fresh tears leaked from Canada's eyes as she recalled rides on the go-round, cotton candy on her hands, the smells of asphalt and fried bread in her nostrils. She opened her eyes and wiped at the tears again. "Okay, okay." She exhaled deeply, stood and went to the window to open the drapes.

"Keep the shades drawn," the shadow whispered.

She stopped, turned. "Why?"

"It's a good habit. Lock the door, too."

She moved to the door and fastened the chain lock. "No one knows we're here. You said as much earlier."

"Yes," the shadow replied. "For now. A few more hours, anyway. But he's in Butte now, and he'll find our trail—*your* trail—soon enough."

Pause. "The machine. The guy you talked about earlier."

"I know I said 'he,' but we're really talking more about an 'it.' Do you know what a golem is?"

Canada thought. "The creepy guy from *The Hobbit*, wasn't he?"

"Close. In name. But a *real* golem is an ancient monster—essentially, a monster made of clay and given life to seek vengeance. You've seen the old Frankenstein movies, right?"

She smiled. "Yeah, Dad. I even read the book."

"That's where the idea for Frankenstein's monster came from—the legend of the golem."

"But if it's a legend . . ."

"You want me to say it's not real. Dead wrong; there's a lot of truth in old legends. Some more than others."

Canada furrowed her brows. "What's it seeking vengeance on?"

Canada almost felt she could detect the undulating shadow

quiver. "There are many—so many—who want to see no change at all. They'd rather sit by, do nothing. So they're threatened by those who want to change the world."

"You already got me. I'm dead, remember?"

"Not to the Nameless One, you're not."

"So on top of dying today, I now have a man with no name trying to kill me."

"As I said, there are many who don't like what we're doing."

"And so what exactly am I doing?" Canada was feeling a bit better now, getting her feet back under her.

"Sharing the secrets of the next world with this one. Helping thousands—millions—abide to warnings from we who see what they cannot."

"The network."

"And now that you're officially dead, you're part of us. We have contacts all over the world, in every government, working with us. You might travel outside our North American borders, but for the most part, you'll be a home operative. I promise you, Princess, you're doing the right thing."

Canada shook her head. Her father, Bud MacHugh, using ten-dollar words. He was a miner, matching the gruff stereotype. Never even graduated from high school. It didn't seem right at all. And yet, it seemed so very right; in her bones, she felt it. "Dad, no offense, but you sound different."

"Different?"

"You don't talk the same. 'Operative' isn't something I would expect to hear Bud MacHugh say."

"It's been eleven years since I died, Princess. I mined before, but I'm working a different kind of underground now."

"You were an open-pit miner."

"A figure of speech. I thought you'd like it."

"Yeah, yeah. I get it."

"Okay, you'll lie low here in Bozeman tonight. Then, tomorrow, you'll go to the airport in Billings and fly to St. Louis for your first assignment."

"My first assignment? What about training?"

"On-the-job training, Princess. Just like the blast crew."

---

The Nameless One stood next to the Travona Head Frame in Butte and listened to the shadows shrieking inside the gaping maw of the tunnel. It was dark, but the shadows refused to leave the tunnel. They wouldn't venture out while he stood here.

He looked at the head frame above him and studied the red lights outlining the structure. The newest addition, a large spotlight, was mounted on the platform at the head frame base; wiring, lumber and some leftover concrete slurry surrounded the base. Obviously, the spotlight wasn't quite ready to go yet.

Once, the city had been filled with head frames, giant towers of creosote-treated lumber reaching for the sky. Miniature towers of Babel.

He closed his eyes, remembering the heyday of mining in Butte not so very long ago. The shadows had quickly established themselves here, especially with a network of underground tunnels stretching several hundred miles.

Indeed, Butte had become something of an operational base for them. But now, he was here to stop that.

Their network had grown exponentially since he'd last been in Butte. Not surprisingly, perhaps. He'd come in search of the woman—the one whose presence had awakened him from his slumber in the deep recesses beneath Chile—but he was too late. She was already gone. It had taken so long for his body to fully awaken. Immediately, he'd become a stowaway, hiding on a cargo jet headed for Phoenix. But shortly after landing in the States, he had felt her leave Butte. He switched to diesel trucks at that point—his preferred mode of travel—only to feel her return to the city several hours later. In Idaho Falls, he'd found another flight—this one a mail flight— and eventually ended up in Butte.

As soon as he was on the ground, however, he knew she was gone again. He could feel it. He could smell it. And so he came here, to the Travona Head Frame, to twist the secrets from the Nothingness that ran beneath the city. The Nothingness would scream, but it would also yield.

It would keep her away from Butte, hoping to keep her away from him. But he already had a rough sense of where she'd gone; he'd visited her trailer, sifted through her belongings like a bloodhound getting a scent.

Yes, he had her scent.

He also had the Nothingness, in a much thicker, much denser concentration than anything in Chile; standing near it like this, he could sense what was happening. She was still somewhat close, maybe only a few hours away. Which pleased him. He was sick of flying; he hated the sensation, and so much preferred the rattle and hum of the giant semis and their trailers rumbling down the highways. Earthbound. Fueled by diesel, refined from petroleum buried deep below the earth's surface. Diesel engines brought to mind deep, buried things. The smell, the taste of diesel reminded him of earth's deep clay.

He sighed. She must be allowed to work with them for a time, because she would be the key to exposing recent plans and secrets. The things he'd missed during his long slumber in Chile.

So she would begin her journey with the Nothingness. But then, he would stop her.

He looked at the city spread out below him, felt the cold breeze coming from the tunnels brushing his face as the Nothingness inside shrieked. He breathed deep, taking in the familiar scent the breeze carried: the scent of approaching death.

Like the smell of clay, it was a scent he knew very well.

————————

Canada picked up her bag at the carousel—a bag containing all her current possessions in the world. She hadn't been given much time to put a lot of things together before dying yesterday.

Well, this was for the better anyway. So many things in that trailer that needed to . . . to . . . be thrown away. She couldn't even say the words in her own mind, even though she knew they were true. Doing this was a way of making a clean break. A new life. She smiled. A new life as a dead person.

She looked around the airport, listening to the metallic whine of the baggage carousel near her. The crowd at the airport was pretty light. It was midmorning here in St. Louis—she flipped open the cell phone she'd been given and checked to see the local time was 10:37—then closed the phone and looked at the few people near her. No nods or gestures from anyone.

The cell phone rang, startling her; the caller ID displayed a number she didn't recognize, a number with a 555 area code. Canada knew there was no such thing as a 555 area code, so officially the number calling didn't exist. That sounded like a shadow network to her. She flipped open the phone.

"Hello?"

A woman's voice spoke. "Meet me at ground transportation. Go out the sliding doors just north of where you're standing, cross the island, take the garage elevator to the third floor. I'll be at row L, stall 33. Black sedan."

The connection went dead. Canada stared at the cell phone, wondered what had happened to her old cell phone. Obviously, if she was dead, her cell phone should be inactive; that would be a loose end.

She put the phone back in her pocket, looked at the sliding doors the caller had mentioned. "Fox Mulder, here I come," she whispered under her breath as she angled for the doors.

So what, exactly, would an *assignment* entail? It sounded so concrete, so solid, for a network of shadows. It was crazy, to be sure. But then, Canada had done more than one crazy thing in her life.

She pressed the elevator's call button in the parking garage just outside the doors. The bell sounded immediately, and the doors opened for her. She stepped inside and pressed the 3 button, which illuminated with a green glow. The elevator moaned and began to move.

As the elevator ascended, Canada thought briefly of her mother and felt . . . what was it she felt, exactly? Certainly not anger, not the bright red flare of rage she'd felt for so many years when she thought of her mother. This was something more like pity. Regret? Yes, she should have said something more to her mother.

The elevator chimed again, and the doors opened on a dark, asphalted floor. Canada walked five rows over to reach the L sign, then began tracing her way down the row. The numbers descended until she came to 33. She looked at the car, a black Chevrolet Impala. Yup, a black sedan.

She saw someone sitting inside the car, but just the back of the person's head.

Canada worked her way to the driver's side door and opened it, threw her bag in the back seat, then slid in behind the wheel.

"You packed," the woman's voice beside her said. "You don't need to, you know. We can get you anything you need. Anything." The woman tilted her face toward Canada. It was sharp and angular, as if drawn with a ruler. The woman's skin was a dull white, and her short, straight hair was dark. Anne Rice with a haircut.

"Nice to meet you, too," Canada said pointedly. "I'm Candace MacHugh, but you can call me Canada."

"Wrong answer. Candace MacHugh is dead now; your name, for the purposes of this little soiree, is Franny Glass. My name is Lisa Harper, *Franny*." She emphasized the last word, and made no move to shake hands or exchange other pleasantries.

"Okay, *Lisa*. Since you and I are becoming such fast friends, tell me what's what."

"Look at the dash. See that GPS unit?"

Canada looked at the Global Positioning System, hit the power switch, and watched it come to life with a low beep.

Lisa continued. "It's been preprogrammed with our route. Any assignment you get, you'll follow the same routine. You'll have a rental car, with GPS, provided for you."

"It's good to be queen," Canada said as she started the car and backed out of the stall.

"First time in St. Louis?" Lisa asked. Canada could tell the question was really a thinly veiled way of saying, *You haven't traveled much, have you?*

"It is," Canada said as she exited the parking garage and made a left, following the GPS commands. "Yours?"

"No, no. I've been here many times."

"Well, maybe they'll give you the key to the city sometime." Canada looked at Lisa, but the other woman turned her head to stare straight ahead.

After a few moments of silence, Lisa spoke again. "Strong blue-collar city. Much like your beloved Butte. Big in meatpacking in the early 1900s. Freight and commerce, that kind of thing. It's tried to go a little fancy now, though, trying to be upscale. Forgotten its roots. So many places, so many people, make that mistake now."

Canada thought it sounded idly like a threat. She made another turn. They were on an Interstate now, and from what she could tell, the GPS was taking them outside of the city a ways.

"So where are we going?" she asked Lisa.

"To a bonfire."

Transcript: Interview with copper miner Gustavos Karakaedos
Conducted May 1960 by [NAME REDACTED]
Collected by [AGENCY REDACTED]

INTERROGATOR: It's May 10, 1960, 9:37 local time in Butte. This
is [NAME REDACTED] interviewing Gustavos Karakaedos.

GUSTAVOS KARAKAEDOS: Call me Gus.

INT: Okay, Gus, let's get started.

GK: Why are we doing this, please?

INT: Why?

GK: Yeah, this [UNINTELLIGIBLE]. Why the interview?

INT: We're attempting to reconstruct some of the important . . .
ah . . . events of Butte's past, and we're conducting these
interviews to—

GK: Who do you mean by "we"?

INT: Ah, the United States government.

GK: The government. What department?

INT: Um, that's classified information, sir. Your participation in
this interview, as I described before, is entirely voluntary.

GK: Voluntary, yes. I discover long ago how government "voluntary" programs work.

INT: If you'd rather not—

GK: No, no, I am fine.

INT: Okay, sir. If you could just start by telling us a bit about yourself.

GK: I was born Gustavos Karakaedos in the old country in 1879—

INT: The old country being . . .

GK: Being *Hellas*, or as it's called here, Greece. Yes?

INT: Okay.

GK: I came to United States in late 1892, and Butte in early 1893, where I start to work in the mines. I start in Silver Bow number two mine.

INT: And so at that time you were..ah . . . how old?

GK: Thirteen.

INT: And today, you're . . .

GK: Eighty years old.

INT: Okay, thank you. You were present, then, on January . . . ah, January 15, 1895, then?

GK: The Big Explosion? This is what you want to ask about?

INT: Yes.

GK: You must understand, Butte eats people. The mines, you know, the tunnels. Now the open pit—they call it the Berkeley Pit, even though it swallows more than the Berkeley mine—but it will eat people, too.

INT: I . . . ah . . . don't understand.

GK: We miners, you see, we know the city eats people. It is part of life in Butte, yes? We step into those hoist cages, listen to the wheels crank us down into the tunnels, we know it might be our last time we go down. We know the tunnels might eat us. Sometimes, men fall down shafts. Sometimes, the hoist cages fall. Sometimes, the Duggans crush them.

INT: Duggans?

GK: Yes. Duggans are giant slabs of rock, yes? The ground beneath Butte, sometimes the rock gets very rotten. At that time, there is a big funeral home named Duggans, and so when men work with these rotten rocks, we call them Duggans because—

INT: Because they would send men to the funeral parlor.

GK: Yes.

INT: Okay, back to January of 1895.

GK: Yes, yes, the Big Explosion. I am down in number two that morning, so I don't see what happens above ground, yes? I hear only from others. But Butte, that day, she eats more people her favorite way: with fire, with explosions.

INT: What happened?

GK: The fire department goes to a fire at the milling company.

INT: The Royal Milling Company.

GK: Yes, yes. The firemen, you see, they go to put out the fire, but they don't know blasting powder is in other buildings near them, yes? This blasting powder, it is illegal to store in these buildings, but this is Butte in 1895, you see. So the firemen, they fight the fire at the milling company, and a giant explosion comes, yes? Joseph Franklin, a fireman I know, later tells me the whole roof of the warehouse comes off, a hundred feet in the air, just like that.

INT: This was the Kenyon Connell Commercial Company warehouse?

GK: Yes. This is the Big Explosion people talk about since then. But this is also how Butte is hungry, how she eats the people who live here, you see. After that explosion, firemen, other people, policemen, they all rush in to help the people hurt, yes? And this is when the second warehouse explodes, the hardware store warehouse. Metal bars, pipes, tools, these kinds of things, you see, they become like missiles. They kill all the people rushing to help. The next day, they find glass in Walkerville.

INT: That's two miles away from where the explosion happened.

GK: If you say so. Long way. They also find metal and such from the explosions, sticking in buildings downtown. That sort of thing. Joseph also tells me, while they are there, that oil—

from the hardware warehouse, you see—rains down on them from the sky, and it is on fire. Many people die.

INT: Ah . . . fifty-seven dead, was the official count, more than a hundred injured.

GK: Yes, well, these are just the people who count, you see? They say fifty-seven, but many more—people who come from Greece, or Ireland, or Slovakia, people like me, yes?—they die also. They do not count, yes?

INT: Okay. What I'm interested in—

GK: No, wait, you must understand this. Many, many people simply—poof!—gone. No one then finds them. One man . . . eh, I cannot remember the name right now. Anyway, he is the fire chief. They discover he dies in the explosion because they find his belt, yes? But that is all they find. The rest of him, gone. So many, gone.

INT: Okay, I'm interested in what happened below ground that day.

GK: What . . . do you mean?

INT: We've been told of . . . strange things happening below ground. In the tunnels.

GK: Who tells you this?

INT: Many people have.

GK: Many bad things happen in the tunnels, yes? I tell you before.

INT: Yes, but specifically, I'm wondering about [INFORMATION REDACTED—CLASSIFIED].

GK: [WEEPING SOUNDS].

INT: Mr. Karakaedos? Gus? Are you okay?

GK: We stop now.

INT: We can . . . ah . . . take a break.

GK: No, we must stop. We speak no more of this. I tell you: Butte eats her people. Today, yes, she is still hungry.

## 11

THE GPS STILL SHOWED A couple blocks to go, but Lisa motioned for Canada to stop the car. "Pull over here," she said. Canada thought briefly of continuing on anyway—something about this Goth Chick Wannabe made her want to do the opposite of everything she said—but she bit her lip and pulled the black Impala to the curb.

"We don't want to get any closer. Yet," Lisa said as she continued to stare down the street.

Canada followed her gaze. "Closer to what?"

"To that." Lisa pointed at an apartment complex a couple blocks away.

Canada studied the complex; things seemed pretty quiet right now in late morning. Had to be after eleven o'clock. "I thought you said something about a bonfire," she said to Lisa, still looking at the apartment building.

Suddenly, a giant fireball mushroomed from the second floor of the building, shattering glass, and the heavy *whump* hit the Impala a few seconds later, rocking it on its shocks.

"There you go," Lisa said, opening the door calmly.

Canada threw open her own door and sprinted past Lisa, who acted as if she were taking a leisurely stroll around the neighborhood and it was all perfectly natural, perfectly normal, for apartment buildings to explode and erupt in flames.

Canada pulled up short in front of the building, panting as she examined the damage. This was only one building in the complex; three others, each forming one side of a square, intersected the first. The fire would definitely spread if help didn't get here soon.

Help. Yes, that was the first thing she should do. She pulled out her cell phone and dialed 911. When the dispatch asked for an address, she realized she didn't know it. No, wait, wait. She *did* know it; she recalled seeing it on the GPS unit in the car, and rattled off the address for dispatch, then hung up without waiting for an answer.

She turned and looked behind her just in time to see Lisa casually amble up. "Hang tight," Lisa said. "Our contacts will be here in a few minutes."

"Hang tight? There's gotta be people in there." She turned toward the apartment building, but felt an iron hand grip her arm and spin her around.

"Look," Lisa said through clenched teeth, "you have no idea what's going on here, and I'm not about to have you go and get yourself killed—on your first assignment, no less. So I'd suggest you stay here and shut up."

Canada felt her Irish temper flaring, and she tried to choke it back. *Calm down, calm down,* she told herself. But when she pulled her arm away, Lisa let go and grabbed her hair instead. Canada's instincts kicked in. She stopped Lisa's arm with her left hand and, without thinking about it, sent a quick jab to Lisa's nose with her right. Immediately, the woman's grip on her hair loosened, and Lisa staggered backward a few steps, both of her hands now over her face. "We're here to save people, and you're *pulling my hair?*" Canada spat. "What is this? Third grade?" Lisa didn't answer; instead, she checked her hands to see if her nose was bleeding.

Canada turned to the building. Her mind returned, again, to the Berkeley Pit and the woman surfacing in the poison water. Her father assured her that woman was a . . . well, a ghost. But still. She wasn't about to stand around in shock for the second time in as many days. Trent had the right idea; it was better to do something.

She took off across the lawn, now littered with debris, heading for the front door of the apartment building. The fire had spread throughout the structure now, but most of it was still on the second floor; Canada knew, from past experience in Butte, that buildings burned down much slower than they burned up.

She felt the front door of the building. Warm, but not searing hot. That meant no fire was burning directly on the other side. She edged the door open and slipped inside.

Sprinklers overhead poured water on the carpets. Canada saw two shadowy figures moving down the hallway to her left, but couldn't make out the faces. Smoke was boiling around her, getting thicker by the second. Upstairs, on the second floor, the fire was obviously raging; it sounded like a tank rolling around up there.

She peeled off her long-sleeved shirt, stripping down to a tee only, rolled it, and tied it around her mouth and nose as a makeshift bandana. Okay, it wouldn't save her from breathing anything really hazardous, but it was something. She picked her way forward, but the first floor, from what she could see both directions, was clear now. She'd seen a few people filtering out, including the shadowy figures down the hall. The fire department would probably do most of its work on the first floor, anyway. Where she would be needed most, she knew, was on the second floor; by the time the firefighters got here, it would be engulfed and impassible.

"Okay, okay," she whispered to herself as she moved up the stairs. She could see a haze of darker smoke hanging in the air of the second floor, but no flames had worked their way to the stairway yet.

She reached the second floor, then dropped to her hands and knees and began to crawl to stay below most of the smoke. The less smoke she inhaled, the longer she'd be able to help. She saw the fire, burning about halfway down the hall and moving fast, its steady roar overpowering all other sound; she tried to yell a few times, but she couldn't even hear herself. She'd only be able to stay in here a few more—

A leg.

Maybe about fifteen yards down the hall, still away from the main brunt of the fire, but there it was: a leg, clad in jeans, and a black skateboarding shoe on the foot. She stopped briefly, wondering if it might only be a body part blown off in the explosion. As a powder monkey back in the open pit mines in Butte, she'd only seen one accidental explosion, but that had been enough. Certainly enough for Murdock, Ten-spot, and Comet.

She continued down the hallway, feeling the overwhelming heat of the flames starting to push against her. She wouldn't be able to stay here long. As she neared the leg, she saw it wasn't detached after all, and she let out a sigh, followed by a few quick coughs. This close to the flames, she was taking in more smoke. The leg belonged to a young man, maybe twenty-five years old, who was half in/half out of the front door of an apartment. No obvious injuries or wounds; judging by the position of his body, she guessed he'd started out of the apartment, but had been overcome by smoke. Kid shoulda crawled.

She grabbed his legs, rose to her knees, and pulled. It wasn't easy to move him without rising to her feet, but she managed to get him into the hallway. She turned back to the apartment and saw a spilled box littering its contents across the floor: compact discs, a few books, file folders. Obviously, he had stopped to collect a few things before trying to get outside. Bad move; it had almost cost him his life.

Down the hallway, Canada saw the fire flare briefly. Above her, she felt a shower of dust coming down. She guessed part of the ceiling had collapsed and fed the flames. In another few seconds, the whole thing might come down on them.

She gauged the distance to the stairs and considered. No way she'd be able to drag this guy twenty yards or so while on her hands and knees. She'd need to stand up. And to do that, she'd have to hold her breath and move fast. Okay. She could do that.

She pulled the guy up into a sitting position, then bent in front of him and draped his arms over her shoulders. She took a breath, held it, then stood, pulling him up with her and dragging him along. Her muscles strained, and already her lungs were begging for more air, but she gritted down and moved as fast as she could. Up here in the smoke, she didn't even try to look. She kept her eyes closed, but she could still feel the smoke stabbing at her eyes, forcing tears out of the corners.

Finally, when she couldn't hold her breath any longer, she dropped back to the floor and checked her position, allowing her lungs to take in new air, but being careful not to pant. The make-shift bandana seemed tighter now, and her tears and sweat had formed a wet sheen that soaked her face and neck. She wasn't quite there yet, but she was close. She repeated the routine with the young man's body, keeping him behind her as she stood, draping his arms on her shoulders like a giant backpack. She took another step, then heard a giant *whoomp* behind her; instantly, she felt as if she'd been hit by a car. She went face-first to the floor, the breath she held knocked out as the young man landed hard on her back. Obviously, something had exploded in the fire.

Dazed for a moment, she wondered if she should just leave the man there in the hallway and scramble for the stairs herself. Maybe he wasn't even alive now; he could have taken a piece of two-by-four in the back with the last explosion. Heck, maybe he hadn't even been alive when she reached him; she realized, woodenly, that she hadn't even checked his vitals. She'd just assumed he was alive.

But she'd come this far, and she wasn't about to give up now. She turned, and noticed the explosion had carried them forward a few feet; just to her left, the staircase descended to safety. She scrambled down a few of the steps, turned and grabbed the young man, cradling his head against her chest and looping her arms under his to drag him down the stairs.

She was panting, no stopping it now, but the air tasted a bit cleaner; down here, they were out of most of the smoke. Still, her lungs rejected the air, and she was coughing steadily. Actually, she dimly realized, she'd been coughing the whole time; she felt as if a thousand tiny needles were piercing her lungs at once.

After a few more seconds of struggling, she bumped into something and felt it shift. Oh no, the stair rail was collapsing and—

But no, that wasn't it. She felt arms around her shoulders, and something was being forced onto her face. Fresh air, unadulterated by smoke, shocked her lungs, bringing on a spasm of ragged coughs. She wasn't consciously walking now, but she felt herself moving, being carried.

Then, she was on the ground. She opened her eyes, but the tears made the world look like a giant kaleidoscope.

A voice came to her: "Can you understand me?"

She nodded, because she couldn't talk; a fresh wave of coughs kicked her lungs into reverse. She pawed at her face.

"No, no. Just relax. You're okay; this mask will give you oxygen. We'll leave it on for a few minutes."

Canada tried to nod, but kept her eyes closed and put her head back. Obviously, she was outside now, and safe. The fire department had arrived.

After a few minutes, she opened her eyes again. Once more, the world swam through the tears, but it was better; she could make out the blue sky above her. She sat up and looked around her. She was on the ground, near the back of an ambulance. A paramedic saw her sit up and rushed over.

"Take it easy. You might be a bit light-headed."

"I'm fine," Canada croaked, then coughed more. She felt as if she were going to hack up a whole lung at any moment.

"We'll take you in, run a few tests to find out how much smoke you got in your lungs, along with who knows what else."

"No, really, I'm okay."

"Somehow, I thought you'd say that. You'll have to sign a form for me." She handed a *Refusal of Care* form to Canada on a clipboard, then hesitated. "People said you went into the building and pulled him out."

"I guess so." Canada had almost signed her own name to the form, but of course that would be stupid. She thought for a moment, then signed *Lisa Harper*. Let her deal with the mess, if one came about. She smiled as she thought of this, handing the form back to the paramedic and smiling magnanimously.

"I think he'll probably be fine, but we'll definitely be taking him in." The paramedic nodded to a nearby stretcher, where Canada recognized the form of the young man she'd dragged out of the building.

Canada stood. Her legs wobbled for a few seconds before she caught her balance. Her lungs felt as if they were filled with lava, but she was already doing better.

The young man began to stir. "Stay right here," the paramedic said to Canada before turning away and going back to him.

Canada nodded, then felt someone else step up to her. She turned her head to see who it was. Lisa.

"That was stupid," Lisa said, unconsciously rubbing her nose. Canada wasn't sure whether she was referring to the earlier punch or her trip inside the burning apartment building. Maybe both.

"That's what we're here for, isn't it?" Canada asked, then cleared her throat. It tasted like the old rocks at the bottom of a campfire.

"Killing ourselves? No," Lisa said. "*Now* we start what we came here to do."

"That doesn't include saving people?"

Lisa narrowed her eyes. "Of course it does. Don't you see? We knew this was going to happen, thanks to the Network, and we managed to evacuate the building. Only a few people stayed behind." Lisa glanced over at the young man on the stretcher.

"Stayed behind why?"

Lisa shrugged. "You'd have to ask him. But my guess is, he was one of the ones cooking."

"Cooking what?"

"Meth. You should know all about that, being in Montana. Meth lab exploded on the second floor. My guess is, your little friend over there had something to do with it."

"But . . ." Canada couldn't think of a response.

A van with an NBC logo parked down the street, and Lisa nodded toward it. "Showtime."

"The news van?"

"We're here for PR." Lisa looked down at her, shook her head. "'Course, some folks would rather be part of the fire department. Don't worry; I've got it covered."

Canada stood. "I'm good," she said.

Lisa looked her up and down, then huffed. "Fine. See that guy over across the street, walking up to the other news crew?"

Canada looked. "Guy in the Buddy Holly glasses?"

"That's Doug Anders. He's the lead operative on this assignment. It's his turn to baby-sit you for a while."

Lisa walked off, approaching the newly-arrived news team. Canada saw a fake smile bloom across the woman's face as she got closer to the newspeople.

Canada wiped off her own face as best as she could, wishing for a mirror, ran her fingers through her hair, and walked—a bit unsteadily—toward the guy in Buddy Holly glasses. He was watching as the television crew recorded a clip of the burning building.

Canada cleared her throat, stifled another cough. "Umm, hi. I'm—"

"The newbie. I can tell. I'm Doug Anders. So far as you know." He held out his hand, and Canada shook it. He noticed the soot and dirt all over her. "Gotta love a woman who gets into her work so much."

Canada blushed, although she didn't quite know why.

"Relax," Doug continued. "I'll show you the ropes. First rule: you don't ever appear on camera. But that doesn't mean you can't be part of the story. Lisa, I see, is talking with the Channel 8 folks, and we got Channel 5 here doing some b-roll." He pointed at the cameraman recording footage of the fire. "Here's an information sheet. I'll go head off the PIO if you'll talk to Julie from the newspaper." He nodded at a short man with balding hair, dressed in a uniform.

"PIO?"

"Public Information Officer. Works for the police department. He's not very good; new position for him. Soon he'll figure out he needs to be controlling the news crews and journalists, and he'll give 'em the old 'no comment' routine and tell 'em he's going to set up a news conference tomorrow." Doug held up another copy of the information sheet. "We'd rather not wait. People should know about meth labs, the dangers."

Doug started walking without waiting for a response. Canada pulled a lock of red hair behind her ear, wished again for a mirror, and followed him.

"Julie, sorry to see you for something like this," he said to the newspaper reporter as they approached.

The reporter looked at Doug, then at Canada and back to Doug again. "That's why I'm here," she said a bit hesitantly.

"Oh, sorry," Doug said. "I haven't introduced you. This here is Franny Glass, who's just started working with us. Does a fair amount with the fire department, as you can see. She was inside the building, and has a few interesting things to tell you."

Julie looked at Canada again. Canada pulled a lock of hair behind her other ear, returning the other woman's gaze.

"Oooh, look," said Doug, ever cheerful. "Looks like the 2 News Crew is here. I'm sure they'd love to talk to our good friend Franny here. Come on," he said as he grabbed Canada's hand and started to pull her away.

"No, wait," said Julie from the newspaper.

"Okay, then," Doug said. He was looking at the PIO, who was fast approaching. "I'm just going to step to the side here and talk with a few folks from the police department. Be right back." Doug took two steps and intercepted the PIO, then pulled him to the side for a conversation.

The newspaper reporter looked back to Canada. "Well, let's hear what you have, Franny," she said. "Before Doug carts you off to the TV vultures." She offered a bitter smile.

Canada nodded, looked back to the apartment building. She had a major headache coming on, and her lungs felt as if they'd been shredded. "Um, well, this fire started with an explosion," she offered.

"A bomb?" Julie asked, her interest flaring.

"No, no." Canada suddenly became aware of the paper Doug had thrust into her hand. She looked at the headline that said, METH: AN AMERICAN EPIDEMIC, then handed the sheet to Julie. "It was a meth lab," she said simply.

## 12

LATE IN THE EVENING, Canada sat in the back of a black van with Doug, waiting as he typed on his computer. She had no idea what he was working on, but she felt like a TV cop doing late-night surveillance. She tried not to breathe deeply, as her lungs still burned from the apartment fire earlier in the day.

"What's with the black vehicles?" she asked. "In the movies, you government guys are always in white cars, and your vans are disguised as some local exterminator's vehicle or something."

Doug looked up at her and smiled, the phosphorous glow of his computer screen bathing his face in a ghostly radiance. For a second, it reminded her of Our Lady back in Butte, and Canada felt a pang of regret. She wouldn't be seeing Butte again anytime soon. "Two things," he said. "One, this ain't the movies, sunshine. Two, it's not 'you guys,' it's 'we.' You drank the Kool-Aid."

"Charming way of putting it."

He smiled, turning his attention back to the laptop's screen. "Late news should be on any minute now," he said, pulling up a screen. "I've got a live webcast."

Canada nodded, going silent as Doug typed in a few more keystrokes, hit the touchpad on his laptop, and pulled up one more screen. "Two of the locals are on now; the other two hit the air at ten o'clock." He toggled between the two broadcasts. "You prefer Channel 2 or Channel 5?" Canada shrugged, and he continued. "Channel 2.

Good choice. That Jonathan Rogers, well, there's an anchorman with a face you can trust, huh?" He tapped the screen with a finger as the newscast intro played, watching for a few seconds.

"Hey, you got any money?" he asked.

"A little," she said. "My 'traveling cash.'"

"Good enough. Bet you five bucks we're the top story on both nine o'clock casts. If it bleeds, it leads."

"But there wasn't any bleeding."

"What are you, a literalist? It's an expression. Shhhh, we're on."

Doug stared at the screen intently as a middle-aged man with chiseled features and impeccable hair took his cue and began to speak. A graphic labeled him as *Jonathan Rogers*.

"Good evening," Jonathan Rogers said on the computer screen. "Our top story tonight: A local apartment complex goes up in flames when a meth lab explodes. Two News Crew reporter—"

"That's one," Doug said as he brought the other feed forward. The lead anchor on this channel was a younger woman with brunette hair, in the midst of her lead story.

"—been talking with fire crews all afternoon and evening, and she joins us now live at the scene. Good evening, Tori."

The newscast showed a young African-American woman standing at the scene of the fire. "Good evening, Heather. As fire crews sort through the burning ruins behind me, all indications point to a meth lab as the source of the explosion, probably on the second floor. The fire and police departments have released no official statements yet, but a news conference is scheduled for tomorrow morning at ten to—"

Doug shut the lid of the laptop suddenly. "Didn't I tell you? Those PIOs are the same everywhere. Don't comment at all during the story, set up a press conference the next day. Oh, and you owe me five bucks."

"I didn't agree to the bet."

Crouched, Doug began making his way toward the front of the van. "So you really are a literalist. Ah, well. Maybe you can buy me a drink at the airport." He slid behind the wheel of the van and turned around. "Come on," he said, patting the seat next to him. "Buckle up for safety." He started the van and waited while Canada slid into the seat next to him, then pulled away from the curb and into traffic.

"Mini Apple tomorrow, eh?" he said as he pulled up to the first stoplight.

"What?"

"Minneapolis. Your next assignment."

"Oh, yeah. I guess. I mean . . . you know what? I didn't know that. How did you?"

"Your GPS in the car. Next destination is always on your readout."

"And where's the car?"

"I took care of it."

"What about you?" she asked.

"What about me?"

"Where you going next?"

He smiled. "Sorry, that's on a 'need to know' basis."

"Oh . . . okay. I, uh—"

"Nah, I'm just yanking your newbie chain. I'm headed out to the California coast, and I think I'll actually be there for a few days. Interstate pileup."

They traveled in silence for a while, then Canada spoke. "Can I ask you a question about the news stories back there?"

"Sure. We got about a twenty-minute drive to the airport."

"We just say that stuff, and the press runs with it? Don't they have to verify the information?"

Doug chuckled as he changed lanes. "'Course they do. Typical journalistic standard on a story like this is independent verification from two different sources."

"Okay, so who was the other source?"

Doug turned and batted his eyes theatrically at her.

"You?"

"Or Lisa, maybe. Heard you met her. Plus we had maybe three or four deep spooks, and a few ghost ops, of course."

"Deep spooks? Ghost ops?"

"Deep spooks are people working the case who aren't identified to others. You and me, we're spooks, just not deep spooks. Ghost ops are—"

"The shadows."

"The shadows? That's what you call them?"

"Yeah," she said. "You call them ghosts. And us spooks."

He smiled. "Yeah. I'm a clever one."

"So that's it, then? We just fly in to talk to the media, then trot off to our next destination."

"In and out. There's a lot of stories out there. I do have to tell you one thing though," Doug said, his tone turning serious. "You have to watch your back. Our ghosts and spooks are good, and the network moves fast, but . . . it sounds like you have a baddie after you."

"I heard that already."

"And you'll hear it again. I'm serious. We're doing good things— protecting people, spreading the word about dangers, the whole Justice League of America speech. You should be proud of that. But you should also be careful, because this guy is bad."

"The golem guy, you mean."

He nodded. "Try to be unpredictable. Don't keep schedules, shake things up. Don't just sit in your hotel—keep moving, like a shark. Make like a mako."

Canada shivered, chilled by Doug's sudden turn to seriousness. She needed to change the subject. "Okay, got it. So tell me what's in Minneapolis."

Doug checked his rearview mirror as he merged into Interstate traffic. "Serial killers," he said nonchalantly.

At the Husky Truck Center just outside of Bismarck, the thing calling himself Keros approached a truck with Alberta plates—a red
Peterbilt hauling boxed freight. The dark-skinned driver was making
his way around the trailer, doing a final check before hitting the
road; the big red Peterbilt idled, its diesel engine chattering. Keros
had been watching this particular driver, had picked him inside the
travel center's diner. The turban-wearing driver, whom Keros recognized as Indian, had caught a few looks from other truckers in the
diner, but ignored those looks and took his time eating.

Keros liked that. Liked a man who wouldn't be intimidated by
unfamiliar surroundings. And so, when the driver paid for his meal
and walked out the door, Keros followed. He had expected to see
Canadian plates on the driver's rig. Many Asian and Middle Eastern
drivers had signed on as over-the-road carriers with Canadian trucking firms; few American firms wanted turban-wearing drivers hauling their freight.

He stood beside the driver's side door to the big Peterbilt and
waited for the driver to work his way back around. Soon, the driver's
head popped around the front of the rig and, even though Keros
detected a slight hitch in the step, maybe even a limp, he continued
his approach without hesitation.

Yes, he liked this driver very much.

"Evening," Keros said as the driver approached.

"Good evening," the driver said, and Keros recognized the
accent immediately.

"Punjab?" Keros asked the driver.

The driver narrowed his eyes, looked back. "I am," he said war-
ily, but not fearful. "And how do you know such a thing?"

"Your accent."

"So you have heard the accent before. You have traveled to India?"

"Traveled many places. Looking to do a bit more traveling right now. Where you headed?"

"I must be in Chicago Wednesday morning," the Punjab driver said, speaking with the artificial formality so many Middle Easterners had learned in their ESL classes. Keros was impressed; this man had a recognizable accent, to be sure, but his English was quite good.

"I'm headed to Minneapolis. Love to be there in the morning, if I could."

"You would like to come with me?"

"Yes."

"Please be my guest." The driver bowed, then motioned for him to go to the other side of the rig.

Keros walked around the truck, taking in the deep, earthy smell of the diesel exhaust. He enjoyed this smell; it reminded him of his time in the Middle East, near the oil wells. He climbed onto the passenger side runner, opened the door, and swung himself up into the cab. "*Bhala Hove*," he said to the driver.

The driver turned and smiled. "Your Punjabi is excellent," he said. "And you are most welcome."

Keros smiled. "I see you have a slight limp, my friend," he said, adopting a hint of formality with his own English to put the driver more at ease. "May I ask how you were injured?"

"Ah," said the driver. "An old war wound. The Pakistanis, you see. They don't know how to stay in Pakistan."

"I know it well."

"The injury is several years old. I feel it most often when a storm is approaching. You know this feeling?"

Keros smiled, gazed out the window at the side mirror. He let his eyes flare red for a few moments, two flashes of crimson in the darkness. "Oh, a storm is most certainly coming, my friend," he said, smiling as he watched his red eyes glow. "A very big storm is coming."

## 13

BUTTE, MONTANA STANDARD
STRING OF LOCAL DISAPPEARANCES BAFFLES AUTHORITIES

August 22—Local law enforcement authorities are investigating a string of unexplained disappearances, but so far have "no solid leads," according to a source inside the Silver Bow County sheriff's office.

In the last month, at least ten Butte residents have seemingly vanished, leaving behind all their possessions: luggage, cars, wallets and purses, and in at least two cases, even the clothing they were wearing. "Two people were last seen at the Copper Camp Inn," said the *Standard*'s source at the sheriff's office, who wished to remain anonymous. "We found clothes, covered in some kind of soot or ash, but no indications of burning or scorch marks on the clothes or anywhere in the room." Authorities describe similar scenes in other cases, including a woman whose wrecked car was found with clothing in the front seat.

So far, authorities have refused to talk publicly about the incidents, or even officially acknowledge a connection. "In a city of Butte's size, a handful of people disappear each year," Sheriff Grant Crowley said in a recent press release. "Most of these end up being explained as we dig into the pasts of the people in question. Usually, if someone runs, he or she has a good reason for running."

The sheriff's office also urged residents to take this opportunity to warn children about the dangers of talking to strangers and teach them strategies to avoid possible abductions.

## 14

THE SUN WAS BRIGHT AND HOT already, but the air was still heavy with morning mist. Canada sat in the parking garage of the Minneapolis/St. Paul airport, listening to the low idle of her rented SUV—a black four-wheel-drive monstrosity she wished she could take off-road back home. She looked over at the GPS unit, studied the address it displayed on the screen. After a few moments, the colors blurred, and she felt tears leaking from her eyes.

She turned off the GPS, killed the engine, and leaned her head back.

A voice came from the passenger seat. "Hello, Princess."

She smiled painfully, yet didn't move her head or open her eyes.

"Rough night?" the voice asked.

"I've had better," she said. She opened her eyes and peeked at the seat next to her. The familiar ebb and flow of her father's shadow occupied the seat. She let out a big sigh, puffing at her bangs. "What are you doing here?" she asked.

"Thought I'd be your local contact for this one," her father said. "I heard you and Lisa didn't hit it off so well."

Canada put the SUV into gear and made her way from the garage. "Oh, I don't know about that. I think I made a pretty big impression."

"On her nose."

"You got it." They made it out of the airport, found the right highway, and accelerated into traffic.

"Ah, you can take the girl out of Butte," her father said.

"Yeah, yeah. She deserved it, trying to push me around like that. Didn't even try to help anyone inside the building."

"She made sure those who wanted safety were already gone."

"Look, let's just forget it and focus on the next . . . the next . . . um, assignment." The GPS beeped, letting her know she needed to take the next exit. She looked down at the display. "We're headed somewhere outside of St. Paul."

"An old industrial section. You'll like St. Paul. Good, honest blue-collar town. It'll remind you of home."

"Butte is good, but I wouldn't go as far as honest." She took a deep breath, then continued. "Okay, I'm ready to be the hero and all that. Let's go nab ourselves a serial killer or two."

"We will, eventually."

She looked over at the seat. Her father had moved into the deep shadows under the car dash, away from the bright sun bathing the front seats. "What do you mean by 'eventually'?"

"I don't think we'll be stopping any of them yet—we're close on a couple, but not quite there."

"Close on a couple? So how many are there, exactly?"

"Exactly? Hard to say. Three active that we know of here in the metro area."

"But if we don't really know where they are in Minneapolis, and if we're not really able to stop them right now, I'm here because . . ."

"You're here because you're learning. Like last night, you'll be working with a few local operatives, getting your feet under you. Talking to some media folks, maybe, distributing some information. Then, you'll be going out to the San Fran tonight—a big freeway pileup will happen out there tomorrow."

Canada paused. "But if we know there's going to be a huge pileup tomorrow, why can't we change it now? I mean, you, we, whatever, probably have contacts with the California Highway Department. Close that section of highway, tell people it's under construction."

"I hear what you're saying. But the thing about all this is: You don't mess with fate. If something's supposed to happen, you have to let it happen."

The GPS bleeped, indicating another upcoming turn. Canada shook her head, frustrated. "So what good is it knowing this stuff ahead of time? I mean, you—the shadows—can tell us when stuff is going to happen, but we never seem to be able to do anything about it. So why bother?"

"Just because you can change something doesn't mean you should. Believe me, we've tried to change the course of events, but . . . ever hear of something called the Butterfly Effect? Each and every event has this ripple effect on the rest of existence. Thing is, if you remove something that's supposed to happen, you always cause a bigger splash, and bigger ripples. Fate, she's a real tough broad: if she wants a pint of blood from you and you don't give it to her willingly, she'll find a way to take a quart."

"So you're saying preventing some of these things would actually make it worse?"

"Look at 9/11, the war in Iraq. Tragedies, right?"

"Sure."

"A whole group of the guys on those planes—six of them—lived together in an apartment while they were planning that. And they were supposed to die from a gas leak in their apartment on September 10."

Canada furrowed her brow. "You mean—"

"Yeah, the day before it all came down. One of our operatives—a new recruit like you—cut the gas to the apartment. He saved half a dozen, for twenty-four hours anyway, but ended up killing five thousand the next day. If I had to guess, I'd say the whole 9/11 thing would have fallen apart, somehow, someway, if those guys had died when they were supposed to."

Canada went quiet for a few moments. "I saved a guy from the apartment building yesterday."

"I know."

"So you think something major is going to happen now? Like he's going to go on a rampage and kill dozens of people?"

"That, I don't know. Even what we *do* know, as shadows, is selective. We don't get to pick all the pieces."

"But then, why do anything at all? I mean, why try to stop these serial killers, why bust the terrorists in Seattle? How do we know what's too much, what's pushing the envelope?"

"It's all too complex to explain right now. In the shadow world, we can sense what should be changed—what *can* be changed—and what can't. And anyway, we're here."

Canada put the black sedan into park and looked at the disintegrating tenement in front of them. Its best days were long behind it; bricks were crumbling to dust, and several windows were cracked and broken.

"Charming neighborhood," she said.

"Good base of operations. No one would think to look in a place like this." Above, the clouds of an approaching thunderstorm began to blot out the sun. Canada leaned forward and peered at the clouds through the windshield, surprised. Just a few minutes ago, the whole sky had been bright blue. The air smelled like dried mud or clay, which made her think the rain was certainly going to come soon.

She saw movement on the seat next to her, and turned to see the shadow sliding through the crack at the bottom of the car door. She stared at the door for a moment before opening her own.

Her shoes clicked on the asphalt as she walked to the front door of the building. Odd, no one seemed to be around; it was as if the building were a shadow itself. A ghost.

She tried the front door, jarring loose some dust as she rattled it. Locked. "Oooh, yeah. Gotta keep the riffraff out of a high-class establishment such as this," she muttered.

Abruptly, her father's shadow materialized on the ground next to her again, free to move under the cloud cover. "Call 602 on the building phone."

"And say what?"

"How about 'Let me in'?"

"No secret password or anything, huh?" She pressed the button for 602; within a few seconds she was surprised to hear a response buzz through the speaker.

"Yeah?" the tinny voice asked.

"I think you're expecting a visit," Canada said.

After a few moments, she heard the buzz and grabbed for the door. The inside of the building did nothing to contradict Canada's first impression. As she walked across the stained carpet, she felt loose floorboards sagging. She passed a tattered couch in a small sitting area and made her way to the elevator, then pushed the call button.

"Elevator's broken. Gotta take the stairs." She turned to look at the voice, saw the back of a figure walking down the first floor hallway.

"Thanks," she called to the figure's back, and the man cocked his hand in the air in acknowledgment, even though he neither stopped nor turned.

The stairs were next to the elevator, and the bannister at least felt solid when she grabbed it. On the wall next to her, she saw a shadow moving. "One advantage to being a shadow, huh? Stairs are much easier."

"There are many advantages," a woman's voice said, and Canada sprung back in surprise, realizing the shifting shadow wasn't her dad. She continued climbing, noticing shadows sliding all around her on the walls and steps. The shadows creeped her out, but she forced herself to act calm. This was her job now, and, well, she was working with her father again. That, and making the world a better place. Unless, of course, she was doing too much and actually making the world worse.

She crossed the stoop for the sixth floor and allowed herself a final breath before moving down the hall. What number was it again?

"You there, Daddy?" she asked. No answer, even though she could still see a few shadows wheeling around her. Okay, so he had something else to do. Wait, 602. That was the number she was looking for.

She began walking down the hallway and noticed a door open. A man came out of the room, tall and lean but somehow puffy-faced. His complexion was a milky white, reminding her, in many ways, of her good friend Goth-Girl Lisa. Maybe she should try to fix up the two of them. They could have vampire children and be a very happy family.

"Six-oh-two, I presume?" she asked as she approached the man.

"Actually, you can just call me Harold. Harold Bleecker." He smiled at his own humor, held out his hand. Canada grasped his hand and wasn't surprised to find it cold. "Most people just call me Bleecker, for whatever reason."

Canada pasted on a smile. She guessed most people called the guy Bleecker because that was a perfect description of him. In Butte, anyway, he'd definitely be a Bleecker; hard to get away from your last name there, unless you had a colorful nickname.

"Most people call me Can—ah, to tell you the truth, I'm not sure what my name's supposed to be right now."

"I've had days like that. Come on in."

Canada stepped through the doorway to room 602 and immediately warned herself not to touch anything she didn't have to. She wasn't much of a housekeeper herself (well, okay, she'd heard the word *hoarder* more than a few times, and realized she fit that label), but this room was . . . grungy. It was as if a thin film of grit covered everything. Maybe from the plaster flaking off the walls.

Bleecker obviously read her face and launched into an explanation. "We're a bit messy here, so sorry for that. But, you know, we don't spend all that much time here. Just a gathering place, really, to trade information. We do most of our work out on the streets."

She did her best to ignore the surroundings. Hey, she'd been on the blast crew once, a long time ago. Boring holes was a lot dirtier and grittier than this place. No sweat.

Two other men were in the room, both of them staring at her.

Bleecker made quick introductions. "This here's Shaw," he said, pointing to a short, squat man sitting at a makeshift card table. "And over there on the couch is Connors." Connors was bald, lanky.

"Evidently you guys don't buy into the first-name basis thing," she said, trying a bit of a joke.

Connors took the bait, standing up from the couch. "Best if you don't know our first names. You understand. And you are . . ."

"Not big on first names myself," she said. "For now, just call me Doe."

"As in scared deer in the headlights, or as in Jane?" asked Bleecker, looking at her with a grin forming on his mouth and in his eyes. She heard one of the others let out a soft chuckle.

She returned his gaze, hard, let a bit of rising anger steam away some of her fear. "As in the sound a man makes when he gets kicked hard in a bad spot," she said, holding him in a stare-down. After a few seconds, he looked away; she turned to the other two men, smiling, and they looked away as well. Now she had some control, which was good because she was terrified. Something about this was so wrong.

On the wall in front of Bleecker, the men had stapled and taped numerous news clippings about area murders, along with photos of crime scenes. Photos of dead bodies. Dead women, more specifically.

Canada forced her eyes away from the photos and addressed Bleecker. "Looks like you guys have been busy in here."

Shaw stood and moved away from the card table, went to the wall and posted a new clipping he'd just cut from the paper. POLICE REFUSE TO COMMENT ON SERIAL KILLER INVESTIGATIONS, the headline of the article read. Shaw studied the wall as he spoke. "Gotta keep it for posterity, you know."

She tilted her head at the wall, still not letting herself look at all of it. "What info do you have for me?"

Shaw spoke. "Check this out. All these victims, see how their eyes have been removed? We should go to the media, call him 'The Optometrist.' This one doesn't seem to have a real signature yet, other than the drop zones: city parks. Maybe 'The Park Predator' or something—"

"You're giving each of them nicknames?"

The three men all stopped and stared at her as if she'd said the oddest thing they'd ever heard.

"'Course," Connors answered, staring at the wall again. "That's part of the whole process. Ever hear of the Boston Strangler? The Green River Killer? Zodiac? BTK?"

Canada swallowed, not liking the direction this conversation was going. She gave a slow nod.

"So tell me any of their real names," Connors said to Canada.

She cleared her throat. "Umm . . . one of them was Ramirez, I think."

"Bzzz. You're thinking of Richard Ramirez, one of the Hillside Stranglers in the L.A. area."

Shaw broke in. "The name's all part of the game, you see? How you position it in the media."

Connors nodded. "You have a meeting scheduled with a reporter from the *Star Trib* in about an hour. You'll need—"

Bleecker didn't have a chance to finish his sentence, because at that moment the front door of the apartment erupted in an explosion of violence. The door didn't simply open, or even rip from its hinges; it seemed to *disintegrate*. With lightning speed, a tall, dark-skinned figure moved into the room, white hair flowing behind him as if in slow motion. But the figure itself didn't move in slow motion; he moved with stunning fluidity, stepping inside, locking his arm behind Connors's head and twisting. Within a fraction of a second, Connors collapsed, and before his limp body hit the litter-strewn floor, the white-haired figure was on Shaw.

Canada's muscles thawed as her brain processed what was happening. This was the man, the *golem* her father and Doug had warned her about. He had come for her, and now she had to get out, had to—

Behind her, she heard glass shattering, and she turned her head toward the sound. Bleecker was breaking the glass in the apartment window, motioning for her to crawl out.

That seemed like a very good idea indeed, since the white-haired man was between her and the front door. She sprinted for the window.

A voice boomed behind her. "You must stop, Candace Mac-Hugh." For a moment that voice, the authority in it, almost did stop her, but then the sheer terror of it had the opposite effect and she knew she had to get as far away as she could.

She wriggled out onto the window ledge, hugging the bricks, looking both ways. A dozen feet away, a rusty fire escape clung pathetically to the side of the building. She looked down, realizing for the first time in her life just how high six stories were, then pressed herself into the bricks as hard as she could and began inching her way down the ledge.

The first few feet weren't bad; she made it to the next window well easily, but then fear started to clamp around her chest. She thought of the pavement, six stories below, and nearly lost her balance.

Careful.

She took a deep breath and made the next stretch of ledge, sliding her feet through the pigeon guano stacked high on the concrete surface. Next window well. Just one more stretch, and she would be at the fire escape.

After another deep breath, she scrambled the last few feet to the fire escape and stepped onto it. It yawed away from the building, teetering for a moment before settling against the bricks again.

Behind her she heard a high scream—a cry of terror and pain she was somehow able to identify as Bleecker's—cut impossibly short.

She was out of time; she needed to do a final sprint down this fire escape and somehow make it to the bottom. The scream suddenly made the idea of splattering on the pavement sound much more appealing than facing the—the thing—that had burst into the apartment.

She was down two flights now, her feet barely touching the iron steps as the whole escape creaked and groaned, swaying with her movements.

Third floor. He had to be out the window now. Had to. But she couldn't look back. Second floor. The escape was seriously swaying, and she heard bolts popping out of the brick. First floor. The whole structure was falling, and she held on, somehow riding the collapsing iron to the ground as the escape gave way. She hit the ground and rolled, fully expecting to feel the mangled mass of iron hit and crush her, but miraculously she was clear.

Without realizing it, she'd closed her eyes. She opened them and sprinted toward her car. By some wonderful stroke of fate, the car was parked on the back side of the building. She finally chanced a look back over her shoulder, and felt a low moan escape her lips when she saw something impossible happening.

The white-haired thing, the golem, was outside the window and crawling down the side of the building, face-first. "You must stop, Candace MacHugh!" he screamed again as he reached the ground, and she kicked her feet into high gear to reach her SUV.

She opened the door, jumped in, twisted the key and started it. She rammed the car into drive and floored the accelerator. The tires started to squeal and smoke boiled out from under the front wheel wells, but the car wouldn't move. Why? Why?

A glance in the rearview mirror told her. The white-haired man's face filled the reflection in the mirror, grimacing as he held the vehicle in place.

Impossible. He'd made it to her SUV in just a few seconds, and now he was holding it—*lifting* it by the rear bumper—and yelling something at her.

Her mind wanted to shut down, curl her body into a small ball and pretend none of this was happening. She was in another world, far away from this. A dream, that's what it was. None of this could actually be happening. This was an illusion; soon she would realize it, and this world would fall away and everything would be happy and bright again, and she would go have ice cream with her daddy, who wasn't dead at all but—

Through the terror, an idea struck her. She opened her eyes, glanced in the mirror, saw the contorted face of the white-haired man trying to scream over the squall of the tires burning on the asphalt. She let her foot off the accelerator. The white-haired man continued to scream, and now she could make out a bit of what he was saying.

"—with me. The heart is deceitful above all things, and—"

He adjusted his hands to get a better grip on the bumper. It was the chance Candace had been looking for. She dropped the transmission into reverse and gunned the engine again. The front wheels bit and the vehicle lurched backward against the golem, throwing him to the ground. Before she could stop, the car had thumped over the top of him. She threw it back into drive and hit the accelerator. The SUV groaned as it moved over the white-haired man's body, and then it was free, whipping erratically down the street as all four tires of the AWD were finally on the ground. For the first time she noticed the sharp, acrid tang of the burning rubber tires in her nostrils. She hoped she hadn't damaged them. A flat right now was the last thing she needed, although considering how this morning had started off, it would fit right in.

She glanced back at the body in the rearview mirror. "He's dead," she muttered to herself as she sped away.

"Oh no. You can't kill him. Not that way, at any rate." It was her father's voice, but she kept her eyes focused on the receding reflection in the rearview mirror.

Now she was mad. "Nice of you to show up. Now maybe you can shut up for a minute. Of course I killed him, I—"

"Turn now," her father's voice said, too calmly.

She hit her brakes and screeched around the corner. But even as the SUV plowed around the corner, she caught a final glimpse of the white-haired man's body in the mirror.

A final glimpse of it suddenly sitting up.

# 15

CANADA THUNDERED DOWN THE INTERSTATE, worries about a speeding ticket the furthest thing from her mind.

"All right!" she said through gritted teeth as she felt her foot sinking on the accelerator even more. "Who—*what*—is that?"

"The one you've been warned about. The Nameless One. The one who now calls himself Keros, even though he's not really a man."

"And thanks for all your help, by the way."

"I would have helped if I could have."

"Of course you could have. You can—"

"I can do nothing against him."

"Well, that much is obvious." She continued to move and weave among traffic.

"You can slow down now," her father's shadow said. He had returned to the darkest shadows beneath the dash. "He will need to find transportation and I think maybe we can misdirect him from here. Do you have the cell phone we gave you?"

"Yes."

"Now is the time to use it. We will make emergency travel arrangements, change your schedule. Maybe something still on the West Coast. Seattle, I believe."

"To do what?"

"Round up some terrorists."

Canada rolled her eyes. "Excuse me if I don't seem overjoyed about this new job."

"In the meantime I'll see if we can do something to slow him down."

Canada saw—no, *felt*—the shadow slip out of the door and outside the moving car. What happened to him? Did he just drop to the pavement? Maybe so, since the thunderclouds overhead still darkened the sky. No rain yet, though.

After a few moments, Canada sighed and fished through her bag to find the cell phone. She hit the 1 for the preprogrammed number. Immediately, a soothing woman's voice spoke on the line. "Good afternoon, Ms. MacHugh. Have a little trouble in Minneapolis, did we?"

———

Mike Wachholz climbed into the cab of his pickup, the one he called his "Four-by-Ford," fired up the big block 401, goosed the pedal a few times, and listened to the dual exhaust rattle.

He reached out, caressed the dash. "You're the best gal I ever had," he muttered. He looked back at his house, the front screen door still flapping. Didn't surprise him; Tricia was obviously too lazy to pick herself up off the kitchen floor, stop her blubbering, and go close the door behind him.

He threw the truck into reverse, backed up, then rumbled out onto the street. The state liquor store was just down the hill. He was out of Aces High bourbon, and needed a little refill. A little juice for the jaws.

He thought of his miserable lot in life as he drove down the street. Odd jobs here and there after the unemployment ran out. Digging, running errands, that kind of thing. Stupid stuff.

And Tricia. How had he ever ended up with such a pathetic excuse for a wife? She'd seemed so quiet, so attentive at first, but then . . . then he saw those thoughts in her eyes. Saw what she was thinking about him. Looking down on him, like the others.

A long, angry honk rudely interrupted his thoughts, and he swerved to avoid the oncoming car, then laid on his own horn as the lights flashed past him. Lots of stupid drivers around Butte. Couldn't even stay on their own side of the road.

Something was wrong with the old Four-by-Ford. He could smell it. A burning smell. Not really the smell of burning oil, or an overheated engine, or anything like that. This smell wasn't mechanical. More like a wood fire. A barbecue.

Maybe it was just someone firin' up the old 'cue, getting ready to throw a steak on the grill. That sounded pretty good right now.

He noticed a wisp of white smoke curling between his fingers. Odd, he didn't remember lighting up. He pulled his hand off the steering wheel, patted the front pocket of his shirt, checking for the Marlboros. They weren't even there; he'd probably left them on the counter at home. Besides, it was early afternoon, and he really didn't like to hit the cigarettes much until he'd had a little more of that bourbon. The bitterness of Aces High and the bitterness of the dried tobacco, they went together nicely.

Meanwhile, where was that odd burning smell coming from? That smoke on his fingers, for that matter? He pulled his hand away from his pocket and held it in front of his face, taking a few seconds to refocus his eyes.

Well. His hand was a dirty gray, as if he'd been running it through some dry, chalky mud. Kinda flaky. And the smoke was curling around the whole hand. He watched with detached interest as one of the fingers crumbled.

Whoa. Maybe he didn't need any of that jaw juice after all. Maybe that last bottle was enough. Or maybe . . . yeah, this was Tricia. Something she'd done. Maybe poisoned him or something.

He put his hand back on the steering wheel, but the hand

disintegrated, gray ash puffing away from the wheel. His other hand was smoking, too, and he felt his face flushing.

Okay, it was hot this August, but not that hot. He jammed his foot on the brake, brought the Four-by-Ford to a quick stop in the street, then felt something snap inside his pant leg. A few moments later, he watched as his pant leg collapsed.

No more bourbon, he vowed. And definitely no more smokes. He tried to look in the rearview mirror, get a glimpse of himself, but he felt as if his whole body were immobilized. He couldn't move his neck, couldn't move anything.

No, wait, his neck moved now. But not in a direction he'd ever experienced. It folded back, straight back, and he was looking at the ceiling of the Four-by-Ford, watching as smoke and ash floated above him like a small cloud of mosquitoes.

Tricia would pay for this when he woke up. This was a dream, of course, one she'd brought on by slipping a Mickey into his whiskey. He knew this for a fact now. Yes, Tricia would have to answer for this when he woke up, would have to answer for everything: the holier-than-thou thoughts, the lost job, the Four-by-Ford rusting away to nothingness. She'd brought all of this on him. All of it. Oh yes, she would do some explaining.

But Mike Wachholz didn't wake up.

## 16

SIX HOURS AFTER RUNNING OVER a vengeful Jewish Frankenstein, Canada deboarded a charter flight in Washington state and
headed up the 405 toward Everett. Once again, she was in a black
vehicle—this time another sedan.

Surprisingly, she felt better. She'd had time to think about all of
it, and it was making more sense. Not total sense, to be sure, but
more sense. Her father *had* warned her about . . . about the
golem . . . and she went into this with her eyes wide open.

Well, maybe not wide open. But open. Mostly.

She did feel bad for losing her temper, exploding at him like
that. He'd understand, sure; she'd inherited that Irish temper from
his side of the family after all. So she wasn't worried about him for-
giving her. Still, she felt she was somehow tarnishing their relationship—her memory of their relationship—by yelling at him like that.
For eleven long years, she had dreamed of someday talking to her
father, getting a chance to be Daddy's little girl again. She'd been
given that chance, and within the span of a few days, she'd gone
ballistic on him.

Now her anger seemed more a response to being terrified. She
could understand why Doug and her dad had been so serious about
the golem. Something about his mere presence gripped Canada's
stomach and twisted. Even now, just thinking of him, replaying her
narrow escape, she felt her whole body tensing.

Yes, she'd do whatever was needed from now on to avoid another run-in with him. And she would make up things with her father, show him she was on his side, by acing this next assignment.

The GPS beeped, indicating an upcoming turn. This would be like the dry-run assignment, where she helped the little girl find her daddy. Rounding up terrorists, that was a Very Good Thing. Talk to the news? You bet; she was a natural talker, knew how to spin a good story.

She remembered all the times she'd tried to talk her father into taking her to Columbia Gardens. Any little accomplishment she'd magnify into a reason—and most times he'd agree.

The sights and sounds flooded back to her once again. Cotton candy and corn dogs. The scream of kids on the rides. Daddy's hand folded around hers, big and warm, making her feel safe.

And the go-round.

Always the first stop when they visited Columbia Gardens. Daddy bought tickets, and they walked down the midway, past the swirls and colors and noises and excitement to the go-round.

Daddy always put her on a horse, swinging her up in his strong arms, placing her in the slick formed saddle, and keeping his arm draped around her back. Up and down, around and around the go-round went, and she never wanted the ride to end. She never wanted to get off, because it was perfect, just perfect, riding that go-round horse and feeling his arm around her. Nothing could reach her there, nothing.

Another beep from the GPS. She was approaching her final destination now.

She sighed. Unfortunately, the gardens were gone. The precious copper beneath it had been its demise; mining companies dismantled the entire complex and turned it into another open pit mine— an open pit where, oddly enough, Canada had worked for a couple years.

Now, even the copper and the mining were gone. All those memories tied to one place.

She pulled her car to the curb and shut off the engine. She rolled down the window, breathing in the salt-tinged air, feeling its cool dampness across her face.

It was a beautiful neighborhood: green lawns, white homes, two-car garages, an occasional dog barking. In fact, the only thing unusual about this cul-de-sac was the fact that three black sedans, and one black van were parked on the street—along with a couple of police cruisers.

She sensed something happening on the seat next to her as she watched the house. Without turning her head, she spoke. "Hi, Daddy."

"Rough day at the office?"

"Might need to ask for a raise."

"At least you're keeping your sense of humor."

Canada watched for activity on the street, but saw none. "Looks like the party's just about ready to start," she said.

"Just about. Waiting for a few folks. Some media."

She nodded, thought about rolling up her window again, then decided she wanted to let the breeze wash through the car. "I just want to say . . . I'm sorry about earlier. I was upset, and—"

"Don't worry about it. You're learning, and this is a lot to bite off at once."

"I suppose. It's just, I can't help feeling like this is all wrong. For me, anyway. I mean, the mining—being on the blast crew—that felt so *right*. I felt so connected to you, in some way, following in your footsteps like that. Even though you weren't around. And now, so many years later, I'm following you again, and I have you sitting here next to me—okay, not sitting, but you know what I mean—but it's so *odd*, so unbelievable. And I just needed to let off some steam. I guess I just don't want to make any mistakes."

The shadow of her father waxed and waned for a few moments before speaking again. "We all make mistakes. Too late to make up for them. You just move on to the next mistake."

"Aren't you quite the optimist nowadays?"

"What I'm trying to say is: you look behind you all the time, you never see where you're going."

She smiled. "Now *that* sounds like the Bud MacHugh I know and love."

"We're doing good here," the shadow said. "Helping round up some terrorists. We managed to get local law enforcement to wait, and we have media coming to capture the roundups. You'll be the liaison with the local media. You have some press releases and other information to hand out—check that big dossier in the back."

Canada turned to fish the briefcase from the back seat, balanced it on the armrest next to her, and popped the top. Several copies of a press release lay in the bottom of the case. The headline read, TERROR CELL DISMANTLED IN SEATTLE AREA; OTHERS AT WORK?

The shadow continued. "You were upset back there in Minnesota. That's natural. But you have a job to do, as well. It's not easy, but it's important—we have to get these stories out there. The people have to see them."

She nodded, still looking down the street, wondering absently how her father saw her. How any shadow saw anything, heard anything, sensed anything. They had no eyes to see, no ears to listen, no skin to touch.

As she sat considering this, another police cruiser pulled onto the cul-de-sac, followed by a white van with a huge logo painted on the side. KOMO NEWS FIVE, the logo said.

The police cruiser flashed its lights, and motion erupted everywhere. Suddenly, officers started pouring out of the black sedans and the black van, some of them wearing body armor and face shields, most of them advancing with drawn guns.

She looked at the house and saw two officers scaling the fence to go around the back.

"Time to go," her father's voice said. The shadow slid out of the car and was gone, leaving her alone again.

She pulled the file folder out of the briefcase, read through the press release quickly a few times, then glanced back to the house. The KOMO News van had parked on the street and elevated its giant satellite dish on a boom; bright lights bathed a reporter doing her standup in front of the camera.

Canada opened her car door and got out. Behind her, she saw another news van turning into the cul-de-sac. Time to go to work. She walked up to the second news van, this one from KING TV, and waited for it to park. A woman with auburn hair stepped out of the passenger side of the van, dressed in dark blue. A fellow redhead. She'd start with her.

"Hi," she said, approaching the reporter, who was busy smoothing her clothes and peeking into the side mirror of the van, clumsily digging through her purse while she examined her face. "I—we—have some information here about today's operation," she said, holding out a copy of the press kit.

The redheaded reporter continued digging through her purse, brought out a tube of lipstick, and applied it to her lips before turning to look at Canada. "Thanks," she said, grabbing the folder from Canada and scanning through it. Her brow furrowed as she read. "Good, good. Looks like names and photos and such, and we can hopefully get some footage." She looked toward the house, where her camera operator was shooting footage of the exterior. "They're in there right now, aren't they? I mean, the police?"

"Yes."

She looked back at Canada. "And you are?"

"Helping," she said. "All the names and places will check when you verify."

"When I verify where?"

"That's your job."

The reporter continued to read. "You guys have obviously been working on this for a long time. So why did I just get an anonymous call this morning? I could have been working with you all along on this. I would have kept it quiet until—"

"Sorry. I just got called in on it this morning myself." Canada started to walk away.

"Wait, wait," the redheaded reporter said. "Where you going?"

Canada nodded at the other news team.

"Look. I, uh . . . if you could hold off sharing this with them. In this business, you know, we're all about exclusives. Maybe . . . maybe we could put you on camera, have you make a few comments about the investigation."

"Sorry. Share and share alike."

A commotion came from the house, and the reporter spun to look. Police were leading people out of the house now, young men who looked to be of Middle Eastern descent. They looked frightened, wide-eyed, stained, and sweaty as if they were deer in the headlights. But in this instance, the headlights were the bright glare of television news cameras.

The redheaded reporter ran toward the house, Canada's presence forgotten now. Canada looked around, noticing neighbors in their yards gawking; back on the street, another car was parking. An unmarked police car, she guessed. The door opened, and a middle-aged man got out and looked around, taking in all the activity.

"Hello, Mr. PIO," she said to herself as she began walking toward him.

## 17

THAT NIGHT, CANADA SAT IN HER hotel room, cycling through the television channels. The terrorist roundup, of course, was the lead story on all four locals, as well as the national broadcasts. In all, local authorities had taken six young men from Egypt, in America on visas to study at the University of Washington, even though none of them had actually enrolled yet. Three of them lived together in the Everett house where Canada had been several hours before.

She turned off the TV and lay on the bed, staring at the ceiling, feeling suddenly overwhelmed. She'd assumed she'd get used to this, get her feet under her. Get her sea legs, as the sailors said. And granted, it had only been a few days, but the whole thing made her edgy, nervous. Her father had said something about her being a natural at this, but it didn't seem natural at all.

Why?

Absently, she scratched at her right forearm. Ever since this afternoon, she'd noticed a steady itch everywhere. She'd assumed it was the Seattle humidity, making her skin feel tacky, and she'd showered as soon as she checked into her hotel room. Before she had stepped into the shower, she was sure her skin was a tone or two darker. Not tan, exactly. Almost like dirt, really. For a moment, she had flashed back to her days on the blast crew, spending hours in the pit, wiring explosives as dirt and wind cycled around her, finding their way through her clothes and onto her skin. By the end of the day, a thick layer of dust always covered her, and the shower was always her first stop after shift. The company had showers and dressing rooms, but of course the women's showers were always uncrowded—only four or five women on any given shift—and she had the time to take long, hot showers, closing her eyes and letting the warmth cascade over her.

She sighed and stood up, making her way to the bathroom. The earlier shower had helped; she swore her skin looked lighter, healthier, afterward. But now the filth had returned.

She walked to the bathroom and looked in the mirror. Yes, she did seem to be a bit darker, a bit more gray. It made no sense. She'd been in the hotel room since the last shower. Unless, maybe, the air-conditioning system had been releasing some dust and dirt. Sure, that had to be it; she'd experienced that kind of thing before.

She stared at her reflection in the mirror, wishing she were forty pounds lighter. Wishing her hair were not red. Wishing her skin were unfreckled. She deserved something like that, didn't she? After all, she'd had a tough life in Butte. Growing up an Irish redhead. Something about being a redheaded girl on the playground seemed to attract trouble. Following in Daddy's footsteps, working her way into the pit mines. Not many women in those positions, and she'd had to do more than anyone else just to prove she belonged there.

And then her mother, throwing out her father. Her father dying. Eleven long years, she'd spent without him.

On top of that, the mining industry, the very soul of Butte, literally collapsed. But Canada hadn't left. She'd stuck it out, made the best of it, done as much as she could without complaining. So why couldn't fate, whatever, smile on her just once and make her life . . . somehow better? She wasn't sure what would do that, but certainly there was *something*, wasn't there?

She stepped into the shower, turned the water to extra hot,

almost hot enough to burn, and scrubbed at her skin. Amazingly, the gray flakes did come off; she was paying attention, concentrating, and she saw them slide off her skin as the water cascaded over her body.

It wasn't dirt, not really. It was more of a . . . a gauzy kind of film. It was gritty, and ashen, and it enveloped her. But when the hot water hit her skin, the film slid off and down the drain.

She closed her eyes and scrubbed, trying not to think too much about what that meant. She had far too much to think about, and she just wanted to listen to the running water, feel its pressure against her skin, and forget for a few minutes.

Finally, she reached to turn off the water and stepped out of the shower. She grabbed a towel and dried herself as she walked into the other room. She only had one change of clothes—a loose tee shirt and jeans, some hikers which she put on right away. The clothes she'd worn on assignment, a professional suit, hung in the closet. She'd leave the suit when she left this room. At her next destination—wherever that might be—she'd have fresh clothes.

She went to her small duffel and dug through it. These were still clothes she'd brought from Butte. Clothes that had hung in the closet of her trailer. She brought them up to her face and smelled them, the scent reminding her of home. Funny, wasn't it, how she'd never been able to part with so many things in that trailer—never been able to part with that trailer itself—and yet, after a few brief conversations with her father (*her dead father*), she'd willingly left it all behind?

Now, her nerves felt jangly and loose. She wanted to be in the trailer again. Wanted to caress the stacks of newspapers, the piles of laundry. Wanted to sit down in front of the old coffee table, be surrounded by the familiar canyons created by her stacks. Was that so much to ask?

She even wanted to see her mother, speak to her. Odd.

She pushed away thoughts of her mother, unwilling to continue down that path. She didn't *need* to keep these clothes, but she *wanted* to. She had some downtime, hadn't heard where her next assignment was going to take her yet, so she decided she could do some laundry. She'd wash these clothes from home: two pairs of jeans, three tee shirts, a sweatshirt, a light jacket. She'd keep them with her, reminders of everything she'd left behind.

She stuffed the clothes into the duffel, checked to see if she had money—not much coinage, but the hotel would probably have a change machine in the laundry room—grabbed her room key, then went to the front door and opened it.

Keros, his white hair flowing freely, stood at the door.

"Candace Mac—" he began.

Canada slammed the door as she felt panic jamming an ice pick into her gut. No, not just one ice pick. Hundreds of them.

Okay, time to think. Wait, check that. No time to think, time to act. She was on the tenth floor of this building; what could she do? No fire escape to save her this time; the room windows didn't open. She'd already tried them. She could probably throw a chair through one of the windows, but why? She wasn't exactly going to jump ten stories. The white-haired golem outside, maybe. But not her.

Knocks came at the door. *Tap tap tap.* Steady, insistent, but not agitated. She could make out her name again, but the door was muffling whatever else he was telling her.

Think, think, think. Maybe a weapon of some kind. Hit him with a chair. No good; she'd run over him with a car the day before, and he was standing at her door now. What harm could a piece of office furniture do?

Now Canada heard the steady sound of twisting metal, and she looked at the door again. The door handle was turning. It was locked, of course it was locked, but that wasn't stopping him. She saw the handle twisting, moaning as the metal stressed and bent, then popping off and falling to the floor.

Decision time. Now.

She stepped forward and folded her body behind the door as it began to open. It was a stupid idea, really. He'd never fall for it; he'd never just run into the room and—

Immediately after the door opened, Keros spoke again, his voice amazingly calm and authoritative. "The heart is deceitful above all things, Candace MacHugh." Then, he rushed in, heading for the bathroom. Maybe he was drawn by the light and the fan, still on.

It was her chance, and she took it. She slid around the door and out into the hallway, then sprinted for the elevator. No, wait, not the elevator. What was she going to do, wait for it to reach her floor? Well, maybe. She punched the call button, and immediately the doors opened with a *ding*. She jumped inside the elevator, punched the button.

But she wasn't stupid enough to stay on the elevator. She backed out, skidded across the carpet to the stairway door, and burst through. Her instincts, her whole body, told her to go down, to get to ground level and outrun her pursuer, but her mind overruled that instinct. She vaulted up a flight of stairs, crouched on the landing for the eleventh floor.

Out in the hallway, she heard Keros bellowing again, saying her name. How did he know her name, anyway? Then, as she expected, the stairway door burst open. It flew into the bottom step of the flight she'd just scaled, sending chips of concrete flying. Immediately, she heard him descending the stairs.

Good, he'd taken the bait. He thought she was on the elevator, and he was running down the stairs as fast as he could to reach the bottom. She peered over the railing, watching him move. What she saw made her gasp: he was descending each flight in brief seconds, as if his feet weren't even touching the steps. He'd reach the bottom floor before the elevator, there was no doubt about that. Good thing she hadn't jumped on it. Now, if she could just plan her next steps, keep her cool, she could be out of this building. Find her black sedan, make a phone call, hit the road. Wait, she didn't need to find the sedan to make a phone call. She had the cell phone with her. She'd put it in the pocket of her jeans when she slipped them on. That was good.

Far below, she heard Keros bust through the doors to the lobby.

Maybe she should make a call now, try to summon help, let them know she needed to shake Keros. No, that would be wasting what little time she had. The hotel was fifteen stories high, so she just had four more floors to scale before—

She heard a door slam open again. The words she dreaded hearing filtered up to her: "Candace MacHugh!"

So much for the elevator misdirection. Now, she had to keep her head down, figure out her next move. She ran up the steps as fast as she could, taking two at a time. Twelfth floor, thirteenth floor.

Below, she heard movement. Not the click of footsteps. Too fast to be footsteps. She glanced over the railing and was shocked by what she saw. He was already up several flights—maybe even at the eighth floor or so now. Not possible, not humanly possible.

But then, she reminded herself, this Frankenstein monster wasn't human.

She vaulted up the last flight and crashed through the door marked ROOF ACCESS. It wedged open, letting in a strong head wind. Immediately, Canada chose misdirection once again. She left the door wedged open and slipped down the last flight of stairs. She opened the door to the fifteenth floor, pulling it quickly behind her and letting it click shut. She noticed a button in the middle of the door handle. Could she really lock the stairway door? She pushed the button. Evidently, it did lock. Go figure.

The elevator was still out of the question. Especially from the top floor. He could be back at the bottom before she was halfway down. She looked down the hallway and saw three maid carts. Perfect. She ran past the first cart to the second and started looking through its contents. The doorway just to the left of her was open, and Canada could see the maid changing bed linens. She rifled through a few outside pockets stitched into the cart's apron. Her hand grasped what she'd prayed was there . . . a keycard. She hoped it was programmed to open all the rooms.

Behind her, she heard the stairway door shaking, and knew she only had a few more seconds. She didn't think the maid changing the sheets had seen her, so she was probably safe if she just chose a random door. Not the one directly across from the maid, though. That would be too obvious. She sprinted down two more doorways to a room with a *Maid Service Requested* sign on it, flipped it to *Do Not Disturb* and slipped inside. The room was empty.

She latched the door behind her, then slid to the floor, panting, her back braced against the door itself. Her breaths were coming in ragged gasps, threatening to turn to hyperventilation, and she felt tears welling at the corners of her eyes. Stupid, stupid, stupid. She'd been so stupid. Doug had told her—or had it been her father?—she shouldn't stay in any area too long. Keep moving, like a shark. Instead, she'd stayed in this hotel all day, and that laziness had come very close to getting her killed. Just like being out in the pits, getting careless about setting the charge: a delayed detonation would turn you into hamburger.

Still.

Keros hadn't seen her on this floor, she was sure of that. He'd been struggling with the door when she slipped into this room, and he had no way of even knowing, for sure, that she was on this floor. As far as he knew, she could be in any room in this whole hotel. And the maids hadn't seen her, so it wasn't as if they'd be able to point him in her direction.

She was out of options anyway, so she'd have to stay here for a few minutes. She needed to catch her breath. Catch her thoughts. Time to use the phone now? No, she needed to stay quiet.

She waited quietly, calming her breathing, clearing her mind, thinking of nothing. She pictured white static, concentrated on the dull noise, made her body go numb. The tactic worked, and she felt her body, her mind, relaxing.

Finally, after several minutes—five, ten?—she turned her head and pressed her ear to the door. She couldn't hear anything other than the steady thrum of the air-conditioner in the room behind her. She kept her hands on the door and stood, sliding her hands against the door's surface. The door had a fisheye peephole, and she looked through it. Nothing in the hallway.

She put one hand up on the door chain and slid it into the cor-responding slot, took a deep breath, then opened the doorway a crack. Still she saw nothing. She tilted her head, listening. It sounded like the maid a couple doors back was vacuuming now. Nothing else, though.

She closed the door, slid the chain out of its slot. Okay, she was far from home free. She still needed to get out of this hotel, and her creepy friend was probably watching all the exits.

That simply meant she'd have to exit a different building.

She peeked down the hallway both directions, then crept out into the hallway again and hurried back toward the elevators. As she reached the end of the hall, she noticed the knob of the stairway door, lying useless on the floor.

She poked her head into the stairwell, listened for a few seconds, turned and looked toward the roof. Nothing. Canada swallowed hard, trying to keep the bitter, dry taste of fear down, and moved up the final flight to the roof. She didn't want to think too much about what she was going to do; it would be better if she just got it over, did it all in one long act.

She turned slowly as she stood on the roof, feeling the wind whistling through her clothes. Still no sign of the golem. If she had to guess, she'd say he was in the lobby, watching for her.

That's what she was counting on, anyway.

She went to the edge of the building and peered over it. There was another building next to it, but it was several stories shorter. No good. She went to the next edge and stared over. This was better. The adjacent building on this edge was only one story shorter, and the distance between the buildings seemed closer. Maybe five feet. She could jump that, couldn't she? She'd read somewhere the average human could jump her height from a crouch. More than that with a running start. The hotel was a new building, made entirely of blue glass, so she didn't have to worry about a concrete or brick lip. That meant she could get a running start. Plus, since the next-door building was shorter, that would help her distance. She backed up twenty feet and breathed.

She was going to get away from the No Name Man, or whatever she was supposed to call him. Even more than that, though, she was going to become his worst enemy, do everything she could to stop him. He'd made her mad, and she vowed he'd regret it.

Canada took another deep breath, closed her eyes and exhaled. *When you open your eyes, you will start to run*, she told herself.

And she did.

Her eyes flicked open, and instantly she was moving across the smooth surface of the glass building, picking up speed as she raced toward the edge.

And then, she was there. Her mind screamed at her, telling her to jump, so she vaulted from her right leg as she swung her arms forward, launching. She refused to look below her as she jumped, but she could still see it anyway, one-hundred-fifty dizzying feet of nothing but air, and—

Her left leg touched down. She tried to keep her feet, but it was impossible. Immediately, she tumbled, tucking and rolling to protect herself. She'd cleared the space a good five feet, juiced on adrenaline. She lay there a few moments, listening to her heart pound in her ears—bam BAM, bam BAM—then moved. Didn't feel like she'd twisted or broken anything.

Bam BAM. Bam BAM.

She stood, brushed herself off, and moved toward the door. She wasn't sure what kind of building this was, but judging from the kind of day she was having, she was sure the access door to the roof was locked. That meant she'd have to find some way to break the lock, or cut through the door, or—

But it was unlocked. She felt the door heft in her hand, and she smiled. She'd finally caught a break in this whole thing. She went through the door and scrambled down the stairs, past the sign marked *Roof Access*. She went through a door onto the top floor access and looked down the hallway. This was an older building, judging by its structure alone. But it had been renovated somewhat recently. Maybe it had been a hotel once upon a time, but she was guessing maybe apartments now, or office space. Whatever it was, the top floor was quiet; she was the only one in the hallway, and all the doors down the hall were closed.

So, should she just press the elevator button and head straight down? Yes, she should. If he'd tracked her this far . . . there was nothing more she could do to escape him. She pressed the call button for the elevator and waited. The doors opened . . . empty. She held the doors for a few seconds, tilting her head, listening for movement elsewhere. Nothing.

Canada relaxed, just a bit, as she stepped into the elevator. Her hand hesitated over the lobby button for a second, then she moved it and pressed 3 instead. Three was a good number. The elevator began dropping instantly, much more quickly than she would have expected in a building of this vintage, and less than half a minute later the doors opened onto the third floor.

She left the elevator immediately, keeping her eyes and ears open as she moved to the stairway again. Still no sounds. She went down the last few flights of stairs and, in the lobby, saw a huge construction project under way. Scaffolding lined the walls. Exposed framing held wire. Rubble from peeled plaster littered the floor. She scanned the lobby and spotted a sign on the front door. It was facing out, toward the street, but Canada was able to decipher its message backwards. CLOSED FOR REMODELING, the sign said. NEW EXTENDED STAY SUITES COMING SOON!

So it was still a hotel, kind of. Canada looked around and found a set of dirty canvas overalls draped over a ladder, a hard hat on top of them. Perfect. She slipped on the overalls and donned the hard hat, tucking her red hair underneath. She spun around, spotted a bucket, picked it up, and headed for the door.

Outside, she didn't stop to look around; stopping and gazing would be too suspicious. She needed to look like a construction worker, someone just cleaning up the construction site, maybe hauling a bucket of plaster to the garbage. She went to the corner of the block and turned, then set the bucket down and picked up her pace as she continued on another block. At that block she started running, checking behind her to see if anyone was following. Up ahead, a bus had pulled over to a stop, and she climbed aboard. The doors hissed shut behind her, and she breathed a sigh of relief.

She had escaped Keros a second time.

She sat down and hit the 1 on her cell phone. A now-familiar voice answered. "Well, Ms. MacHugh," the voice said in a pleasant tone. "Looks like Seattle's not your kind of town, either."

## 18

"I'M GOING AFTER HIM," Canada said. She turned to the shadow on the seat next to her, wishing yet again she could gauge any kind of reaction or emotion. "I have to."

She was uncomfortable staring at the shadow, so she turned and looked out the window instead. The clouds at 35,000 feet were soft and puffy, like beds of cotton. She could get used to this charter jet.

"I knew you were meant for big things," her father's voice finally said. She smiled; a buttery ribbon of pride warmed her, hearing her father say such a thing. "But you're going to need help."

A voice spoke from behind her. "Ms. Franny Glass, I presume?"

She turned in the chair. It was Doug, the operative she'd worked with at the apartment fire.

"What are you doing here?" she asked.

"Following orders, being a good boy."

Her father spoke. "To tell you the truth, we anticipated this. We thought, perhaps, your . . . let's say your prime directive would be stopping Keros."

She turned back to Doug, arched an eyebrow. "You have something to do with this?"

He shrugged. "Nah. I just work here."

She smiled. She'd been surrounded by so many new faces; it was good to see a familiar one again. Even if it was a face she'd only seen a day or two before.

He sat down in the seat next to her. "Sure you want to do this?"

"No."

"Good, good. Angst is a good thing."

She put her head back on the seat. "So can he be killed? Can he be stopped?"

Doug smiled. "He can. Will he? is another question." He opened his notebook computer and pulled up a web page for a site requiring a username and password. "Now, I doubt there's a website called *howtostopascaryguywhostalksyou.com*, so we'll just have to make our own plan."

He clicked on a site link and downloaded a flash animation. "I've been plotting the movements of Keros—over the past several years. How he seems to work, what he seems to do. You'll notice, first off, how he travels. Rarely flies, which we can use to our advantage. It'll give us a head start. Because we know what he's after . . ." His voice trailed off.

"Me," said Canada.

"You, Princess," Bud MacHugh's voice said, rejoining the conversation.

"We've concluded," said Doug, "the best way to find him is to use bait. And, if you don't mind me saying it, you're the ideal bait for him."

Canada looked to the shadow of her father, than back to Doug. "Okay, I can see that."

"You can see it, but are you fine with it?"

Canada thought for a moment. This golem, this Keros, scared her at some deep, elemental level. And that was reason enough for her to face him. Exorcise her demons. Or at least exercise them. "Yeah, I'm more than fine with it."

Doug nodded. "So here's the plan, then. We send you on a fake mission. We're thinking Jacksonville. Touch down at the airport, keep you there. We'll send it out through our network of ghosts and spooks; that's how he gets his information, anyway. But here's the thing: you'll be in an airplane hangar at the Jacksonville airport. We've had it in our network for a couple of years, retrofitting it for . . . um, for something just like this."

She nodded slowly. "For . . . the golem."

"We've been working on a place to trap him. That's the hangar. But we've also been waiting for the right person."

"What exactly constitutes the right person?"

Doug shrugged. "Someone we know he's after . . . who survives long enough to make it to Jacksonville."

She smiled. "Comforting to know I'm the first." She felt the plane banking, turning.

Doug pursed his lips, seemed deep in thought for a few moments. "Look, maybe I should just show you some of this on the computer," he said. "It sounds too crazy for me to say it." He opened a new web browser page on his screen.

"Crazier than dead spirits in the shadows?"

"Pretty close. Here it is." He pointed to a screen. The headline at the top said, JEWISH MYSTICISM: THE GOLEM. "Your mission, should you accept it," Doug intoned dramatically, "is to kill a monster."

## 19

BUTTE, MONTANA STANDARD
RECORD SUMMER FIRE SEASON SURROUNDS BUTTE

August 25—Yesterday, the National Interagency Fire Center in Boise confirmed this year as the worst fire season in more than fifty years for the State of Montana, with more than one million acres burned. That exceeds the 800,000 acres burned in the 2006 and 2005 seasons, and a similar season in the famous Yellowstone fire season of 1988.

A spokesman for the National Interagency Fire Center, who wished to remain anonymous, said, "This is easily the all-time worst season in terms of acreage burned. And many of the major fires are still burning—especially in southwest Montana." The center coordinates local, state and federal firefighting efforts.

The fires the spokesman refers to surround greater Butte, including three major fire complexes threatening to converge and surround the city: the Pipestone complex to the southeast, Ramsay Ridge to the west and the huge Opportunity fire to the north.

"The important thing for the people of Butte to know is, they need to stay calm and stay in their homes," said the spokesman. "Don't venture away from the city into the surrounding wilderness or forest areas. At this time, Butte is in no danger of burning."

## 20

"OKAY," CANADA SAID TO DOUG. "A golem is a clay guy, a monster—kinda like Frankenstein. I already heard that pitch."

"Frankenstein, right. Good first step. But you need the crash course. We're talking a *real* golem here—an almost immortal figure made out of clay, then brought to life by prayer."

"Brought to life by prayer?"

Doug took a deep breath and let it out. "I'll give you the thirty-second overview, then let you read the background information. There are some legendary elements worked into this story, but the essential idea of the golem—from Jewish mysticism—is intact."

Canada turned to look for the shadow of her father. He seemed to be gone for now.

"Okay," Doug began. "The word *golem* literally means, in Hebrew, 'cocoon.' And that's kind of what a golem is: a cocoon, usually made of mud or clay, that holds a spirit inside. This spirit is breathed into the golem by a Rabbi speaking Hebrew incantations.

"The stories of the golem go way back, but the most famous is the story of Rabbi Judah Loew, the Maharal of Prague. You can read more about him on this site." Doug indicated the screen with his hand. "Basically," he continued, "sometime in the sixteenth century—we don't know when, exactly—the Maharal created a giant golem out of the mud of the Vitiva River in Prague. He made this golem to protect the Prague ghetto where he lived. He built the golem, wrote the word *Emet* on the golem's forehead—which means 'truth' in Hebrew—then said the special incantations from the Jewish Kaballah to breathe life into his creation.

"Only problem was, the golem grew, and the Maharal lost control of him; soon he was killing innocent people. To stop him, Rabbi Loew had to confront the golem and erase the first letter from the word *Emet* on the golem's forehead. This changed the word to *Meit*—this is in the Hebrew alphabet, remember—which means 'dead.' When he did that, the golem died, and he crumbled instantly."

Canada stared, letting her mind process all the information.

Doug stayed silent for a moment before speaking again. "I'll leave you alone for a while, let you read through some of this stuff." He moved toward the back of the plane. Canada watched him disappear behind a curtain.

She slid into Doug's seat and turned her attention back to the computer. The headline continued to loom: JEWISH MYSTICISM: THE GOLEM.

She put her finger on the trackpad and scrolled down the page.

*The rabbi's son-in-law walked around the clay figure seven times, reciting a cabalistic formula he had composed. When his son completed seven rounds, the figure of clay began to glow red like coals. Then the rabbi told his son to do the same thing in reverse, walking around the figure seven times while reciting a different prayer. After this, the figure stopped glowing; instead, vapors spewed from it, nails sprouted on its fingers, and hair grew on its head. Finally, the rabbi himself walked around the golem, reciting a sentence from the story of creation in Genesis: "And the Lord God formed man of dust of the ground, and breathed into his nostrils the breath of life; and man became a living soul" (Genesis 2:7).*

She clicked a link and moved to another article.

*Historical texts record several variations on the creation of golems.*
*However, there are three main elements common to all stories:*

*(1) Soil: The body of the golem is formed of soil (sometimes clay*
*or dust)—particularly "virgin" soil which has not been*
*plowed.*

*(2) Incantation: A verbal ritual or prayer is used to reshape the*
*soil into a human form.*

*(3) Name: At the end of the prayer or ritual, a name is given*
*to the creature to activate it.*

Another link, another story.

*The golem is most often characterized by inhuman strength and is*
*essentially indestructible by natural, physical means. In some cases, the*
*golem is infused with supernatural powers that help it carry out its*
*mission of protection or revenge. This may include invisibility, a*
*heated touch, or the ability to summon and control the spirits of the*
*dead, forcing them to tell all their secrets. . . .*

Canada felt cold prickles on the back of her neck; she went back
and read the last part again: *the ability to summon and control the*
*spirits of the dead, forcing them to tell all their secrets.* A heavy pit was
forming in her stomach; so much of this was fitting the scheme. The
inhuman strength, the indestructibility. And yes, this bit about dead
spirits. It was ludicrous, of course it was ludicrous. But it seemed to
be true nonetheless.

"Interesting reading?" Doug's voice asked.

She looked up from the screen to see him sliding into the seat
beside her. The plane banked again, causing him to stumble a bit as
he sat.

"The shadows. He—the golem—can control them, can't he?
That's why they're so scared of him."

Doug nodded, returning her stare. "They don't even like to
talk about him very much. Notice how your father zipped out of
here."

She took a deep breath. "And that's why they call him the Name-less One. They don't know his name, because—"

"Because only the one who activated him knows his name."

She pondered this. "I suppose this is the part where I'm sup-posed to say this is all a bunch of bunk, that there's no way a guy made of mud is summoning dead spirits."

"Which means this is also the part where I show you this." He reached across her lap and spun the computer screen to face him, then typed some words into a new browser window. "The name he's been using—Keros—I was a little curious about."

"I was kinda wondering that, too. Sounds, I dunno, Greek or something."

Doug shook his head. "That's what I thought, too. But then I thought, let's look at Hebrew, where it's actually spelled as 'cheres.' Hebrew. Take a guess what it means." Canada shook her head, waited for the answer she knew was coming. "It means 'mud' or 'dirt.' Evidently, just naming himself 'Clay' would have been so twentieth century, I guess."

She bit her lip, twirled a lock of red hair around her finger. "Okay," she said, "I'm listening. I want this guy—this thing, this Frankenstein, whatever. He scares me, which is why I need to face him."

Doug smiled. "Now, you've been reading some of the back-ground information about golems on here. Like anything, there's some misinformation, some legendary parts that have sneaked into the truth."

Canada interrupted him. "Who made him?"

"What?"

"Who made the golem?"

Doug shook his head. "Don't know. In all likelihood, he's been around for centuries, not a recent creation. For all we know, he might actually be Rabbi Loew's golem—revived, growing stronger, doing more over the years. No one who has seen the attic of *Alt-neuschul* Synagogue in Prague has lived, so we don't know that his golem is dead. Not for sure."

"And no one's tried to kill him all these years?"

Doug smiled bitterly. "Ah, I didn't say that."

"So he could have killed several other people who tried to stop him over the centuries."

"Maybe dozens. Hundreds."

"You really know how to give a pep talk. You should go into life coaching or something."

Doug shrugged yet again. "You're the one with the death wish. Why should I sugarcoat anything for you?"

Death wish. Canada shuddered, thinking of her time on the blast crew. Yes, deep down, she'd always wanted to make a wrong move, get caught in the explosion. Maybe that's why she couldn't get that recent dream out of her mind—the dream in which she was swallowing the boiling, sulfurous water of Old Faithful, feeling the water flail away the skin of her face and scorch the folds of her throat. Yes, she had a death wish. She might as well use it. "Okay," she said. "What do I do?"

"Well, like I said before, we've been preparing a hangar. Not really a hangar, though. A bunker, more like. We've carved a huge bunker under this hangar in Jacksonville: thick cement walls, the whole bit, a couple dozen feet beneath the ground. No building is going to hold this golem, but maybe a fortress will.

"So the plan is, we put you down there. We send out word through our ghost and spook network that you'll be doing some underground work in Jacksonville. He'll figure it out."

"Because he can command the shadows to tell him."

"Yup. And when he figures it out, he'll come for you. When he gets into the fortress . . ." Doug cleared his throat, a little uncomfortable. "Well . . ."

"You'll need to lock me in there with him."

"Yeah."

"Which means only one of us comes out."

"Well, either you or no one."

"So you think this fortress will hold him if he . . . um . . . kills me?"

"You want the truth? No. I don't think it will hold him. But it's all we got. The hope is, you can kill him. Deactivate him. Then we don't need to find out."

Canada felt the plane starting to decrease its altitude now. "Deactivate. Yeah, I was reading about that."

"So here's where it gets a little more difficult," Doug said.

"Good. I was hoping for a challenge; it's been way too easy so far."

"When he gets into the room, you have to walk around him, counterclockwise, seven times."

"Okay. I read something about that on that website you showed me."

"That's the easy part. Then, you have to approach him and wipe his forehead. In the legends, the golems have words written on their foreheads. Sometimes on their arms, but usually their foreheads. That's not the actual case here, from what I've been able to gather, but the action—rubbing his forehead—is part of what needs to happen. When you do that, he should crumble to ash."

"Meanwhile, he'll stand there calmly, letting me do all this."

"Now you know why we've had such a hard time finding volunteers."

Canada heard a whirring sound, and felt the landing gear on the plane lock into place beneath her feet. "We're landing," she said. "Any particular place?"

"Jacksonville."

"So you just assumed I'd agree to all this?"

"Saved us a lot of time, don't you think?"

## 21

TWENTY MINUTES LATER, Doug parked another black sedan outside a giant metal Quonset hut. Just that quickly, the plan was in motion. Canada wasn't sure how she felt about being so easy to read; obviously, everyone knew she'd agree to go after the golem. On the one hand, it made her a bit mad, frustrated. Why would they assume she'd do something like this? Another part of her, however, a deeper, more essential part of her, was saying *bring it on.* She was ready to swallow the boiling water.

"So," she said as she opened the door and stepped out of the car.

Doug followed suit. "So."

Canada really had no idea what to say. The situation bordered on absurd. But she needed something to break the tension and noticed he had his computer case slung over his shoulder. "Someone really ought to talk to you about that Internet addiction," she said. "Can't go anywhere without your computer."

"Once a geek, always a geek," he said, patting the case. "Might come in handy. You'll see."

Doug slid open the door of the Quonset hut; it gave way with a painful creak and a shower of dust particles.

"He opens doors for ladies," Canada said, stepping through. "I love an old-fashioned guy."

He followed her into the darkness of the Quonset hut, then went to the wall and flipped switches on a breaker. Feeble lights glowed in the darkness overhead. "You're sure we're in the right place?" she asked.

"Hey, you want a place that looks well-used? Invites suspicion. Don't you ever watch spy movies?"

He led her to an office door toward the back of the hut, their footsteps harshly echoing off the concrete and metal. The door opened to reveal a mundane-looking office with dark paneling on the walls and an old-fashioned steel desk. A half inch of dust covered everything in the office; it looked more like a crypt than anything. With another flick of the switch, he turned on some suspended fluorescent lights. He went to the back of the office, found a seam in the paneling near the corner, and pushed; the entire wall slid into the adjacent section, neatly disappearing on hidden tracks. Behind the paneling stood a giant door recessed in concrete.

"*Voila*," Doug said as he reached for the door handle, twisted the knob, and opened it. Behind the new door, lights—warm, modern halogens, in contrast to the sickly fluorescents present in the rest of the hangar—illuminated a stairway. He motioned with his arm. "Remember, I'm one of those old-fashioned guys. Ladies first."

Their shuffling paces echoed off the concrete of the narrow passageway as they descended the steps. With each breath, Canada smelled the chalky earthiness of the cement and felt the temperature dropping. Obviously, they didn't heat this underground bunker or whatever they wanted to call it.

After several steps, the stairway opened into a large, circular room with a domed ceiling. To Canada, the shape looked a lot like the grain silos she'd seen across the Montana countryside. She quelled a quick pain in her chest, brought on by thoughts of home.

Inside the cavernous room was a small couch, a table, and lamp.

"Someone's quite a decorator," Canada said, surveying the room.

"Hey, the closest IKEA is miles from here."

"So this is your handiwork?"

"Part of it. Not the decor, really. But the design of the chamber, all that kind of stuff. I had a hand in it, anyway."

"So now I just wait around for our friendly neighborhood golem to show up? That's the plan?"

Doug hesitated. "We're on the complete opposite end of the country now, and we know he likes to travel by truck. So most likely, he's over a day away." He walked to the small table, set the computer case on it. "In the meantime, *we'll* wait for him to show up."

She looked at him, furrowed her eyebrows. "You're gonna get all chivalrous now, stay and protect me?"

He smiled. "Something like that."

She couldn't help it; she had to return his smile. In a way, it did make her feel good. It would be nice to have company. She'd kick him out of the underground concrete silo long before the golem showed up. This was her battle, after all, not his. Something personal. The golem had probably killed dozens of people, and now he had tried to kill her. She intended to return the favor.

"So," she said, "how much time you thinking? How long until he's here?"

"Well, it's about three thousand miles from here to Washington. If he got started immediately and could travel nonstop—we're still probably a day ahead. Maybe more."

A new voice joined the conversation, deep and rich: "You won't need to wait nearly that long, Candace MacHugh."

They both turned to the voice at the doorway. Staring back at them, his long white hair flowing behind him, was the Nameless One. Keros.

The golem.

Keros moved into the large concrete room and pulled the heavy door shut behind him, sealing the three of them inside.

She heard Doug gasp.

"Evidently, that wasn't part of the plan," she said.

Keros walked across the floor toward them, surprising Canada with his silence. Every scuffle, squeak, and click of her shoes—and Doug's shoes—had reverberated off the concrete surfaces. But Keros made no sound; it seemed his feet weren't even touching the powdery cement surface. As if to prove it to herself, she glanced at his feet while she backed away toward the far side of the circular room. Yes, they were touching the floor. They just weren't making any sound.

Keros came to the small couch, turned his back toward them, and sat. "Do what you must," he said. His voice, as loud and authoritative as ever, more than made up for the silence of his footsteps.

Both Canada and Doug cringed at the booming sound. She looked at him and arched an eyebrow; Doug shrugged. Well, might as well get started. Maybe golem guy wanted to play games; let him play games. She was going to do her business. She began moving toward her right.

Doug stopped her. "Counterclockwise," he said through clenched teeth, still looking at the back of Keros. Even though the golem sat motionless on the couch, his hair continued to move slowly, rhythmically—as if he were underwater.

She switched directions, moving the other way, taking side steps and keeping her back to the wall as she moved. After a few seconds, she came into Keros's line of vision. He smiled. It was supposed to be comforting, she supposed; instead, it made her shudder. She swallowed hard and continued her route, turning and picking up the pace. His gaze followed her as she made one circuit. For a moment, she thought his head might revolve a full 360 degrees, which would have been even more unnerving, but it did not. When she passed out of his line of vision, he simply faced forward again.

She began a second circle, now breaking into a jog, then starting to run. Keros kept watching; this was, indeed, disconcerting. Surely he knew what she was doing, didn't he? She completed her second and third circuits, bypassing Doug each time.

Fourth circle, and still Keros didn't move. Fifth circle, sixth circle. She stopped. This wasn't what she'd expected. But then, some of that website stuff talked about golems being dim-witted, unable to grasp complex subjects. Maybe that was the case.

"I believe you have one more circuit to make, Candace Mac-Hugh," Keros said, still facing away from her.

She glanced back at Doug, then walked another complete circle around the exterior of the room. Finally, she moved another 360 degrees around the exterior, until she was facing the seated man.

Another smile. "Careful," he said. "You don't want to make eight circuits; that will break the pattern."

She needed to move forward now, but her legs didn't want to work. For the first time, fear set in, and she realized it was because Keros was being so *calm*. She'd expected a fight, a struggle of some kind. But this . . . this calm sense of knowing was so much worse.

Abruptly, Doug broke the tension, sprinting up behind the seated golem. "Go! Go!" he screamed at Canada as he reached from behind the golem and rubbed at its forehead.

Canada felt herself pressing against the cool concrete, waiting for an explosion of violence from the white-haired form. Instead, Keros simply sat, letting Doug rub at his forehead for a few moments.

Doug finally hesitated, then stopped and looked up at Canada, a questioning look in his eyes.

Then, it happened. Keros's arm came up and over his shoulder in a lightning-swift motion. It was like watching a cobra strike. He grasped Doug's face in the palm of his hand briefly, and Doug's body went limp, falling to the floor.

During the whole struggle—if it could really be called that— Keros had moved no other part of his body than his arm. His gaze had never left Canada's face. And the creepy smile had never left his own.

Had he really killed Doug that easily? Could such a thing be possible?

She was sitting on the floor now, her knees drawn up toward her chest, and she realized she was curling into a ball, trying to make herself as small as possible. This was too much. She felt a tear beginning to trickle down her cheek.

Keros stood, walked toward her.

She heard herself utter a small moan that became a squeak. She wasn't so tough after all. Butte chick or not, she was literally scared stiff by the figure looming over her.

Slowly, ever so slowly, Keros leaned toward her. He dropped to one knee and took her right hand in both of his. Then, he brought her hand to his forehead and rubbed with it—softly at first, then harder. His touch was oddly comforting, as if an electrical current were coursing beneath the skin. Still, her body wanted to withdraw from his presence.

"Always wrestling," he said at last. His voice seemed softer, more personal.

She tried to speak, but her throat was too dry. She swallowed the bitter taste of fear rising up from her stomach and tried again. "You're . . . you're not a golem, are you?"

The smile returned. "All creations are golems. But not all are born of dust."

Now his hand was moving toward her own forehead, and she didn't have the strength to resist. She felt his touch against her forehead, a brush of the fingers, and spokes of warmth began to radiate away from the point of contact.

He spoke a single word: "Sleep."

And she did.

Valeria Cimino had lived all her life in Butte—had, in fact, lived in the same neighborhood all her life—and now she hated going out of her way to avoid that . . . that . . . *bischero* on the corner. But she really had no choice. For the last few weeks, he'd camped on the corner at Mercury Street, just two blocks from her house, holding up a sign and begging for money. Something on the sign about being a homeless vet.

A vet? Please. More like a *pigrone*: a bum. Definitely a drunk; she could tell just by looking at him. Maybe even a drug addict, collecting the money for a fix.

Valeria shook her head, checked her deep red lipstick in the rearview before looking back to the road. Three times a week, she liked to go down to the Lucky Lass Casino, drop ten dollars in quarters in the keno machine.

Up ahead, the sign of the Lucky Lass glittered with golden brilliance, a string of yellow bulbs outlining a giant horseshoe.

Well, okay. More like five times a week. And more like twenty-five bucks in quarters.

Not that she played for money. No, no, no. She did it to take her mind off things such as her sorry lot to be married to the now-dead (thankfully) Frankie Cimino, the many good friends she'd lost over the years, and that bum on the street, who was forcing her to detour her regular routes. And did he care what he was putting her through? He did not; he was, like everyone else, blind to her misery.

She glanced in the rearview mirror again, but couldn't see the beggar on the street.

*Covolo*, it was getting hot. Even inside the car, with the air-conditioning turned up full blast, she felt the heat. She glanced in the mirror again, checking her lipstick, hoping she hadn't sweated and smudged some of it off. No, the lipstick was still there, but her skin. It seemed so gray, so . . . *dry*.

Now, as she turned into the parking lot of the Lucky Lass, such

incredible thirst overtook her. She needed a nice glass of juice perhaps. Something to take off the parch. Just as soon as . . .

Her leg didn't seem to be working. She was trying to brake with
her right foot, but when she looked down she saw both her legs were
smoking, smoldering, crumbling to ash like twin cigarettes perched
on the side of an ashtray.

This . . . this was not possible. Hallucinations, yes, probably
brought on by the heat. She hadn't been taking care of herself so
much lately. She'd actually put off her trip down to the Lucky Lass
a few hours more than usual, and here was what she got for that: the
heat had gone to her head, made her think she was seeing things
that plainly weren't there.

First thing she needed to do was stop the car, and maybe she
could just do that by shifting into park. She wasn't moving fast,
so . . .

But her arms would not work either; they, too, had joined her
legs as smoldering, wispy stalks of ash. And now, Valeria Cimino saw
the sign for the Lucky Lass Casino looming above her, and it became
clear she was going to hit the sign.

As she crashed into the casino sign, as she succumbed to the heat
pressing in around her, as she crumbled into dry flakes of nothingness, Valerie Cimino thought again how this was all the fault of that
bum down the street.

## 22

CANADA RETURNED TO CONSCIOUSNESS, feeling movement beneath her. She didn't open her eyes yet, wanting to get her bearings, to find out as much as she could before she signaled she was awake.

Yes, she was moving. And there was a steady whine. She was back on the plane, she guessed. Certainly on an airplane of some sort, if not the same one. She'd expected to feel as if she'd been put through a meat grinder, but oddly enough, she felt perfect. No headache, no aches or pains of any kind.

"You are awake, Candace MacHugh." Keros. A statement, not a question. So much for being covert. She opened her eyes.

Yes, she was on the same aircraft. Keros stood in front of her, unmoving even though the aircraft seemed to be jostling a bit in turbulence. She looked to the cockpit to see who was flying; all she could see was the back of the pilot's head. No copilot, though, unless Keros was filling that role.

"How long have I been . . . unconscious?" she asked, not really meaning to say it out loud.

"Several hours," Keros replied. "We've been airborne almost as long."

The events in the bunker came flooding back. "We were sealed inside that concrete—" she began.

His voice cut her off. "What is concrete but dried mud? Mud has no power over me."

She was sitting in the same seat as before, and Doug was strapped into the seat next to her. Dead.

"No, he is not dead," Keros said, as if reading her thoughts. "He's merely sleeping while we talk."

"Talk about what?"

"You."

"What about me?"

"You're a tough one, Candace MacHugh. No wonder it singled you out."

"It?"

Keros's eyes studied her face, never wavering. Canada didn't want to back down from him, but looking into his eyes was too unsettling. She dropped her gaze.

"The Nothingness."

"The Nothingness?"

"The shadows. What you've been calling your father."

She pursed her lips, shook her head. This monster knew nothing about her father, about how he was helping people, warning them of impending disasters.

"You're right, Candace MacHugh. I know very little about your father. Your real father. I know much about the Nothingness, though. As do you. As does every human, when it comes down to it."

"Who are you?" she finally asked. It seemed a good way to get the subject away from her father, a good way to get her mouth going and push her away from the fear she felt revolving inside.

He smiled. "You've been told that one. Call me Keros."

"Great. That clears up everything."

Keros smiled. "You want to understand everything. This is human nature. But most humans can't accept they'll never truly understand everything. Also human nature.

"This, however, isn't what we need to talk about. What we need to talk about is you. Your work with the Nothingness."

"And then you'll kill me."

"I kill no one. People kill themselves well enough."

"Oh, yeah? What about those cops in St. Paul?" She thought back to the three men she'd met in the run-down apartment, her precarious flight down the fire escape.

Another smile, an all-knowing smile that rubbed Canada the wrong way. "Tell me why you think they were police officers."

She stopped. "Well, because . . . well, we were there to work with them, track serial killers. Until you showed up."

He shook his head. "I know what you were *told*. But you still haven't said why you think they were police officers."

She was being backed into a corner. She didn't like it, but she had nowhere else to go. "Because . . . I guess that's what my father told me."

One crisp nod of his head. "That's what your father's *voice* told you."

"Same thing."

"Is it?"

"Okay, just quit with all the psychobabble and tell me what you're getting at."

"What I'm getting at, as you put it, is simply this: What you see isn't always what's real. Often isn't, in fact. Go back to the three men in St. Paul and think. Did you ever see a badge proving any of them was a police officer or other law enforcement official?"

Pause. "No."

"You've undoubtedly been around police officers before. Did any of those men seem to fit the mold of what you know?"

She bit her lip, not liking where this was going. "No," she admitted.

"So tell me, then, what you did see."

She blew out a deep breath. "I saw . . . three guys who . . ."

"Before that. The building."

"I saw an old abandoned building. No one living there, from what I could tell."

"Okay."

"And inside, I saw three guys who were . . . I don't know . . . cutting out newspaper articles and photos of people who had been killed. Women, mostly. And they were hanging the photos—" Canada stopped, a revelation lighting in her eyes.

"Ah," Keros said. "I think you may be seeing the truth now."

"Are you saying *they* were serial killers? Those three, the guys in that apartment?"

Keros raised his eyebrows, said nothing.

"I don't get it. Why would they send me to meet with serial killers?"

"You said it yourself: the press. My guess is, you would have left that meeting with a few new photos and juicy details, and zipped right over to the newspaper or one of the TV stations."

"Okay, so they get an article in the newspaper. I get it, I guess. I don't know why, but—"

"You'll figure it out soon."

"Okay, let's just set that aside and look at the facts: serial killers, working together?"

He nodded. "The Nothingness can be very convincing," he said. "Wouldn't you agree?"

She swallowed hard, nodded.

"You'll find the common thread; I'll leave it to you to think about your other assignments. But tell me, why were you in Florida just now?"

"For you."

"Yes."

"To be . . . well, to be bait, draw you to the bunker."

"Yes. Did you pause to consider why, specifically, it had to be Florida? So far away from your hometown of Butte?"

She shook her head. "That's where they had the abandoned hangar, where they built the bunker. Nothing mysterious there."

Keros smiled, ever patient. "You think that is their only bunker, those who hide in the earth? They have many locations; their network runs deep. Why, then, Florida?"

She thought some more. "I don't know. But . . . I do remember Doug talking about how it would take you a long time to get there by truck. I . . . wait a minute."

"Yes?"

"We're flying. *You're* flying. They said you wouldn't fly."

"You're trusting the Nothingness for your information." He moved abruptly, sitting on the floor of the plane. Everything he did, it seemed, was instantaneous, too fast to follow with the naked eye. "I prefer not to fly, Candace MacHugh. But there is a big difference between being unwilling and being unable."

"Okay. Point taken. You'll fly when you need to." She was getting more uncomfortable now; a fine sheen of sweat had begun to dot her forehead. She felt as if she were on the verge of something big. Very big. Something, oddly enough, she was afraid of knowing.

"It is a frightening thing, is it not?" Keros asked. "When you discover the truth doesn't agree with what you've been doing?"

"What do you mean?"

"Four days now, you've been in four different cities. This morning, you were clear across the continent from your hometown of Butte. Why?"

"I told you, to work with the shadows, to help people, that kind of thing."

"No, that's what the Nothingness told you. I want you to tell me what you're now knowing, inside, to be the truth."

And he was right. Deep inside her, she felt something—first a trickle, then a stream, then a torrent—rushing to the surface of her consciousness. But she couldn't say what thought that torrent was bringing to her. Not yet.

Canada felt the plane descending, obviously preparing to land. She glanced at Keros, still unable to meet his gaze. Would he go to the cockpit? He made no move to do so.

She reached for her seat belt to buckle it, realizing she'd never been unbuckled. She turned and looked at Doug, who remained buckled, as well. Well, if Keros was taking them someplace to torture them, get information from them, he was being very conscientious by buckling them so they arrived safely.

"You are only seeing things with your heart right now, Candace MacHugh. But the heart is—"

"Yeah, the heart is deceitful above all things. You said that before."

"Many times."

Now Canada turned to look out the window. "Where are we?" she asked, but even as the question left her mouth, she recognized the city skyline: the head frames, the Berkeley Pit above the downtown, Our Lady of the Rockies overlooking the city. "You brought me back to Butte."

"Consider what you've been doing on these 'missions' you've been assigned. Why are they so far away from Butte? If you're really talking to dead spirits, and if those dead spirits are really imparting important information, don't you think the ghosts of Butte have plenty to share?"

Canada stared at Butte, rising up to meet them, and found tears forming in her eyes. For some reason, she felt she'd never see the city again. Now, she was back, and she had to admit it felt good. In fact, she felt she never should have left in the first place. This was part of the torrent of thought that had been rushing through her mind.

"So once again, I ask you: what else might explain these assignments?"

Now she couldn't keep it in. "They . . . wanted to keep me away from Butte."

"And me. They knew I would follow you."

"But why would they do that? I'm just . . . I'm just a trash collector. Or a copper miner. Or . . . I'm not sure what I am."

"But they are. Think what happened on your first assignment. When the apartment building blew up, what did you do?"

"I went into the building and pulled the guy out. The guy who was cooking meth. But now, worse things may happen because of it."

Her voice trailed off as Keros's icy blue eyes stared her down again.

She swallowed hard, felt the bump of the landing gear as the plane touched down. "You're saying that's not true either, are you?"

"I'm saying you went to a disaster, and while everyone else wanted to stand and watch the building burn, you went into the fire and saved a man."

She felt a lump in her throat now. "I'm sorry. It's just . . . this has all happened so fast. I don't know who to believe, what to believe anymore. Just a few days ago, it all made sense."

Keros nodded. "The best lies always make sense."

The plane coasted to a stop, and Canada listened as the jet's turbines began to wind down.

"Now what?"

"Now you really step through the looking glass."

Canada felt an uneasy dread overcoming her. "What do you mean?" she whispered.

"I mean, this isn't the same Butte you left a few days ago. It's not the same precisely *because* you left."

The pilot was up now, and he unlocked the door, dropping the steps to the tarmac. Outside, Canada could hear . . . nothing. Just the wind. Odd. Even though it was early evening, Butte should still have some air traffic. She peered down through the oval window next to her. Other planes were on the tarmac, but none had landed recently; nor did any seem to be leaving.

"The other planes," she commented, her voice little more than a whisper.

"Grounded," Keros replied. He made no move to get up or leave the plane. "No air travel in or out of Butte. It's been quarantined."

"Quarantined? If that's the case, how did we get in?"

"Ah, well, this is a charter of the Nothingness, is it not?"

"Yes, I suppose so."

"The charter service is based in Butte, so the plane, as far as the Nothingness knew, was just returning to its home base. Certainly, the Nothingness did not realize I was on the aircraft when this flight started. But it will certainly know in a few moments. When we landed, the fragments of Nothingness aboard slid off the plane to report."

"The shadows, you mean."

"Yes."

Next to her, Doug remained unconscious; she noticed also, for the first time, that his laptop case was on the floor beside him. "What about him?" she asked, tilting her head toward Doug's form.

"He tried to help you in the bunker, when all was said and done, did he not?"

She thought of Doug, scrambling to stop Keros. "Yes, he did," she said.

"You will need every ally you can get for what's to come."

Canada shook her head. "Okay, let's just back up: why is Butte quarantined?"

"Friedrich Nietzsche once said, 'When a man stands and looks into the abyss, the abyss also looks into him.' He did not know, at the time, how correct he was."

Now Keros motioned her toward the door; she stood and went toward it, bent to keep from hitting her head on the ceiling. She peeked through the door and saw the pilot walking across the tarmac to the terminal. The wind whipped at her hair, and she brought her hand to her face to hold her red locks at bay.

"Your hometown of Butte is looking into that abyss now. You, yourself, are looking into it. I cannot tell you what to do, as this is your free choice: you will do what you will do.

"But remember this, Candace MacHugh: when you saw the fire, you did not hesitate before plunging in and saving a life. There are others like that in Butte, Candace MacHugh. They just need someone to lead them through the flames. The Nothingness knew that, and took steps to remove a leader. I think you now know that, as well."

With that, he turned, still crouched, and moved toward the back of the jet.

"Wait—" she said, but he stepped through the curtain in the back and disappeared. She scrambled back into the plane and stuck her head through the curtain. Keros was nowhere to be seen. Somehow, she was unsurprised.

What should she do now? She could try to revive Doug, she supposed, but what would that get her? She needed to check out the city, find out what was going on, and Doug, she had to admit, would only weigh her down right now. Still, she wanted to talk to him later. She went to him and checked for his pulse. He seemed to be okay. She looked around, found a pen and a piece of scratch paper, then wrote her new cell phone number (she had to pull it out of her pocket to check) and a note: CALL FRANNY GLASS. She turned back to the door and spotted Doug's computer, still on the floor. It would be good to have that.

Five minutes later, with Doug's laptop in a carry case strapped over her shoulder, Canada walked through an eerily deserted Bert Mooney Airport. The ticket counters and car-rental desks were unoccupied, the baggage carousels quiet, the television monitors dark.

Even though she was wearing soft-soled hikers, Canada heard every footstep echoing off the concrete and granite of the airport's interior.

Where was everyone?

*"This isn't the same Butte you left,"* she heard Keros's voice tell her. She shuddered, adjusted the strap on the computer case, and walked on.

## 23

Transcript: *Angela Franks Phone Conversation*
Date: October 10, 1995, 13:47:17—13:52:08 [Elapsed Time 4:51]
Recorded by: [NAME REDACTED]
13:47:17 [BEGIN CONNECTION]

AF: Hello?
CALLER: This is Angela Franks?
AF: Yes.
CALLER: This the Angela Franks heading the committee to build
    a memorial at Granite Mountain?
AF: Who's calling, please?
CALLER: A friend. Someone who wants you to stay . . . safe.
[:05 SILENCE]
AF: This isn't funny. If you don't tell me what this is about right
    now, I'm going to hang up and call the police.
CALLER: Go ahead. We already have a couple of them sitting out-
    side your house right now. To protect you, of course.
[:07 SILENCE, :11 UNIDENTIFIED NOISE]
CALLER: You're checking, aren't you? Pulling back those curtains,
    maybe?
[:04 SILENCE]
AF: Yes, they're . . . ah . . . on the . . . what do you want?
CALLER: We want you to get the story straight.

AF: Granite Mountain, you mean.

CALLER: Yes. We know of your . . . ah . . . research into the fire.

AF: I . . . don't know what you're talking about.

CALLER: Of course you do, Ms. Franks. You've been told the fire was caused by [INFORMATION REDACTED].

[:07 SILENCE]

AF: How . . . did you know that?

CALLER: You don't need to worry about that. You need to worry about . . . what people will say. Who's going to believe what you've been told? You likely can't quite bring yourself to believe it, Ms. Franks.

AF: I . . . I know. You're right. It's just—I interviewed so many people. Families of the miners, you know? And they swore— they said the men down there that day just suddenly—

CALLER: Well, certainly the miners would be traumatized. You understand, 168 of your fellow workers, burned alive below ground. Stories start, and it's easy to believe those stories. But really, they're legends you understand. Mining lore. So much more interesting to talk about than the truth.

AF: And I'm guessing you're calling to tell me the truth.

CALLER: Of course. The fire was caused when an assistant fore- man accidentally ignited a power cable with his carbide lamp.

AF: Yes, I know what the official story is, but—

CALLER: I think, Ms. Franks, that's really all of the story you need to know. All of the story anyone needs to know. The true story, you understand. Something you need to consider as you build the signage—the interpretation—at the memo- rial.

AF: So you're telling me I should—[UNINTELLIGIBLE].

CALLER: I'm telling you, you shouldn't be sucked into these fan- ciful stories the miners and their families have told over the years. Partly because I'm concerned for your safety. But I'm more concerned for your daughter's safety.

AF: My . . . daughter?

CALLER: Yes. Melissa Franks. Mrs. Cheney's class at Central Elementary. Loves animals, wants to be a veterinarian. It would be indeed tragic if . . . well, let's not even think about it.

[:07 SILENCE]

AF: I . . . you . . . she's just eight. She has . . . you can't bring her into this.

CALLER: No one wants to bring her into anything. As I said, Ms. Franks, we're only concerned for her safety. For the safety of all of us. You understand. After all, that fire at Granite Mountain Mine . . . how many years ago now? Almost 70? You see how that was started by someone who wasn't careful.

AF: The assistant foreman and his carbide lamp.

CALLER: Yes, yes. Someone who didn't have safety on his mind, so he killed 168 men underground. And after that, well, a few men above ground died, too—Frank Little, Butte's beloved martyr for unions.

AF: Someone hanged Little, then pinned a note to his shirt warning other miners to beware.

CALLER: A warning they wisely heeded. That assistant foreman didn't have safety on his mind. Frank Little didn't have safety on his mind. You, I'm sure, do. You see how important it is to us to get the correct story memorialized. For your safety. For Melissa's safety. For everyone's safety.

[:11 SILENCE]

CALLER: Why, Ms. Franks, are you crying? I didn't mean to upset you. As I've said all along, I'm only concerned about the well-being of you and your family.

AF: I . . . understand.

CALLER: Good, good. I'll look forward to the memorial dedication next year.

13:52:08 [END CONNECTION]

TRANSCRIPTION NOTES: See file on "Franks, Angela" for photos and obit (Deceased 19 January 1996).

## 24

SINCE THERE WAS NO WAY Canada could rent a car in Butte, she decided she could just take one. How was anyone going to trace her, anyway? She was dead. She knew, from past experience, that the car companies always left the keys to the cars above the visors at the Butte airport. Surely, under normal circumstances, they brought the keys inside and locked up all the cars after each evening's last flight.

But something told her these weren't normal circumstances.

She walked out of the airport and to the row of Hertz cars parked across the drop-off lane. The first car was a black sedan. No. Not this time. Next to it was a blue Jeep. She'd driven enough black sedans in the last few days.

Sure enough, the keys were above the Jeep's visor. She took them out, started the Jeep, then threw it in reverse and backed out of the parking spot. A familiar *beep* sounded from the dash. A GPS receiver.

She smiled, reached down and turned it off. This was Butte. *Her* town. She didn't need a GPS.

She spun the wheel and drove down the slight incline toward the airport exit, now becoming aware of the odd smell blowing in the breeze for the first time. It was a scent she'd often smelled in Butte during the summer: fire.

Each summer, when the blazing sun scorched the forests of western Montana, and when lightning storms invariably strafed those bone-dry forests, Montana found itself in the midst of fire season. That always meant the scent of smoke, along with a fine haze that painted the sky blood red during sunsets. Sometimes even the moon.

She rolled down the window, looking across the city. The familiar burning smell was there, but the sky looked clear; it wasn't forest fires. At least, it wasn't just forest fires. She knew fires were burning around Butte, but the sky wasn't dark enough for the smell to be this strong.

She turned north on Harrison Avenue, heading toward uptown. Now she had to decide where to go. She wanted to head to her trailer, but that was probably a bad idea. She needed to go somewhere untraceable; Keros hadn't killed her, as she'd imagined he would. In fact, he'd said some things that made sense, some things that were making her question her role in all this.

Right now, she just needed to hide. She needed to collect her thoughts, plan her next steps, and find out what was wrong with her city. In that order, most likely.

The Copper Camp Inn would probably have a vacancy. She'd head there, check in. She passed a few other cars on the street, but there seemed to be so little activity. What day was it? Didn't matter. This was too quiet for any day of the week. She wanted to get to the hotel and flip on the TV, find out what was going on.

Wait, wait. The Jeep had a radio. She could flip to the local news/talk station. She punched the power button, hit AM, and chose the Seek button. On the first station, she caught a caller in mid-sentence:

"—telling us what this is about at all. Some sort of contamination or something?"

The show's host answered: "There's been no official word, sir. The CDC, I believe, has scheduled a press conference for tomorrow to talk about the quarantine."

"Rightchere in Butte?"

"Well, no, sir. It's scheduled for DC. National press would not be able to attend a conference in Butte because of the quarantine."

"See? Thisere's what I'm talkin' about. Here in Butte, we been getting this kinda thing since the beginnin'. We 'lectrified America with our copper, ya know."

"I do."

"And then, whadda they do? They shut them mines, put a lotta good folks outta work. That's the thanks we get. Jus' a few years ago, Montana Power Company goes belly up, and we're left holdin' the bag again. I mean, when they gonna stop stickin' it to us?"

"That's a question for the ages, sir. You're listening to the Mark Meyer Show on KOPR-AM News Talk, and we'll be right back."

Canada shook her head. Sounded like no one in Butte knew what was really going on. She'd have access, though, wouldn't she? She could find out? Yes, she could, just as soon as she got to the hotel and did a little exploring with Doug's computer and her cell phone.

She was in front of the Safeway now, just a few blocks away from the hotel. On the sidewalk, an older woman was carrying a canvas bag, walking down the hill to—

Abruptly, the woman burst into flames.

No, wait. Canada couldn't have seen that correctly. It wasn't possible. She slammed on the brakes and steered the Jeep toward the curb, throwing it into park before it had rolled to a complete stop. She opened the door and went around the front of the Jeep. The woman pitched forward, dropping her canvas bag filled with groceries from the Safeway. A few apples spilled out of the bag, one of them bouncing off the curb and into the street.

Canada hurried toward the hunched form, but she could see that, yes, curls of smoke were spewing from the woman. Canada pulled off her own jacket, folding it over the woman and trying to smother the heat. For a few seconds, she felt the woman's shoulders beneath her, but suddenly the shoulders collapsed as if Canada had been hugging a sand sculpture: the form was there, but then it crumbled.

She pulled her jacket away, and now all she could see was a pile of clothing—a jacket marked with COPPER LANES BOWLING, jeans, a pair of Nikes smoldering behind her. Tendrils of smoke continued to lick out of the shoes; Canada was reminded of those black snake fireworks she'd seen young kids light around the Fourth of July: acrid, black-gray smoke oozing from a tiny orange flame.

She grabbed at one of the sneakers, then dropped it. It was hot, too hot to hold, but the sneaker itself wasn't melting or misshapen. Neither were any of the other clothes. It had only been seconds, and the woman she'd seen walking had disappeared, as if she were part of some giant illusionist's act. Now you see her, now you don't. Just swirling smoke and ashes, and a feeling of amazement as you tried to figure out how the trick was done.

But this wasn't a trick. And Canada didn't feel amazed; she felt nauseous.

The burning smell was thick in her nostrils now, and it wasn't the smell of summer fires. That smell was thick and woody, inviting thoughts of a cozy campfire. This smell was sweeter, but not in a good way. It was repulsive.

She felt her stomach flip-flop, and she rose to her feet. Black-gray ash was on her jacket, and she wiped it off, wanting to remove all traces of what had just happened.

But what *had* just happened?

She looked up and down the street. A few other cars were driving by, but none slowed or stopped. The drivers went on by, as if they didn't see her. No other pedestrians were on the sidewalk.

Numbly, Canada returned to the Jeep and shut the door. The radio show was back on, but she needed a bit of silence now. She put the Jeep into gear and wheeled out into the street again, only slightly aware of what she was doing. The hotel was just a few blocks away. One thing at a time. Check in at the hotel, get a room, get her bearings.

She pulled into the hotel parking lot, noticing the bright neon YES sign indicating vacancy. She shut off the Jeep, grabbed the computer and went inside the lobby. The door chimed softly as she opened it, and the smell of coffee rolled toward her. Coffee, yeah. That would be good.

An older gentleman shuffled out from behind the desk. "Didn't think I'd be seeing anyone tonight," he said in a phlegmy voice. "Quarantine's not exactly good for overnight tourists."

"Oh, yeah, yeah. Well, I'm from here. I mean, originally."

"And you just came in today? How'd that happen?"

"No, no," she lied, not wanting to get into a conversation with the man. "I've been here. Just needed to, um, get out of the house."

"Yeah, well. You're one of the few. Smoking or nonsmoking?"

Canada shuddered. "Nonsmoking. Definitely nonsmoking."

"I hear ya." He slid a registration card across the desk at her and turned to get a room card.

Canada, still feeling herself on the street with the woman who had collapsed into ash, numbly fumbled through her things and found one of the credit cards she'd been given by . . . by whom, exactly? She realized she didn't even have a name for who she was working for now. She'd simply thought of them as the shadows, but what was the organization? The government network her father had referred to?

No time to think about that now. Just get to a room. She filled out the registration form and took the room card.

"I put you in 107," the old man said. "It's a suite. Don't think I'll be having a rush on those the next few nights."

"Um, okay. Thanks."

She slid the computer case off the counter, went outside, and walked a few doors down to 107. She thought, for a moment, of putting the Jeep in a true parking spot; she'd only pulled it up to the lobby area. But why bother? As the registration guy had said, Butte hotels wouldn't be getting much traffic during a quarantine.

Inside her room, she set the computer on the small table, turned on the TV, and sat down on the bed to flip through the channels to one of the newsers. Both Fox News and CNN were running nonstop stories about the Butte quarantine. Theories abounded, but all agreed it all came down to an infectious disease of some sort. Butte had been sealed off to all incoming and outgoing traffic that morning, and experts suggested the complete lockdown would last at least another two days. After that, with deliveries supervised by the military and the Centers for Disease Control, a limited quarantine could stay in effect for another week.

Canada watched until the faces began to blur and she realized she was crying. She shut off the television and sat, zombie-like, letting the tears well. This was all so incredibly, unbelievably stupid. How could such a thing happen right now? A widespread disease of some sort, in Butte?

Darkness fell over the city, and Canada lay down on the bed, trying to clear her mind of all thoughts. But it was impossible. After several minutes, she sighed and sat up again.

She stared into the corner for a few minutes before standing and going over to her jacket. A thin film of ash still coated it, and she avoided touching it. She felt inside the pocket, grabbing her government phone. First things first. She dialed her mother's number.

"Hello?"

"Hi, Mom."

Several seconds of silence. Then: "Candace?"

"Yeah, it's me, Mom."

She heard a sob from her mother on the other end of the line. "They told me . . . they said you were dead."

She smiled bitterly. "Well, I kind of was."

"Where are you?"

"I'm here in Butte. I made it back in."

"Even with the quarantine?"

"Don't ask."

"Well, can I see you?"

"I'd like that, Mom. Just let me take care of a few things here, and . . . I'll be by soon."

"Okay. Is this the number I can call to reach you? The one on my caller ID?"

"Yeah. That should work."

Canada hung up, then turned to Doug's computer. She needed to figure out whom she could trust. She opened the laptop and launched a web browser. After a few seconds, she decided to access Doug's hard drive. A password prompt came up. Well, she'd expected that, but it was worth a shot.

She went back to the browser, pointed it to a search engine, keyed in *apartment fire St. Louis*, and clicked to search news feeds. Soon, news stories started popping up as results, including a story from the local *St. Louis Dispatch* headlined OFFICIALS: FIRE CAUSED BY METH LAB. She clicked the story and glanced through its contents, finally finding what she was looking for: the name of the man she'd saved from the flames. Robert Montrose.

She backed up, did a search for "Robert Montrose" and "St. Louis, Missouri." She found a phone number and, even though she thought it hopeless, dialed it. After a few rings, an automated voice told her the number had been disconnected.

No surprise there.

The newspaper said he'd been released from the hospital after overnight observation—but, in his condition, he almost had to have gone home with some kind of medication. She found the name of the hospital where Montrose had been kept for observation: Missouri

Baptist Medical Center. She dialed the main switchboard number and asked if Robert Montrose had been discharged yet.

"Yes, ma'am, he has," the switchboard operator told her. But of course, Canada already knew that.

"I thought so. Say, what was the name of his attending physician again? I talked to him, but I can't remember." Canada winced, hoping the attending physician wasn't a woman.

"Lancaster?"

Canada smiled. "Yeah, Dr. Lancaster. I knew it was a movie star kind of name. Could you forward me to his office number?"

"One moment please."

Canada waited patiently until a new operator picked up and asked how she could help.

"Hi, I'm hoping I can talk to Dr. Lancaster, or maybe his nurse. I have a prescription here for a Robert Montrose, and I'm not able to read the writing."

"I'll connect you to his nurse, Linda."

"Thank you."

Another thirty seconds of waiting, and then another woman's voice. "This is Linda. You're asking about a prescription for Robert Montrose? I already called that in for him."

Canada closed her eyes. "I know. I have it at the pharmacy over here. I just can't quite make out the writing. Some of the people around here, you'd think they were doctors, the way they write."

"I'll bet. Lessee, looks like fairly mild smoke inhalation, and the doctor prescribed Albuterol to help open the airways. Two inhalations, four times a day for ten days."

"Yeah, that sounds right." She paused, licked her lips. "So nothing for chemical burns or anything?"

"Chemical burns? He didn't have any chemical burns."

"That's what I was trying to tell Lorrie over here, but she was convinced the prescription was for chemical burns."

"Well, you win the bet, then."

"I guess I do. Thanks."

Canada hung up the phone, stared at the wall for a few seconds. She was no expert on meth labs, but she'd read about homes being condemned for chemical dangers. If there were really a meth lab in Robert Montrose's apartment building, what were the chances of him escaping an explosion without any kind of chemical burns whatsoever? Slim to none, she guessed.

The cops searching for serial killers in Minneapolis . . . she already had serious doubts about that after her talk with Keros. She'd put them aside for now. What about the terrorists in Seattle? Were they really terrorists? She couldn't say right now.

A thought occurred to her, and she did a search for "Berkeley Pit car accident" in news headlines. Sure enough, a story about her in the local Butte, Montana *Standard* popped on-screen. She clicked on the article, finding out a body had not been recovered at press time two days ago. The article went on to say a Trent Gibson had been on the scene and had made it to the water and attempted to save the driver before being overcome himself; he had been transported to St. James Hospital.

Canada remembered Trent, the young man who had hopped the railing and the fence, then moved toward the Pit to help. She'd forgotten about him, but he'd evidently made it to the water. That surprised her, yet she was touched; if it really had been her in that car, Trent Gibson would have tried to save her.

She hung up, then tapped her fingers on the phone a few times as she thought. Her mind called up images of the Auditor, a mangy mutt who made his home in the area surrounding the Pit for more than a decade. Mining officials and the media had made him out to be some kind of miracle dog, living in an area where no animal could logically survive. But he'd lived to 119, in dog years.

How was such a thing possible?

## 25

IT WAS AFTER DARK NOW—the digital clock on the Jeep's dash said 9:27—and Canada parked a quarter of a mile away from her trailer. Maybe she'd find nothing at her trailer with the quarantine and other recent activity. Maybe she'd find her trailer gone, but the last thing she wanted to find was a police cruiser. Or worse.

She walked down the road, paying attention to the sights and sounds around her as she went, then sneaked into the line of small trees surrounding the trailer court where she'd lived since pulling Daddy's trailer onto the lot. She followed the tree line, moving closer to her own trailer, then crouched down and watched. Everything was still. She needed to try something.

Picking up a rock from nearby, she threw it at the trailer, smashing it against the tin siding on the end. The sound bounced back to her, louder than she'd expected. She quickly stooped down again and waited, watching her old home.

After several minutes of no activity—no lights inside, no alarms, no barking dogs—she felt safe enough to creep close to the trailer. At the front door, she found a sticker on the door, telling her that NO TRESPASSING was allowed and that the trailer would be part of an upcoming ESTATE SALE. Yeah, that would be quite the estate sale.

She tried the door, but of course it was locked. No matter, she always kept a spare key under the steps, and she found it easily. She opened the door and reached, by force of habit, for the light switch before stopping herself. Wouldn't that invite suspicion if the trailer of a dead woman suddenly lit up at night?

In normal circumstances, probably. But Canada guessed it wouldn't be high on anyone's list during a citywide quarantine.

She flipped on the lights. Somehow, she'd expected to see a giant mess inside her home, as if some enemy had ransacked her house in search of a buried secret. Instead, the place looked as if it had been untouched since she left. Probably had been. After all, why would the rusty trailer house of a dead woman be that interesting for . . . well, for anyone?

She moved back to her bedroom to retrieve a new duffel and some clothes—she was wearing the only ones she had currently, after leaving behind her duffel and clothing during her mad escape from Seattle—then found some canned food in the cupboards. She had no idea what was going to happen to her in the coming hours or days, but she guessed she might be a dead girl without a job soon.

She lugged the duffel back to the living room, thought for a moment, then went back to her bathroom. She pulled a box of photos from the cupboard, catching a glimpse of the photo she'd thrown in the white trash can just a few days ago. It was the photo of her and her mother at Yellowstone, smiles on both of their faces.

Yellowstone. Old Faithful. The hot, scalding water sliding down her throat.

For a moment, she thought of grabbing the photo, but who was she kidding? She and her mother had never been close, would never *be* close. Not like she and her father had been. And, somehow, letting that rift between them heal was a betrayal of her father's memory. There. She admitted it to herself. It sounded crazy—it *was* crazy—but it was how she felt. Sure, she could be nicer to her mother, maybe drop by and visit more often, put on a civil face. But her mother was never going to be her father.

She turned off the bathroom lights and closed the door behind her, the Yellowstone photo still in the trash.

Back in the living room, Canada stuffed the photos into the duffel and set it on the floor next to the door, then decided maybe she should grab one more pair of shoes. She turned around to head back to the bedroom again when she clipped one of the giant piles of newspapers. It teetered for a few seconds, all five feet of it, before toppling away from her.

Canada heard a sickening crack, and realized immediately what had happened. The falling newspapers had hit and broken the ugly, spindly coffee table her father insisted she have. Two thoughts hit simultaneously. One, a deep regret that she'd broken the only thing her father left her. And second, relief. It really had been a very ugly, fragile table. You could barely put anything on it.

She moved to the table, pulled off the newspapers that had scattered everywhere, and picked up the top of it, now split cleanly in half.

Something fell as she picked it up.

At first she thought it was one of the newspapers, but the size was wrong. It was a small envelope, sealed with a ribbon. She looked at the piece of broken tabletop still in her hand; the break had revealed a false bottom with a small compartment, and this envelope had obviously fallen out of that compartment.

Canada set down the broken table piece and picked up the envelope. For some reason, she found herself looking around, making sure no one else was there, making sure no one else was seeing her at this moment as she opened the envelope. This was a secret sent across a decade from her father, and she both dreaded and anticipated what it might say.

Inside, she found a handwritten note. She recognized her father's writing immediately: printed letters, no cursive.

*Princess—*

*This is a letter about you and your mom. But I tried to make it about me.*

*I know you look at me as someone wonderful, but I've hurt your mom so many times. The other women. Every time she forgave me and believed me when I said I'd change.*

*Sometimes I even believed it myself. I wanted to change. You should know that.*

*Your mom begged me to stay, but I had to move out. Someday I think you'll figure out that when someone loves you no matter what you do, you either have to love them the same or you have to run away.*

*I ran away, and a few months later I found out about the cancer. Your mom asked me to move back in. For the past month maybe we've been the best we've ever been as a family, you back from college. All together because of your mom.*

*I've been thinking about it though. And I think I've had the cancer for a long, long time. I gave it to myself because I always thought about myself first. And I have to say that's the worst cancer.*

*I guess that's just what I wanted you to know more than anything, Princess. Whatever you do, don't make it all about you. It'll eat you alive.*

*I want to give you this letter now, while you're right here in the house with me. But for some reason I can't. It doesn't seem like the right time. So I will put it someplace safe and trust you'll find it when you need to read it.*

*I love you,*
*Daddy*

Canada finished the letter, reading through blurry vision, then wiped her hand at her cheek and read it twice more. She remembered her dad coming back home right before he died. She remembered it well, how he seemed so happy. So calm. She had started college at MSU in Bozeman, but when she got the news it seemed important to come back to Butte.

To be home with Daddy.

And with Mom, yes. She had always resented her mother, hoped her mother felt remorse for hurting her father. As she'd just admitted to herself, that was part of what made those memories fond for her: picturing her mother in anguish.

But why? Why was it so important for her mother to suffer? And now, her father had truly spoken to her across the years—across eleven years of death—and said her mother had suffered infinitely more than she'd ever known.

All of it in silence. Never once had her mother said anything bad about her father. Never once had her mother tried to correct her mistaken assumptions.

Never once had her mother put herself first.

Canada returned to the bathroom and flipped on the light. She went to the white trash can and retrieved the photograph of Yellowstone, stared at it a few moments, then put it in her shirt pocket.

Back in the living room, she moved toward her new duffel.

"Hello, Princess."

She stopped, surprised. She hadn't been paying attention, so she hadn't noticed the shadow on her couch next to the broken table.

What should she say? This wasn't her dad. Couldn't be her dad. She saw that now after reading the note. All along, the way the shadow spoke, the way it acted, wasn't anything like her dad. But she'd ignored that, because she *wanted* it so much to be her dad.

She wanted that for herself—wanted it because she'd had so little.

The words of Keros echoed inside her mind: *"The heart is deceitful above all things."*

"What do you want?" she asked, trying to keep her voice from breaking.

"We want you to come back to work," he said. "There are other things to do, other places to go—"

"Why is it always other places?" she asked. "Why not here in Butte?"

"We have other operatives in Butte."

"Why not me?"

"Maybe sometime. We could see about getting you moved, but you're just starting."

"He was right. You're trying to keep me out of Butte, because you're afraid of me."

"The Nameless One, you mean?" She had no facial cues to read as the shadow spoke, but she thought she could hear disgust in his voice. "What do you know about him? Nothing. I know so much more, so many things you would be terrified to discover. I don't know how you survived your encounter with him, but I can help you now. I want to protect you, Princess. Just like when you were little. I wanted to protect you from the problems between me and your mother."

Canada drew in a deep breath and felt her resolve, her certainty, melting. Coming on top of the note, this put her back on her heels. The note had been from Daddy, she had no doubt of that. She recognized the handwriting, even the way he wrote it—he always spoke in short sentences like that. Nothing like this shadow.

But.

But the shadow had told her how much he'd changed since dying. He'd been training, of course. Working with other people, rather than drills and rock. It would only be natural that he'd change in eleven years, become more people-focused. Speak differently, act differently. If it was possible that shadows moved and talked, it was possible that her father had changed since dying, wasn't it?

And the note. In the first line, it had said he trusted she'd find the note when she needed to read it. Knocking over the stack of newspapers may seem coincidental, but was it? Was it really?

"I . . . uh . . ." She stammered, searching for words.

"A father always wants to protect his daughter from harm, Princess," the shadow said. Canada felt the shadows growing, expanding to fill the room. And that was okay; it was warm and comforting, as if it were reaching out to embrace her. Maybe that's what it *was* doing.

"I . . . I didn't know much about what happened with you and Mom," she said.

"Of course not," the shadow said. "Parents always try to hide their problems from their children. It's only natural."

Canada felt something shift inside her head. *Parents always try to hide their problems from their children.* That was true, but it was a generalization. Something you could say to anyone. Just as you could say *I'm sorry for what happened between me and your mom.* That was nonspecific; what couple didn't have problems, didn't want to hide those problems?

She exhaled slowly, readying herself. "You wrote me a letter," she said.

Pause. "Yes."

"Tell me about it."

Another pause. "I apologized for not being a better father."

She stopped. Well, yes, that had been part of it. But that was also general, something anyone could guess. She closed her eyes. The thing was, he'd been a wonderful father, really; her mind was filled with vivid memories, and she could easily call them to mind even now. She thought again of Columbia Gardens, the amusement park, the smell of cotton candy.

Columbia Gardens. Yes, that was it.

She opened her eyes. "When I was young, very young, we had a favorite place."

"Columbia Gardens. We already talked about that."

She had asked that at the beginning, and she'd let herself be convinced this was her father because he'd provided the right answer.

But really, that was an easy guess, too. Whenever she talked to any-one roughly her age who had grown up in Butte, the conversation invariably turned to Columbia Gardens. It was a shared experience for all of them, a reminder of childhood made especially bittersweet after its destruction. Everyone loved Columbia Gardens.

"But it was a special place at Columbia Gardens." She brought back the memories, holding the sticky caramel apple in her hand while she went round and round on the horse.

The pause grew. "Everybody loves the carousel," he said.

She smiled, bitterly, closed her eyes. "Yes, everybody loves the carousel," she answered. "But Bud MacHugh—my *real* dad—loved the go-round."

She bent to pick up her duffel. "You're not my father," she said through clenched teeth.

For a moment, all the sound, all the color, all the sensations in the small trailer collapsed into darkness. And then, Canada felt the world shift—like air from a punctured balloon, the color began to drain away from everything around her.

The shadow really *was* growing. But it was doing more than growing; it was coalescing, changing shape. Canada gasped when she recognized the shape, and she felt her stomach melt.

A giant shadow spider now loomed over her.

It reached out with one of its spindly legs and brushed against her skin, leaving a trail of gray ash. The spider spoke, but now her father's voice was gone; his voice had been replaced by something deeper, darker, more guttural. "You think any of that matters, *Princess*?" The spider leaned on the last word derisively. "It's too late now. Too late for you. Too late for all of you."

The shadow spider began shifting, expanding, multiplying. Instead of one giant spider, it was becoming a million shadow spi-ders, all of them scuttling across the ceiling, the walls, the furniture, the stacks of laundry and newspapers. All of it.

Even across Canada's skin, leaving ash trails and rippling her flesh in goose bumps.

"I ATE YOUR FATHER!" the spider's voice boomed, impossibly loud now, rattling her brain.

Canada smelled fire again; something in the trailer had been ignited. The place was a tinderbox.

Grabbing her duffel, she ran for the door and crashed through it, brushing hundreds of ash spiders from her arms as she ran. And now, the shadow spiders *were* solid; they had dimension, and weight, and long scrabbly legs that burned everywhere they touched.

Canada turned back to the trailer and gasped as she saw its entire shell engulfed in shadow spiders. Not millions of them, but *billions*.

She turned again and sprinted toward the tree line. Behind her, something clanked, and she chanced a peek long enough to see the entire trailer glowing in a cocoon of gray ash. Burning, but not in flames. Smoldering like a wet cigarette.

She kept running toward the Jeep, but it wasn't the spiders that kept her running, or even the burning trailer. It was the screams of agony and anguish inside the ash.

The screams contained in the shadows.

## 26

FILE ITEM: ANONYMOUS NOTE TO KXLF-TV, BUTTE, MONTANA
[UNPUBLISHED]
DATED: 17 OCTOBER 1974
FILED: 15 SEPTEMBER 1975
LEAD AGENT: [REDACTED]


To Whom It May Concern:

I know how the Pennsylvania Block fire started a couple
nights ago. I know YOU will want to know about it because the
FIRE has been on your news since then. But you need the WHOLE
story. Because its not just the Pennsylvania Block burning down.
Its the Penneys store and the OTHER buildings burning a couple
years ago and the Medical Arts building last year and all the
buildings that have BURNED around Butte. The fire department
and the police are telling you it is faulty wiring or some lone guy
lighting the fires but you know that is NOT TRUE dont you. Its
alot bigger than that.

I know this because I seen who REALLY set the last fire and I
know people who seen the other fires start.

You might think a person started the fire at the Pennsylvania
Block. Your right, but not the way you think. It was a person that
started ONE fire and not with a match or cigarette or lighter or

anything like that. I will tell you EVERYTHING I saw but not in this letter. This is a BIG story and you'll want it on your news I know it. Its worth A LOT of money at least a THOUSAND dollars. I think someone is FOLLOWING me maybe one of the things I saw that night before the woman caught on fire so we should meet secret. Send your reporter Jodi Haynes to meet me at 1:30 at the M and M on Thursday with a thousand CASH and I will tell you about the woman who caught on fire. I will recognize Jodi because I know her from TV and she seems real nice when I watch her.

ARCHIVE NOTES: LETTER INTERCEPTED AT TELEVISION STUDIO OFFICES 18 OCTOBER 1974; CONTENTS SUPPRESSED. LETTER AUTHOR JONATHAN FINCH (DECEASED 02 NOVEMBER 1974; SEE FILE UNDER "FINCH, JONATHAN" FOR PHOTOS AND OBIT). ARCHIVE IN 1974 OPERATIONS.

## 27

CANADA PARKED THE JEEP outside her mother's house and turned off the engine. She wasn't easily rattled, but the shadow spiders still had her shaking. All the way over, she'd been brushing them from her skin. They weren't there of course, but she still felt them. Their spindly legs, scuttling everywhere.

She sat in the Jeep, collecting her thoughts. She needed to stop the shadows from doing . . . whatever it was they were doing. But she didn't know if she could . . . and if she couldn't, then one thing seemed more important: She needed to talk to her mother. For eleven long years, an unspoken animosity had simmered between them, and Canada needed to set it right. Whatever might happen to her—and she had an idea some very bad things could happen—she needed to take her next steps with a clean slate. She needed to ask Diane MacHugh to forgive her.

Canada looked toward the house. Even though she knew she was wrong, even though she knew she had so much to apologize for, a part of her still felt betrayed. After all, her mother could have said something; not once in the last decade had she tried to talk to Canada about it. About anything, really.

Okay, time to wipe out those thoughts. The only one who had been wronged—truly wronged—in all of this was her mother. She needed to make that right. She opened the Jeep's door and walked to the front door to ring the bell.

When Diane opened the door, glass in hand, Canada could see she was trying to keep her composure. Her mom had always acted that way, hadn't she? Show no emotion. Keep it inside. Until now, Canada had never understood how much she kept inside.

"Hi, Mom," she said. "Can I . . . um . . . come in?"

Diane stood away from the door, tipped her glass to her lips. "Mi casa es su casa."

Canada walked into the living room, sat on the couch. No, that was stupid. Why was she doing that? She was over-thinking all of this; she just needed to let her mom know how she felt. She stood and went back to Diane, who was still shuffling her way into the living room. She hugged her mother before she had a chance to protest. "I love you, Mom," she said, and now the tears were welling again. She held the embrace, whispering into Diane's ear. "I know I haven't said that for so long. Maybe not ever. But I can tell you I've always felt it, whether I wanted to say it or not." Now the tears were turning into a cascade, and she felt her body sobbing.

Her mother stayed stiff for a few moments, but then Canada felt a hand on her back—the hand not clutching the glass of sugared gin—rubbing at her shoulders.

It was the most wonderful thing she'd ever felt in her life.

She broke the embrace, but still held her mother by her shoulders. "I'm sorry for not being here for you. I'm sorry for . . . sorry for only being here for myself."

Diane furrowed her brows, puzzled. "You started drinking?" she said. Her face was close, and Canada could smell the astringent gin, only slightly masked by the sweetness of the sugar.

"No, Mom. I'm not a drinker."

"Well, thank God for that."

She fished into her pocket and pulled out the letter from her father. She handed it to her mother.

"What's this?" Diane asked without looking at it.

"Letter from Daddy."

Diane stopped in mid-sip, cocking her eyebrow at Canada.

"I found it in my trailer. Maybe half an hour ago." Canada motioned with her hands, telling her mother to open the letter and read it.

In her jacket pocket, the cell phone rang. She pulled it out and looked at the display, recognizing the number from Doug's phone. Her mother was sitting down now, reading the letter. "Sorry," she said, moving her finger to shut off the phone. But Diane seemed lost in the letter, so she answered the call instead. "Hello?"

Silence on the line.

Once more: "Hello?"

The silence continued a few seconds more before the connection ended and pushed her back to a dial tone. She looked at the phone, considering, then keyed *69. Immediately, the phone went to voice mail.

She shook her head, putting the phone back into her pocket and turning back to her mother.

Diane was still reading. Or maybe rereading. The glass of sugared gin had slipped from her hand, now on the floor between her feet; the sticky clear liquid had pooled in a puddle and was working its way into her mother's rug.

Canada went to the kitchen to retrieve the roll of paper towels on the counter, then came back and bent in front of her mother, tearing off towels and cleaning where the gin had spilled. She bunched together several of the paper towels, letting them soak up the liquid as she listened to the ancient wall clock in the corner and the steady rasp of her mother's breathing. She continued to clean the floor, and then her mother's feet, which had some of the drink splashed on them.

Finally, she felt a touch on her shoulder. From her knees, she looked up into her mother's eyes, something she hadn't done from this vantage point since she was a very young girl. Streaks of mascara trickled down Diane's cheeks.

"You never told me," she said to her mother and it came out a whisper. Not an accusation, but a statement of wonder. For so many years, her mother had kept those secrets locked up inside.

Her mother smiled. "Why ruin a daughter's love for her father?"

"I thought he was something different."

Her mother nodded. "He was. I saw it, even if he never did. You saw it, too. That's why you loved him so much."

"But you . . . I mean me and you . . ."

"Yeah," her mom said, suddenly looking very tired. "Hasn't really been a me and you, has there?"

"No." Canada smiled. "Not yet."

Diane returned the smile, patted Canada on the shoulder. "Well, normally I'd say an occasion like this calls for a drink. But I don't feel much like a gin right now."

Canada stood and went to the kitchen, threw away the soaked paper towels in the garbage can. Back in the living room, she thought briefly of going to sit down on the couch. But no, she couldn't do that. The shadows were outside. The shadows were everywhere. And she, somehow, had to stop them.

"I know this is a bad time, and I want to stay and talk. But I'm in the middle of something I don't understand, and I should get going. But later, if I make it through this, let's maybe . . ."

Diane smiled. "Yeah. Let's."

## 28

OUTSIDE, CANADA SMELLED THE FIRES again. The ash. Part of it was the forest fires that had been making headlines—forest fires threatening to surround the city—but it wasn't just that. Butte was burning, and so far all she'd done was play the fiddle.

She went to the Jeep, slid into the seat and fired it up. She was just putting it in gear when she heard a voice from behind her.

"Don't you know you're supposed to check the back seat when you're getting in? What, they don't have urban legends in Butte?"

She jumped, then recovered when she realized it was Doug. "Plenty of urban legends in Butte," she said, looking at his reflection in the glow of the interior lights as they faded. "One about a guy who hides in the back seat of a woman's car, and ends up singing soprano after he surprises her."

"Hmmm, that's not the version they tell in Pittsburgh." She could tell his voice was hard, controlled. "The version I know, the guy is supposed to kill the woman for being a Benedict Arnold."

Canada held her breath for a moment. "You've got a gun on me?"

"Then you've heard that one, too."

She moved to turn on the lights, but he stopped her. "No need to do that. Don't need to see me to talk. Besides, these warm summer nights in Butte are so nice. Least that's what the brochure down at the Chamber said."

She tried to see him in her rearview mirror. His rough shape was there, but no features; she shook her head, realizing he looked much like the shadow form of her father. "Look," she said. "I'm sorry if you think I've turned on you. I mean, I *have* turned, I'll admit that. But I think you're on the wrong side of this, Doug. I . . . I think we should talk about it."

"Not here, though," he said. "Somewhere nice and quiet. But not one of your regular hangouts. They know your patterns, and they'll have those covered."

"I know a place. Bar called The Mint."

He seemed to consider for a second before answering. "I don't think I remember seeing that in your files. Should work."

She put the Jeep into gear and pulled out onto the street. They drove in silence for a few minutes before she spoke again. "You're from Pittsburgh, then?"

"Yeah, originally. Haven't been there for a couple years, though."

"So how did you find—" she began, but then remembered his call.

"Yup. Cell phone," he said, reading her mind. "Amazing what you can do with technology nowadays. Incidentally, if you haven't turned it off, you should. Now."

She pulled the phone from her pocket and hit the power button.

He sighed—a long, heavy sigh. "You'd better pick up the speed a bit," he said. "There will be others if you don't get a move on."

"Others? What do you mean?" she said as she pressed down on the accelerator.

"You can ask your questions later. Right now, you can answer *my* questions. Starting with Keros."

She nodded, then realized it would do no good because it was too dark for him to see her. Then she launched into a quick recap of her airborne conversation with Keros. When she finished, he turned eerily quiet, saying nothing for the rest of the drive.

Finally, when she parked the Jeep in front of The Mint, he said, "For me, the first Ghost was my brother—I know you call them Shadows, but I always thought of them as Ghosts. He died five, six years ago. Leukemia."

"I'm sorry."

"Yeah, well." She heard him shifting, then his door opened in the back, turning on the interior lights. For a second, the light blinded her; then she opened her own door and got out of the Jeep.

He was looking at the neon sign down the street. "This the place?" he asked. "Looks dead. Pardon the expression."

"Up here it's definitely dead. The bar is actually below us." She turned and headed toward the door and stairs, not waiting for him to follow but knowing he would. As soon as they were down the steps and through the entrance, she saw Joe. Good old dependable Joe was behind the bar as usual, as much of a fixture as any of the stools.

"Well, if it ain't Canada Mac."

"If it ain't, then what, Joe?" she answered as she led Doug toward a booth in the corner.

"Just if it ain't. I heard you was dead. On the news, you know."

"I was dead."

"Well then," he said. "Welcome back." He sauntered over to where they were sitting. "What can I get yous guys?"

"No cranberry juice?" she asked.

"Whatchoo think?"

"Diet Pepsi for me, then," Canada said.

"Shot a fine Kentucky bourbon in that?" Joe asked.

"Just the Diet Pepsi, Joe."

"Tch, tch. You're always gonna waste those mixers, aintcha?" He turned to Doug. "Same for you?"

"Not quite. Make it a regular Pepsi, and put a shot of that bourbon in it for me. While you're at it, put her shot in mine, as well."

"Now yer talkin'," Joe said and smiled before he turned and made his way back to the bar.

When he left, Doug looked at Canada again. "Canada? Your real name is Canada?"

She shrugged. "Real name is Candace. Canada's a nickname. Which, I suppose, is your real name when it comes down to it."

He nodded. "My real name was Terence. Before . . . before all this."

"You want me to call you that?"

He stared at the table a moment. "Nah," he finally said. "Terence is dead now. I'm just Doug." A bitter smile.

Joe approached their table with the drinks. "One regular and one unleaded," he said. "On the house. City goes under quarantine, I buy a free drink for anyone comes in. Kind of a tradition."

"How many times has Butte been under quarantine?" Doug asked.

Joe looked at him. "Counting this time, once."

Canada smiled. "Joe, I'd like you to meet a friend of mine. This here's Doug. Doug, this is Joe, who has been here pretty much as long as the bar has."

"Pretty much," Joe said, offering his hand. They shook hands, and Joe returned to his place behind the bar. In the corner a TV was blaring; more coverage about Butte on one of the news channels, and the discussion was getting frantic. Experts and analysts traded predictions about major epidemics.

In The Mint, though, things stayed the same as always. A few regulars, alternately sipping beers and shots. A couple guys over in the corner playing cribbage. The sound of work boots shuffling on the floor.

"My dad used to come here all the time," Canada said. "I came in a while after he died."

"For Diet Pepsi?"

"For . . . I dunno. For lots of things. Place still looks pretty much the same. It's like . . . I know this seems crazy, but just because this place hasn't changed, I can still picture him here. I mean, even now, I wouldn't be surprised if I saw him wander in and belly up to the bar after tonight's swing shift." She caught herself. "Well, if there *were* a swing shift, that is." She sipped her drink. "Not a day shift or a graveyard either, but in here, it still feels like there is." She turned toward him. "That make sense?"

"It does. Here's the thing, though." He looked her in the eye. "Operatives are all over this city—couple dozen easily—and right now their number-one priority is you. You've been lighting up the whole network; someone wants you out of the game bad."

She stared for a few moments, then narrowed her eyes. "How do you know about all this?" she asked. "I've got your laptop."

He huffed. "What, you think that's my only toy?" He took another drink. "Now, if you could just tell me what you've been up to since we landed, I'll be able to figure out whether I need to help you, or whether I need to shoot you with the Glock I have strapped to my thigh right now."

Across the bar, she heard Joe yell "Tap 'er light" to a couple of folks leaving the bar. She smiled. Tap 'er light. Yeah, that's what she needed to do here; she was handling major explosives.

"Okay," she answered slowly. "Not much of a choice from my end, but I'll tell you what's been going on."

She took a deep breath and told him of her adventures in her mobile home; he sat listening patiently, asking a few questions. When she finished, he took a long drag on his drink, grimaced, and nodded slowly while he looked down at the table's surface.

"So the Ghost wasn't really your father at all," he said quietly, almost as a whisper.

"No. Not at all."

He nodded, kept staring at the table for several seconds. "I saw him jump once, you know," he said.

"What?" Canada said. This wasn't exactly the response she'd expected.

"Evel Knievel. I saw him. You're younger than I am, so you were probably too young to remember any of his jumps. But I saw him when I was pretty young. Maybe five. In Ohio, a place called King's Island. Big amusement park. He was huge then, you know. I was probably a little too young to understand the whole Evel Knievel thing. But my older brother . . . man, Evel Knievel was the King of Cool. That's why we went to the King's Island jump. Not all that far, drive-wise, from where we lived outside of Pittsburgh."

She wasn't sure why they were on the subject of Evel Knievel, but she nodded. It seemed important. "I remember posters of him at Muzz & Stan's, when Daddy took me there," she said.

He continued, as if he hadn't heard her comment. "I think his appeal was that he was . . . I don't know. Dangerous. You knew he could die doing those jumps. You knew part of him almost *wanted* to die."

*The Death Wish*, Canada thought. "I can see that," she said. She waited for him to continue. He needed to talk about it, get something out.

"Anyway," he said. "I don't remember the exact day. I was maybe five or so, my brother would've been ten, I guess. Our dad took us, made a day of it. The amusement park, this big jump . . . I don't know, auditorium or stage or something out in front of the park. I remember Evel coming in, he was in a *helicopter*—like the president or something. And he came out, talked to the crowd. This was the first time for me, you understand, and, even though I was just a punk kid, I could tell: he had all those people in the palm of his hand. I don't know how many there were, fifty thousand maybe. But he had them, and he *knew* it.

"That was . . . amazing." Doug looked up at her, a vacant, glassy gaze in his eyes.

"Anyway," he continued, "when Evel did a jump, he made a few test runs first, popped a couple of wheelies, ran up the ramp to take a good look, that kind of stuff. Looking back at it now, I realize, man, what a *show*. It was all part of the act, the anticipation, the buildup. It started with his little talk ahead of time, and continued with all this.

"And then, he just went for it. You could tell he was gonna do it on that pass. And part of you was screaming at him to go faster, go faster, and part of you was screaming for him to stop and not even try it at all, because, really, if he screwed up, he could *die*, right there in front of you, you know? And I was five, so it's not like I was really thinking in those terms, not like that, you know, but I can still remember, and that's how I'm trying to describe that thing now, that feeling."

Canada could tell he was reaching a breaking point. She saw tears streaming from his eyes, and he was babbling, running his sentences together.

"And then, *bam*," Doug said. "He was up that ramp, and he was in the air, and it seemed like he was up there for minutes, in a way, and you could just feel the crowd, the whole crowd, the fifty thousand people there, holding their breath, up there on that motorcycle with him for that time. And he *knew* it. That's the amazing thing. It was all so calculated, but it was this incredible power, and this guy—this blue-collar guy from a blue-collar town—understood that it was so much more than just jumping motorcycles. It was being part of something bigger than yourself."

Doug went quiet, and Canada waited. When he didn't say anything for several seconds, she finally spoke. "So did he make that jump?"

"Huh?"

"Did he make the jump, or did he wreck? I mean, he was probably more famous for his wrecks."

"Oh, yeah. Yeah, he made it. He was like way back—I almost thought he was going to flip over backwards for a second, but he hit the landing ramp, and came down solid, and it was . . . *beautiful.*"

She nodded, took a sip of her Diet Pepsi.

Doug bit his lip, wiped at the tears still streaming from his eyes as he stared at the table again. "I know you're right," he said casually, as if he was recalling some long-ago dream. "You're right about all of it. I mean, I knew it myself—I knew it a long time ago. But I couldn't ever admit it. I . . . well, I *needed* that shadow to be Bobby. That was my brother's name, Bobby. Even right now, I want the Ghost to be Bobby. Sometimes, your heart wants something so much, and you just believe it." He looked back at her, his eyes glistening.

She nodded, put her hand on the table and touched his. "I know exactly what you mean," she said. "But if it helps any, I don't think I told you what Keros said to me at one point; I didn't even think of it until just now. He said, 'The heart is deceitful above all things.'"

Doug didn't pull his hand away. He smiled, wiped at his eyes again. "Knows his Bible."

"What?"

"Evidently, you don't. It's from the Bible. Book of . . . um, I don't remember. Guess I don't know my Bible all that well, either."

"So I'm safe from the Glock, then?" she asked.

"Always were. I never had a gun."

"I didn't think you did."

He smiled. "So here I am, in Evel Knievel's hometown, throwing in against the network of Ghosts that brought Bobby back to me— or I thought brought Bobby back to me. But Bobby, he'd want me to do like Evel do, now wouldn't he? Take that jump."

Canada laughed. "He would."

"When I first joined the network," Doug said, "and they figured out I was kind of a tech geek, I started setting up communications for them. And Butte, it kept showing up all the time. I mean, it was huge in the world of the Ghosts and Spooks. And I always thought to myself, 'Why Butte? Why this place out in the middle of Montana?' But then I started doing a bit of research, finding out about the city's history, and that's when it hit me: the mines. Not the open pits you worked in, but the underground mines."

"Sure," Canada replied, enjoying talking about her city, her heritage. "The head frames are still all over town. Like a dozen of them, I think. I know they put spotlights on them, but I haven't seen them lit up yet."

"Anyway, the Ghosts need, well, they need darkness. And it hit me: that's what the tunnels are. That's like the home base for the Ghosts, the tunnels beneath Butte."

Canada nodded. "Their lair," she whispered, thinking.

Doug sipped at his drink and made another face. "I *did* tell him two shots of bourbon and the rest Pepsi, didn't I? Or did I get that backwards?"

She smiled. "Never tell Joe to put in double shots."

Another drink, another grimace. "So I think we've safely established the Ghosts aren't really the spirits of dead relatives. And I don't really think they're just a bunch of spiders, like you ran into at your trailer. So what are the Ghosts?"

"I don't know. I'm working on it."

"How do we stop them? I mean, that's what this whole quarantine is about, obviously. And the forest fires—I mean, Butte is literally surrounded by forest fires now."

"Working on that, too."

"Well, first things first. You can't use that phone you have again. Ever. Each and every phone we hand out has GPS tracking. When it's on, we—I guess I should say *they* now—can tell where you are. So just give it to me now."

She pulled out the cell phone and handed it to him.

"Also a credit card," he said. "Give me that." She did as instructed and Doug paused to snap the card in half.

"Now," he continued, "I'm not one to be unprepared. I have a couple phones from outside the system, as it were. They're clean." He handed a thin, black cell phone to her. "Use this one instead from now on. Sometimes it's good to be the tech guy."

"Thanks."

"Now then, here's the thing. Like I said before, there are at least two dozen operatives in Butte right now. I think they were here to spread the quarantine story. Make it sound worse than SARS, worse than bird flu. A modern plague. Now you're the primary target. That means no more visits to places you normally go. Everyone's gonna have files on you, and they'll know where you hang out. Like I said, I didn't see this place in the file—"

"My second time here in eleven years." She paused. "Although . . ."

"Although what?"

"This is where the Shadow—what I thought was my father— told me to meet him."

"Your father hung out here a lot?"

"All the time."

"That's it, then. The Shadow found that bit of information, knew it would ring true, knew it would bring you down here."

"Fine," she said. "But how come I haven't seen them here? Why don't they come into this bar?"

"Well, they may not know about it."

She nodded, but was unconvinced. "Maybe."

"In any case, the fact that we haven't seen them here is good enough reason to think there may be something . . . I dunno . . .

special. Like I said, it wasn't in your files, so the other Spooks probably won't be coming by." He took another drink. "Now, we may stay away from the Darkness a day or two, maybe ride out this whole quarantine thing, but to tell you the truth, I think we're dead."

She smiled. "You keep saying 'we.' Does that mean you're on my side now?"

"Yeah. For being a tech geek, I never was too smart."

"I'll take the heart over smart every time. We just need to figure out what to do about the Shadows, the Ghosts, and Spooks in the darkness . . ."

Her sentence drained away as a thought bloomed in her mind. The darkness. The darkness. When Doug said it, it struck a nerve, and when she said it, it started rattling around inside her. As if the name held some meaning, some clue. But she hadn't been able to say just what it was until now, until she'd just spoken it herself.

Doug was looking at her. "And . . . what?"

"I think I just came up with the 'and,'" she said slowly. "A way to get rid of the Ghosts, the Darkness, whatever you want to call them. Keros called it the Nothingness."

"The Nothingness. That's probably the best name for it."

"Probably." She turned to the bar. "Hey, Joe," she yelled. "Think you can round up a few of the old gang?"

"Whatcha mean by a few?" he asked.

"As many as possible."

He shrugged. "I could probably get eight or ten in here."

"Like now?"

"I dunno. Eleven o'clock on a Tuesday night, I'm sure they're all probably in bed with their teddy bears by now."

She shook her head. "Just start callin', will ya?"

"Awright. See what I can do."

## 29

AN HOUR LATER, SURROUNDED by ghosts of her past, Canada smiled. But these weren't shadows; these were real. They were men she'd worked with in the pits. Gumbo was there, and so were Lucia and Binkowicz. Hambone, Disco, Pumpkinhead . . . Yeah, your nickname was your real name. Half these guys, she probably couldn't remember their given names. But their nicknames, that's who they *were*.

"Well, yous guys," she said, sliding naturally back into Butte-speak. "Been a while since we all been together. Last time, we were mining in the pits. Suppose it's only fitting that our little reunion here takes place in a pit."

Joe spoke up from behind the bar. "I heard that."

Chuckles all around.

She became serious now. "Okay, I'm about to tell you some unbelievable stuff. Some out-there-in-woo-woo-world stuff, but it's not out there at all. It's here, right here, in Butte, and I think maybe we can all stop it."

She had their attention.

"Awright, you know about the quarantine. Nobody in, nobody out, all that. Tomorrow, you're gonna hear about it on the TV, and they're gonna tell you it's some new virus, something worse than SARS, something that's killed a lot of people. But here's the thing: it ain't SARS at all."

She looked from face to face, continuing to speak. "Long story short, Butte's a prime place for what I been calling Shadows—Doug here calls 'em Ghosts. You pay attention to the Shadows around you, you'll maybe see them moving, like they're alive."

Binkowicz spoke up from the back. "I think I seen something like that, just the other day in my car."

There were murmurs among the men assembled in the bar, and then Lucia said, "I think we've all seen it."

Canada nodded. "Probably, since more and more is happening recently. The shadows are ... they're ..." She looked at Doug. "What are they, exactly?"

Doug shrugged.

"Okay," she said. "We gotta admit we don't know exactly what the Shadows are yet. We're working on it. But the important thing is, this whole virus story is just a cover. There's a reason they're shutting Butte down. There's a reason the fires are closing in on us. It's like they're hungry. I think they're making a huge move. They've been here since the beginning, in the tunnels underground, and I think now is the time.

"During the day, they have people working for them. Operatives. Spooks, as Doug says. Doug and I, we've been Spooks. Tomorrow is their big press conference to make sure everyone is scared of Butte; that's what happens during the day. But when night falls, I think they'll try to take over the whole city."

"Take over the whole city how?" Lucia asked.

She shrugged. "I don't know, exactly. Maybe burn it. I know I watched them burn down my trailer. So we've got maybe twenty-four hours. Now they don't do much in the day. They can go out, but they're restricted to the shadows, see? They can't do anything in bright light." She paused, took a sip from her Diet Pepsi. "And that's what I been thinking. They're in the tunnels under the city, and they hate bright light."

Hambone, a hulking mass of a man, spoke now. "The spot-lights."

"Bingo, Hambone. I think if we can use the spotlights the city of Butte so conveniently mounted on the head frames for us, point them straight down . . . I think the light may kill the Shadows. Get them before they get us."

The whole group was quiet for a few moments. Then Disco, a tall, thin man with kinky black hair, said, "So whatcher tryin' to tell us, essentially, is these shadows are ghosts, and we gotta play ghost-busters by shining huge spotlights on 'em? That's yer story?"

Canada cringed. What was she thinking? Of course they'd never buy it; she wouldn't. She sighed, looked down at the floor. "Yeah, Disco," she said. "It sounds crazy, I know, but that's my story and I'm stickin' to it."

"Well, then," Disco said. "If Canada says it's true, that's good enough for me. I'm in."

Canada looked up; all around her, the miners were nodding, murmuring in agreement. She smiled, looked at Doug.

"Hey, I was in a long time ago," Doug said. "Least two hours."

She laughed. "I know, I just . . ." She turned to face the other miners again. "Thanks, guys. Thanks for believing. Thanks for trying."

"What can we say?" Lucia said, looking at her with his dark eyes. "We're from Butte."

"Okay," she said. "Let's meet—ah, at the Natrona head frame early tomorrow morning. Six o'clock sharp. Disco, I know anything before noon's early for you, but I'm countin' on yas."

Disco smiled as a few more chuckles went around. Someone ordered a final round, and the mass started breaking into smaller groups to chat.

Canada looked at Doug, who was studying her intently. "You're a natural," he said.

"Natural what?"

"Natural everything, I guess. I can see why the Ghosts wanted you out of Butte."

She smiled. "That's what Keros said. Thanks. But I'm back now, and unfortunately for them, the Ghosts are gonna find out about it real soon."

"Unfortunately for us," Doug replied, "they already know."

They left The Mint together, wanting to call it a night so they'd be ready for whatever tomorrow might bring. Six A.M. would come quickly. Canada mentioned the Copper Camp Inn was likely empty, and Doug, with no other place to stay, nodded.

They drove in silence, Canada enjoying the lull; she'd been going on adrenaline and panic for several days straight—since leaving Butte in fact—and it felt incredibly comforting to just drive and not think.

Even so, she could smell a thick, cloying smoke in the air, and the scent brought back images of the woman on the street. She'd collapsed into nothing more than a pile of ashes. Spontaneous combustion. She was sure the Shadows were probably behind that, too, but she wasn't sure how or why it all tied together yet.

She pushed those thoughts from her mind and slowed down as the Copper Camp Inn loomed ahead.

Or rather, where the Copper Camp used to be. It was a smoking pile of ash now, and Canada saw outlines of shadow spiders scuttling across the glow of the ashes.

She gulped, amazed at the site. She'd been gone no more than three or four hours, and now the hotel was reduced to nothing more than soot.

"That's what I was afraid of," Doug said quietly.

"You knew this was going to happen?"

"No, but I suspected. Keep going. Don't slow down."

She did as instructed, swallowing and feeling the back of her throat click.

"You used the card to pay for the room," he said. It was a statement, not a question.

"Yeah."

"Here's the thing: with so many operatives in the town, as well as the Darkness, you can't really hide anywhere. I mean, they can trace you with the phone, with the credit card. We've taken care of those. But even without those, they can track you. And they will. After the hotel, I think I know where they'll start."

She felt her stomach knotting. She didn't want to ask the question, but she had to. "Where?"

"Your mother's house."

## 30

TEN MINUTES LATER, Doug asked her to pull over.

"Are you kidding?" she said.

"No. I'm being smart. We need to drive by there unnoticed; I can pull it off, if the place is being watched by other operatives. You can't. You show your face anywhere near your mother's house—which is exactly what they'll be expecting now that you've turned against them—and we might as well have a giant target painted on this Jeep."

She bit her lip, considering. He was right; it was a good idea. She pulled the Jeep to the curb, and they switched spots. But when they were on the street again, she felt as if the Jeep were crawling; she had to stop herself from telling him to speed up.

"Now when we get there," he said, "like it or not, you're going to have to crouch down. Stay out of sight."

"What if the Shadows try to slide into the Jeep with us? They'll see me, and you know they'll be slipping into every car that comes close to the house."

"Been wondering that myself."

"And?"

"And I don't know. I guess we just have to hope it doesn't happen. They don't know what you're driving, and we got rid of your cell phone, your credit card, basically everything you got when you started your job."

She bit her lip again. "No good. We can't risk it. You'll have to drop me off before we get there."

He paused. "You sure?"

"No, but it's the only way."

"Okay." He wheeled the Jeep to the curb, just down the hill from Montana Tech. Canada got out of the car, looking up the hill at the giant concrete M above the school; like the head frames, it was lit up at night.

She closed the door, still looking at the M, and heard the whir of the electric motor as Doug lowered the window. "You think, on some level, Butte has known about the Shadows for some time?" she asked.

"Whaddya mean?"

"Look at the M up there. The head frames all over town with the strings of light, and now the spotlights." She turned. "Over there, Our Lady of the Rockies, lit by spotlights." She bent down and looked through the window now, but could barely see Doug in the darkness. "It's as if Butte's been struggling against the Shadows, the Nothingness, whatever you want to call it, without realizing it."

Doug nodded.

Canada patted the door. "You have the number for this new phone?" She felt the phone in her pocket. "The clean phone?"

"'Course I do. I told you, I'm the tech geek."

"Call me when you find something. I mean, when you drive by her house."

"Will do."

"And . . . you be careful, too." She paused, licked her lips. "I don't want anything to happen to you."

"Makes two of us."

She chuckled.

He turned on the dome light so they could see each other's faces. "Canada," he said, his voice sounding eerily calm, out of place.

"You've come this far. Even if it's bad news about your mother's house—and I'm not saying it is—that doesn't necessarily mean anything, all right? They wouldn't do anything with her; she's too valuable, because—"

"Because if she's alive, they can use her as bait for me. I was the bait for Keros, and now it's my turn to take some bait."

"I was searching for a more delicate way to put it, but yes. So just try to relax, try to breathe, and hang tight."

"Okay."

"Now, here's the thing. We don't know what's going to happen, so we have to plan for that. Something goes wrong, one of us gets lost or something, the other one has to keep going. Has to meet the rest of the guys in the morning, try your little spotlight trick. Deal?"

"Deal."

She stepped back from the Jeep and watched it roll away, the taillights fading down the street. She began walking, aware, for the first time, that the sky was completely dark now. The moon had set long ago. Anywhere in this darkness surrounding her might be Shadows.

Spiders.

She felt her breath and her pulse quickening as she walked. That sickly sweet burning smell hung heavily in the air, so she tried to breathe through her mouth instead. The city around her was quiet. No sounds of traffic or industry; the only sound, in fact, was an odd, deep thrum. It sounded as if it was coming from somewhere in the ground beneath her. A giant wheel, turning slowly, perhaps, cranking out new Shadows with each revolution.

*Spiders.*

She shook her head, as if shaking off imagined shadow spiders. She had to get a handle on this panic before it spun out of control. The first step was to find some light. Light would be comfort.

Where was she? She didn't have a definite sense of her coordinates; she didn't often come this close to her mom's.

She broke into a light jog, heading down to the next corner to get a look at the streets, but didn't recognize either street name. She stood on the corner, panting, considering her next move. Why hadn't Doug called yet? She took the clean cell phone from her pocket, looked at the time. Okay, only four minutes had passed; maybe he hadn't even reached her mother's house yet. She thought briefly of calling him, but realized she didn't have his number.

Canada turned a slow circle, looking all four directions and deciding her best path. A couple blocks up the hill, it looked like a gas station was open, with bright lights bathing the parking lot. Okay, with the quarantine and all, it probably wasn't open, but at least its lights were on. And if it wasn't open, she could continue up the hill toward Montana Tech. There would be a place to hide there.

She hoped.

She forced herself to walk the first block, but then her panic and fear took over, forcing her to run. Just as she feared, the gas station, a small hut-like structure with a sign on it proclaiming PUMP 'N GO, was closed. But she stepped into the overhead lights, welcoming its milky glow on her skin. She bent over, putting her hands on her knees and forcing her breathing to slow. Part of it was the running, yes, but most of it, she knew, was adrenaline pumping her lungs into overdrive. She was on the verge of hyperventilating again.

Canada closed her eyes, tried to count to five with each breath. One two three four five. Breathe. One two three four five. Breathe. One two thr—

Her eyes were closed, but she could sense something happening. Something shifting around her. She wanted to keep her eyes closed, but there was no way she could; she had to open them and see what she knew was there.

The darkness surrounding the service station was rippling, moving like a living creature. A whisper came to her ears, which became

a chorus of murmurs as its volume steadily increased. No, not murmurs, but moans, growing to shrieks of terror and screaming.
Thousands of voices, maybe even hundreds of thousands, converged
in a sea of violence, pressing against her.

Canada put her hands to her ears, but it did no good; the
screams came through just as loud, just as clear. Slowly, terribly, spiders began to swarm around the circle of light she occupied; almost
immediately, the spiders began pressing in on the patch of light
where she stood.

Overhead, she heard a popping sound, followed by a short buzz;
she looked up and saw the PUMP 'N GO sign had burned out, and
skittering spiders now overflowed it. Within moments, the sign
began to glow, fading to ash.

Canada looked around, but saw nothing that could easily help
her. The front door of the service station was glass, but she'd have to
cross a ten-foot patch of darkness to get there. She looked at her
feet, saw the ever-shrinking pool of light being devoured by a million nightmare spiders, and decided she really didn't have a choice.

Canada took a few deep breaths and then went for the door at a
full run. As soon as she passed from the light to the darkness, she
felt as if her chest were being compressed; the spiders were in her
hair, on her arms and face, everywhere, instantly. Their hot, prickly
legs moved across her skin, burning as they went, trying to force
their way into her nostrils, her mouth.

After a few more running steps, she had to close her eyes to keep
the spiders at bay, and she jumped blindly, like she was jumping into
a slide for second base in high school softball (*"A dinger, Canada!
Looking for a dinger!"*), aiming her feet where her memory told her
the door would be. For a split second, her mind pictured thick
bulletproof glass, but then that thought was shattered by the sound
of glass exploding, raining away from her and dropping to the
pavement.

She was on the floor, thrashing about, wiping away spiders but feeling more, thousands more, instantly replace any she brushed away. Dimly, somewhere in the distance, she heard a sound, a repeating, throbbing, high-pitched whine. She couldn't concentrate on that sound, though, because she was gagging; she was trying to force breath into her lungs, but the air wouldn't come.

Canada ran her hands over her face, wiping enough of a clear spot to open her eyes. And now she saw the spiders all over her, retreating, skittering away in the bright fluorescence of light coming from . . . somewhere above her, and, no no no, her mind wouldn't let her think it but it was true; she was gagging on those spiders, coughing them up like phlegm and feeling them run away from her, and she was crying but breathing now, her lungs filling, so she stood and ran her hands over her entire body and screamed and screamed and screamed, and now the spiders seemed to be retreating and she couldn't remember when she'd closed her eyes again so she opened them once more.

An alarm.

The steady, repeated whine was an alarm, strobing in time to huge security lights flashing inside and outside the service station. The shadows dissolved, falling away, and as her senses returned to her, Canada realized for the first time that she was wet. Above her, the sprinkler system was running, drenching the entire service station.

Now her sense of smell was back, filtering through her numbed brain, and she detected the acrid tang of an electrical fire. The PUMP 'N GO sign, that had to be it; when the shadow spiders shorted out the sign, they tripped the sprinkler system.

For a few moments, Canada stood in the wetness. Then she slowly turned, letting the spray wash off the remaining spiders, the ash trails they left behind on her skin.

She looked outside. Through the mist of water, she saw nothing but night. No scurrying spiders, no swarming sea of blackness enveloping the building. The shadows had retreated. At least for now.

In one of the service station bays, Canada found a truck with keys on the dash. Yes, the keys were there; the service station's owner would of course leave the keys in the pickup. It's not like anyone was just going to jump through the front door, set off the alarm and sprinkler system, then drive the pickup away.

Until tonight.

It was an older Ford, maybe mid-70s, with oversized rims, beefy tires, and a lift kit. In other words, a little piece of heaven after so many black sedans. But mostly it was a set of wheels, and between the shadows who likely still lurked and the inevitable police—they had to be coming, right?—Canada knew she needed out of there.

She nodded, forced her muscles to relax, and pushed the garage door button. She cranked the key, listened to the Ford rumble to life, and put it into gear when the garage door topped out.

By the time she hit the edge of the parking lot, she was already going thirty; she bumped across the curb—nothing more than a small blip on those big, meaty tires—and fishtailed out onto the street. Only then did she realize she'd been holding her breath, and she took in a few quick gasps. Her lungs felt raw, sore, and that made her think of *why* they were raw and sore. Her stomach tumbled again in response.

A block away, she let herself slow down. The darkness outside was just that: darkness. No rippling, no undulating. She checked the rearview mirror. No one behind her. She eased her foot off the accelerator and made a right turn, not quite sure where she was going but needing to keep moving.

She looked at the clock on the pickup's dash as she drove. It read 2:32 A.M. What time did it get light this time of year? Six o'clock maybe? No way she'd make it to daybreak.

Worse yet, she hadn't heard from Doug. Quickly, she fished the clean phone out of her pocket, now slick and wet from the sprinklers. It was still charged and working, but she hadn't missed any calls.

That was bad. It meant something had happened to him.

She started to put the phone back in her pocket, but then an idea occurred to her. She pressed and held the display button on the phone, then scrolled to Contacts. After a few seconds, the word *Doug* appeared on the display with a number attached. She smiled as she hit the Send button. He'd programmed his number into her autodial. Tech geek indeed.

After a few rings, the phone picked up. "Doug?" she said. A bit of static answered. "Doug, can you hear me?"

The static cleared, and a voice rasped, "Doug's with us now." She recognized it immediately; it was the same voice that had spoken to her earlier at her trailer house. The voice of the Shadow posing as her father. "So is your mother." Then, Canada heard the rising murmur, the babble of a thousand voices, crescendoing in screams before the connection went dead.

She managed to bring the truck to a stop in the middle of the street before she dropped the phone. Tears streamed down her face, and now her stomach wouldn't be denied any longer; she opened the door and stumbled out of the big truck, falling to her hands and knees as her stomach emptied itself. She closed her eyes, feeling the tears stream out of them as she cried and vomited at the same time, everything pouring out of her at once. This was too much, too much, and she couldn't make it four more hours until dawn.

She opened her eyes, only slightly encouraged to see that she'd not thrown up any more spiders, and realized lights were approaching from behind.

It had to be one of the operatives. The Shadows had pinpointed her at the service station, and the operatives would know she had stolen this truck, and now they had found her and maybe that was better because all of her senses were on overload and her body was shaking uncontrollably and she was sure she couldn't even stand if she wanted to and the Shadows the Ghosts the Nothingness had her mother and Doug and what else was there for her?

She heard air brakes as the vehicle stopped, followed by the clatter of a diesel engine idling, but she was too weak to lift her head. It was better if she didn't see it coming, anyway. She hoped it was a bullet to the head, quick and easy and painless.

She heard nothing else, but when she opened her eyes again, still looking at the ground, she saw a pair of work boots in her field of vision. Water dripped from her long hair to the pavement.

A voice from above spoke to her. "Rest now, Candace Mac-Hugh."

Only two people called her Candace, she thought numbly as she lost consciousness.

Her mother.

And Keros.

## 31

THE LIGHT WAS WARM, comforting, enveloping. Canada felt it first, and she chose not to open her eyes.

Then, the terror of the last several hours hit her, and her eyes came open on their own. She gasped, stirring up suddenly. Had to check for shadow spiders, she could feel them on—

"Be still. You are safe." It was the voice of Keros, somewhere in front of her.

She did as she was told; it was nice to follow orders for a change, to mindlessly do what she was told to do. She looked around, familiarizing herself with her surroundings. She finally realized she was in the sleeper cab of a large diesel truck, on a small bunk surrounded by padded walls. On a shelf next to her sat a mini-TV, and on the floor a small box plugged into an adapter on the wall. She put her hand down to the box and felt cool air blowing from it. An AC unit.

A curtain behind the TV and shelf moved, revealing the face of Keros. He smiled, and suddenly, for a reason she couldn't explain, Canada was crying. Tears were streaming down her cheeks and falling onto the bunk, so she sat up and wiped at the tears.

"You are safe," Keros repeated.

Canada nodded, still unable to speak, and numbly remembered it was light that had awakened her. At least, she had awakened to light.

It was day outside, she could tell by the light filtering through the curtain.

She tried to speak, but her throat was raw and watery and she had to clear it first. "What time is it?"

"You've been sleeping," he answered. "It's early afternoon, about two o'clock."

Two o'clock? She'd slept . . . almost twelve hours?

"You've slept about eleven hours," he said. He was doing that odd creepy thing again, as if reading her mind and responding to her thoughts. "Your body needed the rest," he continued. He sat on the bunk next to her and waited quietly.

She sighed deeply, testing her lungs. They actually felt pretty good, but she could feel fresh smoke in the air. "I'm really late," she said. "Gotta meet them. The spotlights." She knew she was speaking in short, unintelligible bursts, but she didn't care, and it didn't matter.

"Your people have been working on the spotlights," he said. "Since this morning. They should be done, I would say, within another hour or two."

Another wave of memories from the previous night flooded over her, but she held back the tears this time. "Is Doug . . . was Doug with them?" she asked.

"He is not," Keros said. "But he is alive. As is your mother. They're unharmed, right now, because—"

"Because they're bait."

"Yes."

"Where are they?"

Keros pointed straight down. "Down there," he said simply.

"In the tunnels?"

He nodded.

Canada swallowed hard. She knew this, her gut knew it instinctively; she hadn't needed to ask.

"You've come far, Candace MacHugh. But not quite far enough."

She put her head back against the padded wall. If more difficult parts were ahead of her, she wasn't sure she could make it. Nothing could be worse than what she'd been through last night. And if it was, she was sure it would kill her.

"Look at your skin," said Keros.

Canada did as she was told, and she was horrified to discover it had an ashy gray appearance, even translucent in some areas. It reminded her of the ash tracks the shadow spiders had left on her skin. She ran her hands over the skin of her arms, but the ash stayed. Memories of the hotel room in Seattle flashed before her again. She needed a shower.

Keros took her hand and held it, holding her gaze with his own. His eyes were hypnotic, and she let herself fall into them. "This is where you are now, Candace," he said. "This is where your mother is, where Doug is, where all of Butte is today. It's an affliction that will not go away by itself. You must stop it."

She was terrified, but somehow felt calm inside Keros's gaze. "So Butte really does have an infectious disease? The quarantine is real?"

He shook his head. "The people of Butte have the same disease every human does. But tonight, it will kill them unless you can stop it."

"The Shadows, you mean? The Nothingness?"

"Yes."

"But how can we stop the Nothingness? It's—"

"It is inside you, Candace."

"Okay, the answer is inside me, I get it. But what I mean is, what are the Shadows? I can't fight them, I can't stop them, I can't find an answer that's inside me unless I know what I'm fighting. Is it demons?"

Keros smiled bitterly. "Humans always want their enemies to be demons, spirits. That blinds them to their worst enemies."

Canada felt herself getting mad now, felt her Irish temper bubbling and flaring. "Just give me a straight answer," she said. "I'm sick of these riddles, these fortune cookie blurbs."

"I cannot give you the answers, Candace MacHugh. I cannot make the choices for you. You will do what you will do."

It wasn't the answer she was looking for, but already she felt the flare dying down, and she let herself be drawn into Keros's gaze again.

"But . . . I'm out of ideas."

"I will give you this: 'Even though I walk through the Valley of Shadow, I will not fear.'"

Canada wanted to roll her eyes, but she couldn't. "Great," she said, trying to sound sarcastic. "A Bible quote." But even to her own ears, her voice sounded more earnest than sarcastic.

"It is. And it's what you must do; Butte is not the first Valley of Shadow."

"Okay." It still didn't make sense, but now a sense of urgency was starting to creep in; if it was late afternoon, everyone would be getting ready to light the spotlights. They would have to do it before dark.

Except.

Except something wasn't sitting right. Something about last night . . . but it stayed just out of her grasp.

Keros grabbed her arm, and Canada immediately felt waves of energy flowing into her arm, radiating from the point of contact and spreading throughout her whole body. "This is not all about you, Candace MacHugh," he said, much more gently than she'd expected. "You have to realize that. All of Butte has to, or you—all of you—will fall into the Nothingness."

As if ignited by Keros's touch, or maybe his word, Canada began to think of Butte and all her fond memories. He was right; she needed to do something. And feeling that need made her feel instantly better. Her skin, she noticed, immediately returned to its normal color.

Keros released her arm and moved out of the sleeper cab, back to the front of the truck; a few moments later, she heard the truck start. Canada felt better, much better, after . . . whatever had just happened with Keros. But she could have used an hour of recharging, and he'd only given her thirty seconds or so. She took a few deep breaths and followed him out into the cab, sliding into the passenger seat.

"I will drive you to your meeting spot," he said, "but I cannot protect you after that. You have another eight hours before darkness falls." He put the giant truck in gear and eased out the clutch. "Before Butte falls."

Canada walked into The Mint, feeling groggy, numb; the energy from Keros was gone. She'd been thinking about that all the way over, how tired she was. How overwhelmed she was. How unready she was. She tripped on her way in the door, then made her way to the bar and sat down.

"Well, if it ain't Canada MacHugh," Joe said.

She smirked. "It don't feel like Canada MacHugh, I can tell you that, Joe."

Joe eyed her. "Seen plenty a people stumble outta here, but you're the first one I seen stumble in."

She raised her eyebrows, leaned against the bar. "Gimme the usual. Any of the guys around?"

He pointed toward the back of the bar. "They been in here the last hour or so, wondering what they should do. Like miners, when they wonder what they should do, they start drinking. Watched the news conference on TV; ultra-SARS or some such nonsense, like you said. I think, if you hadn't wandered in here, they woulda gone and tried to do it all themselves in another hour or so. 'Course, by then, they mighta been too schnockered to do much good."

Canada took her Diet Pepsi, tipped it to Joe in a toast, and drained it. "Gimme another," she said, putting the glass on the bar. "Make it a double."

She took her second drink toward the back of the bar, the words of Keros ringing in her mind: *"They just need someone to lead them."* Well, like it or not, she was that leader.

She pasted on a smile, feeling the caffeine in the soda doing its work. "Well, guys," she said, "what'd I miss?" She looked around; the numbers had actually grown. At least two dozen people stood around her now, including four or five women.

"You missed all the work, for one," said Disco. "You should try being a foreman."

They all laughed at that, Canada included. Black humor. Same kind of humor that prompted miners to dub Butte's head frames "gallow frames." There was an uneasiness among them, a nervous tension; they knew something big was about to happen, something that might be bad, even fatal, for many of them. But in the face of it, they had to laugh. She understood this.

"Spotlights all ready?" she asked, smiling.

"Yup," said Hambone. "Had to hook up generators at a couple locations, and jerry-rig the mountings and fittings on others. But they're all pointed straight down. Our candles are ready to light."

She nodded at Hambone. "All right then, since I'm the appointed foreman now—and 'foreman' will do, thank you very much, I'm not a 'foreperson'—I'd say it's time we split up and headed for the lights." A few more chuckles. "Let's get a crew of three at each head frame. And, uh, do we have walkie-talkies?"

No one answered, but Canada was shaking her head now anyway. "Wait a minute, what am I saying?" she said. "We don't need walkie-talkies; we got cell phones. Let's make sure each crew has a cell phone, and let's trade numbers. We'll pick a go time right now." She pulled out her cell phone and looked at the time. "About 2:40 right now; let's give everyone an hour to get into position and call it 3:45. We all light our candles at 3:45, agreed?" She winced, suddenly thinking of Doug again. If he were here, he'd figure out how to conference them all together on their cell phones.

Something twinged in her chest. She'd pulled both Doug and her mother into this mess. She looked at the display. No recent calls. Should she call Doug's number again? She shivered. No, she wouldn't do that. She guessed Doug was nowhere near his cell phone anymore.

Or was he?

Now that she thought about it, he'd said something about tracing her cell phone with his, hadn't he? GPS capabilities? Well, he'd said it about the other cell phones—the cell phones they gave all the operatives—but Doug was a tech guy, after all. She guessed these new phones had GPS tracking built in.

She pressed the menu button, then chose Contacts. One of the options, something she'd never seen on a cell phone before, was Trace. She chose the option and waited while a color display brought up a street map, then zoomed in on an address up near Walkerville. "Thank God for those tech geeks," she muttered under her breath.

Disco was standing in front of her, and she glanced up from the phone display. "Hey, Canada," he said. "Which head frame you going to?"

She shook her head. "Got some other things to do right now, Disco," she said. "I'm the foreman now, remember? I don't actually work." Disco laughed and moved out the door.

Something inside was still gnawing at her. Something big, a 500-pound gorilla sitting in the room with her that she still couldn't see. She was missing a key component with their current plan, but she didn't know what it was. Which was frustrating, because they didn't have the luxury of time.

Lucia walked by, turning her attention away from inner thoughts. "Hey," she said, grabbing Lucia's arm. "Can you and I make a little detour on the way? I need some things, and I think you might have them." Lucia and Binkowicz had always been famous for squirreling away mining paraphernalia. For Binkowicz, it had been simple pyromania; he was born to be on a blasting crew, and Canada guessed he liked to conduct his own experiments outside mining hours. For Lucia, however, it had been the pack-rat syndrome. A fellow traveler, of sorts, as she'd struggled with that compulsion herself. Lucia had collected numerous things from jobsites over the years. Things she would need now.

Lucia smiled, showing teeth yellowed by years of chewing tobacco. "Canada, I got everything."

## 32

A FEW MINUTES LATER, they were at Lucia's place, just west of town off Excelsior Street, in an industrial section. Lucia's home was five acres, half junkyard, half abandoned mine tailings, nestled among warehouses, storage yards, and other industrial properties. He lived inside one of the tin buildings on the property, a building that looked, from the outside, like an abandoned shed. Canada had never seen inside the shed; she wasn't sure she wanted to.

He parked his car, an old green Plymouth Satellite, and sat surveying the area. "Home sweet home," he said. "Wanna see some of my goodies?"

Canada could tell Lucia was bursting with excitement and anticipation, knowing someone was interested in his collection. Few, if any, people had probably asked about it before.

"That's why I'm here, Lucia," she said, opening the Satellite's door and climbing out.

Lucia vaulted out of the car and practically skipped to the nearest shed as Canada followed. "Okay," he said. "You asked about safety equipment. I got some of that in here." He slid open the creaking metal door, reached inside to flip on the light.

"No locks on anything?"

"Locks? Nah. Who's gonna bother this stuff out here—doubt anyone would even think something's in all these sheds."

Canada had to agree. The property looked much like it had for the last decade: overgrown weeds, abandoned junk dotting the land-scape, and rusty metal warehouses whistling in the wind.

"Okay," Lucia said, venturing inside his storage shed.

Canada followed, shocked by what she found inside: rows and rows of . . . everything. Clothing, tools, equipment, supplies, all stacked in neat rows and separated by framing.

Lucia grabbed a clipboard off a rusty nail on one of the framing beams. "Let's start with that lit hard hat," he said, looking over the top sheet on the clipboard. He scanned, turned to the next sheet. "Here we go. Row J." He put the clipboard under his arm and started to walk deeper into the building, then turned and stared back at Canada again for the first time since opening the doors. A pan-icked look came across his face when he looked at her. "What? What's wrong?" he asked.

Canada shook her head, still taking in the warehouse. "I . . . I had no idea, Lucia," she said. "I mean, everyone always talked. But, you know, I thought it was just talk. I didn't know you had this much."

Lucia beamed, obviously pleased at her reaction. "And this 'ere's only one warehouse," he said.

She began to follow him as they made their way to Row J. "If you don't mind my asking," she said, "I'm just wondering . . ."

"Why?" he said, finishing the sentence for her.

"Yeah."

He shrugged as he set the clipboard down and inventoried a few boxes in Row J, selecting one box and slicing it open with a utility knife he produced from one of his overall pockets. "Thought a lot about that, Canada. And I guess the answer is: because no one else is. I mean, at first, years ago, it was the thrill. This is stealin', when it comes down to it. No way around that. So I'd be stealin' from the comp'ny, carting away stuff here and there. Mostly worthless stuff at first, but then bigger 'n bigger things, just to see if I could get away with it."

He pulled a hard hat with an attached headlamp from the box. "We'll getcha some batteries for this," he said, interrupting himself. He made a mark on his clipboard, then turned and began looking for a different row.

"C'mere," he said, motioning to her. She followed him to a different row, this one filled with file boxes. "Pick a box. Any box."

She stepped forward, pulled the front drawer of the box open; inside were several legal-sized files overflowing with papers.

"Go ahead," he said. "Start reading. I think . . . maybe that explains it as much as anything. Why I have this all here."

She nodded and pulled a folder from the file. It was a transcript of a phone conversation recorded in 1983—some miner named Jim Livingston, being threatened by an unidentified caller. She scanned the transcription, skipping to the end. Notes at the end said SUBJECT DECEASED and gave a date only about a week after the call was recorded.

Canada looked back at Lucia. "I don't get it," she said.

"Pick another box, another folder. Keep reading. I'll get the rest of your stuff and be back in a few minutes."

She watched him walk off, then opened another box. More stuffed legal folders. She picked a file at random and scanned the papers inside. This was a report on a mining accident in 1972, which had killed twelve miners.

Another box, another folder. Fires in downtown Butte. More people dead.

More folders, filled with interview transcripts, filed reports, newspaper clippings, letters and correspondence—much of it blacked out with markers or transcribed as INFORMATION REDACTED. And all of it, somehow, related to deaths and mining in Butte.

"See the pattern?" Lucia asked.

Startled, Canada looked up from the letter she was reading. "This is like . . . every shady death in Butte's history," she said.

He nodded. "Well, far from every death, I expect. But enough of them.

"It's not just death, though," he continued. "It's the mines. The mining. It's all tied together. And a lot of it . . . explosions, fire." He paused. "I found all this in storage at the mining offices—in *secret* storage, you understand. But for me, when it comes to those buildings, there ain't no secrets."

She smiled, and he returned the smile before turning and surveying all the boxes in the warehouse. "So yeah, maybe I started as a thief or whatever. Just for the thrill. But when I found these, when I found all this, I knew it was something more than that. I was . . . saving it all, I guess. 'Cuz no one else was. I mean, it got kinda obvious the way things was goin'. We knew the party was endin', din't we? Seemed like someone needed to keep this stuff to . . . to prove it was real, I guess. To remember."

Canada saw his eyes starting to water. "'Cuz you look at all those papers, you start to realize, they ain't just wanting to take away our jobs. They want to rub us out, make it like we never existed." He wiped at his cheek and gave her a hard stare. "Make sense?"

She thought of her trailer, stacked with newspapers, laundry, meaningless objects she'd somehow imbued with her sense of loss and isolation. Lucia was a fellow pack rat, yes, but he was a master. His hoarding had a noble purpose, while hers was just a mental tic of sorts. She smiled. "Makes perfect sense, Lucia."

Outside, the sound of a car pulling in made both of them stop their movements. They froze, becoming statues as they strained to hear the light moan of the brakes engaging, the engine idling for a few moments.

"Lucia, you out here?" Canada recognized the voice. Binkowicz, Lucia's odd partner in crime.

Lucia quick ran to the door and waved him in.

Binkowicz looked surprised to see Canada in the warehouse. "Canada," he said, "I thought you were going to one of the head frames." He checked his watch. "We'll light 'em up in about half an hour."

"I'm going," she said. "Just needed to stop by here for a few supplies first."

"Yeah," Lucia said. "How about you shake a leg here and help us fill up Canada's list." He handed a slip of paper to Binkowicz, who studied the list for a moment.

Binkowicz looked up from the list, staring at Canada. "Sure you don't want a few bricks of ANFO?" he asked, a gleam returning to his pyromaniac eyes.

"Bricks of ANFO?"

He shrugged. "Ammonium Nitrate Fuel Oil. We used—"

"I know what ANFO is, Binkowicz. I was on the blast crew, remember? I'm asking about the bricks."

"Oh. Yeah, kinda my own design. Keeps it stable. Form it in five-pound bricks, dip it in wax to seal it. Tape a tube of gelatinous dynamite to it, along with some kind of triggering mechanism. I don't got many bricks, but I got tons of fifty-pound bags a fertilizer; we could whip up a few."

"I suppose I shouldn't ask where you get the gelatinous dynamite."

"I suppose," he answered. He waved Canada's list of items at her. "But I don't get it. What are you gonna do with all the stuff on this list?"

Canada smiled. "Still workin' on it, Binkowicz. Still workin' on it. But I got a whole half an hour to figure it out."

Five minutes later, Canada realized she had no transportation. She'd been working on this grand scheme in her mind and forgotten one of the most important details: how she was going to get there.

Lucia simply smiled and handed her the keys to his Satellite, then he and Binkowicz helped her load the supplies into the car's passenger side. Canada jumped in and started it, then turned onto Excelsior and began making her way back toward uptown. She pulled the cell phone from her pocket, hit the Trace option again, and began following the map.

She made a right on Mercury Street and pointed the Satellite up the hill toward Walkerville. She looked at the phone on the seat and caught her breath as she saw a shadow on the floorboard shifting and moving. She waited for it to speak, but it didn't. Instead, it rippled out the crack of the door and was gone. Canada checked the rearview mirror, looking for the shadow, but it was nowhere to be seen.

She took another right and checked her mirror. Within seconds she saw a car pull on the street behind her.

Okay, then. Another right. The car followed. She had almost made a giant loop now, but she didn't turn back up the hill on Mercury; she didn't want the car tailing her to see where she was really going. Instead, she did a quick left, then pulled into a blind alley. She put the car in reverse, held her foot off the gas, and waited. In a couple of seconds, the tail followed her, a big black sedan. Newer model. As soon as she saw the smear of black passing behind her, she floored the accelerator and spun into the street, hitting the sedan with the Satellite's rear bumper.

The black sedan didn't have a chance against the heavy iron of mid-'70s Mopar, and it crumpled like a beer can, collapsing in the middle where Canada T-boned it. She kept her foot on the gas, pushing the car across the street and into a light pole on the other side. Only then did she shift the car into drive and pull away. The small sedan came away from the curb, caught up on the Satellite's bumper for a few feet, then fell away. Canada saw the driver, unconscious behind the wheel of the other car. She didn't know whether the impact had knocked him out or the air bag, now slowly deflating as she pulled away. But it didn't matter; she had one less Spook tailing her.

"Think I might owe you a new bumper after this, Lucia," she said, smiling to herself as she turned onto Mercury Street again. It felt good, doing rather than waiting, acting rather than thinking.

The thought of shadow spiders, and the tunnels beneath the city, terrified her. But her mother and Doug were in those tunnels somewhere, and she needed to find them.

## 33

THIS WAS WHERE THE PHONE'S GPS had brought her. She knew, somehow, she would end up somewhere like this.

Canada stood before the bulkhead of the abandoned Corra mine shaft. The timbers of the bulkhead had rotted and begun to fall away, and cool air from the tunnel's bowels—fueled, likely, by water a couple hundred feet down—pushed at her face.

The cool air also, however, brought the constant murmur of moaning and wailing, which chilled Canada's skin far more than the temperature of the breeze. Maybe worst of all was the ever-present smell: that sick-sweet burning odor. Like barbecue, she realized, but how it would smell if the meat were rotten and putrid.

According to the directions on the cell phone, this is where she would find Doug and her mother. Or, at the very least, this is where she would find Doug's cell phone. She let go of that thought, not wanting to think about finding a lonely phone, abandoned on the hard floor of an old mine.

She also let go of thoughts of shadow spiders crawling on her skin.

She checked the clock on her cell phone. About fifteen minutes left before everyone lit those spotlights and pointed them into the shafts beneath Butte. She had no idea what would happen.

Between now and then, however, she intended to find her mother and Doug.

She was prepared this time.

She wore a lit hard hat, coveralls, gloves, and steel-toed safety boots. The boots were a little big, but they would work for this. On her face she had safety goggles and a respirator, and she carried two more respirators. Earplugs sealed her ears.

Lucia, she had to admit, had put her own pack-rat skills to considerable shame.

She walked past the rotting bulkhead, reached for her helmet to turn on its light, and went into the mine. This horizontal tunnel wouldn't last long—maybe a couple hundred feet. Even though she'd never worked the underground mines in Butte, she knew how they operated; the head frames, the giant towers that dotted the Butte skyline, once housed giant engines that powered trams, moving miners up and down to deep shafts hundreds of feet below the ground and hauling the mined ore back to the surface. The head frames, in effect, were giant elevators, making stops at the several underground floors of each mine through a central vertical shaft.

Most of the horizontal tunnels, then, were totally below ground; only a few, such as the one here, came to the surface. If her mother and Doug were truly in this mine, she'd run into them within the next couple hundred feet; there was simply no way to get them into the deeper tunnels without an operating head frame. And she wouldn't want to venture too deep into the tunnels anyway; many of the deep ones would be flooded by water. Others would hold lethal fumes and gases leaking out of the mined rock. That's what the respirators were for. The air was probably fine in this short tunnel, but a respirator was a good safety precaution.

Okay, so that wasn't the only reason for the respirator. Canada also wanted to keep the shadow spiders away from her mouth. She knew, sooner or later, they would show up.

She slowly moved forward, turning her head back and forth to sweep her helmet's beam across the tunnel surface.

Even with the earplugs in, the sound of the moaning and screaming attacked her eardrums. It should be quiet in this rough granite hallway, she should be hearing the shuffle of her feet on the rough surface, but that was all drowned out by the murmuring.

Her heart was pounding louder, threatening to trip-hammer, and she felt her lungs shifting into the next gear. Her mind flooded with images of the previous night as she continued forward. She stopped, forced a few deep breaths through the musty cartridges on the respirator, made herself continue.

What time was it now? Maybe five minutes had passed. Hopefully, no more than that. She turned around; the entrance to the tunnel, still bathed in light, was maybe a hundred feet behind her. She guessed, at most, that another two hundred feet were in front of her before the tunnel met a vertical shaft of some sort.

The light of her helmet caught a glint of something. She stopped her head, moved it back, took a few more steps forward. It was small and metallic.

A phone. Doug's phone. Just close enough to the entrance to still catch its signal.

Her heart sank when she saw it; that meant Doug was, indeed, separated from his phone. The Shadows had put the phone here as a trap, and anytime now, they would—

Wait. Her light caught something else on the floor of the tunnel, just twenty feet or so farther on. Someone on the floor. She retrieved Doug's phone, slipping it into her pocket as she rushed to his body on the floor.

Yes, it was both Doug and her mother, tied with rope and lying on the floor of the tunnel next to each other. The floor's surface was wet here; a trickle of rusty water ran away from them, back toward the darkness.

Her light found Doug's face. He was conscious, but he seemed listless; his eyes dilated in the light's beam, but he said nothing when

Canada bent down to touch him. She scanned her mother's face; her eyes were closed, but she could see her mother's chest rising and falling in quick, jerky gasps, as if she were having a nightmare.

Canada didn't hesitate.

She put down the bag she'd brought along and unzipped it. Two extra masks were inside, along with extra goggles. Also a pocketknife from Lucia's vast collection. They were bound with simple baling twine, so she sliced at the knots between Doug's hands and feet, then repeated the process with her mother.

Out came the respirators and goggles. Doug swatted at her hand groggily as she put the respirator over his face, but then he relaxed and breathed normally once it was on. He offered no struggle as she strapped on his goggles.

Her mother had no visible reaction to either the goggles or respirator; her entire body was limp, even though the quick hyperventilations continued, interrupted every few seconds by an involuntary muscle spasm. Canada hoped it wasn't a result of fumes or poisons built up in the tunnel; it was unlikely just a few hundred feet in, but certainly not impossible.

Doug was moving now, voluntarily moving, and he sat up, looking around. Canada took off her helmet, pointed the beam toward her own face to show him it was her, and took his hand in hers. She could tell he was trying to communicate, saying something through the respirator, but she couldn't hear it over the steady moans in the tunnel.

She pointed the beam of the light down at the space between the two of them, then tried to communicate with her other hand by pointing a gloved finger first at him, then at herself, and finally at her mother before motioning toward the cave entrance; she swept the beam toward the light of the entrance a few hundred feet behind them. In the glow of the beam, she saw him nodding quickly, so she returned the nod and replaced the helmet on her head. She scrambled on her hands and knees to her mother, then lifted her to a sitting position.

That's when she felt the shift beginning.

For a few seconds, the murmurs, the moans, halted. Then, the darkness around her rippled, taking on dimension and weight. She glanced back at the tunnel entrance and saw ripples across the surface of light, like heat coming off hot pavement. Except these waves weren't heat. They were bands of darkness.

Now the darkness began moving through the tunnel like a river, swirling and eddying around them.

Canada saw her light weakening instantly, as if running out of battery, but she knew that wasn't what was happening. The Shadows were overpowering her feeble beam, eating away at it like acid eats away at steel. Within a few seconds, the beam winked out, plunging them into total darkness.

That's when the horrible realization returned. The shadows, the spiders, had eaten away the light at the service station—just as they'd done now.

Light wasn't the key.

Her whole crew was about to point giant spotlights into the darkness of the tunnels beneath Butte, and it would do nothing to stop the Shadows.

Then, she felt the spiders.

Even through layers of clothing and coveralls, she felt the prickly spider legs swarming, moving across her body, looking for openings in what she wore. Within seconds, she realized she'd been stupid to think she could even begin to stand this sensation, and the clothing was no real protection from the spiders at all.

*I can't do this. I can't do this. I can't do this.*

She rolled to her stomach, curled into a fetal ball, but still the spiders were all over her. Consuming her.

*I cant do this I cant do this I cant do this.*

It became her mantra, her escape from the white-hot flashes of terror exploding in her mind now. She realized, at once, that the term "losing your mind" was entirely appropriate; she felt large sections of her brain shutting down, going dormant, unable to cope with the terror coursing through her body.

*IcantdothisIcantdothisIcant—*

Another flash exploded in her mind, but this one was different. Instead of going dim, the flash lit up an awareness of something new. A memory. A connection she hadn't made before.

*"It's inside you."*

Keros had said that. She'd assumed he meant the answer was inside her. Maybe he had meant that, but she felt sure he'd also meant it more literally: the problem was inside her. The *shadow* was inside her.

*"'When a man looks into the abyss, the abyss also looks into him,'"* Keros had quoted.

Yes, the abyss was the shadow. But the abyss wasn't just the shadow.

Canada opened her eyes and felt her mind coming back online. "It's me," she whispered into her respirator.

## 34

CANADA FELT ENERGY COURSING through her again, as if Keros were here and touching her. The shadow spiders were there, yes, but they were . . . nothing. They were shadows.

*Though I walk through the Valley of Shadow, I will not fear.*

She brought her knees up under her and rose, staying on her knees as if in prayer. It was difficult to move, as if she were in a large body of water. No, not water; more solid than that. Gelatin. She could see nothing, could hear nothing but the steady mix of moans and screams, but she had to find Doug and her mother.

She dropped to the floor of the tunnel and began searching, exploring. Nothing but hard granite, a bit of dampness. She adjusted, rotating her body a few degrees, and repeated the procedure.

There, her hand brushed against something. Clothing. She patted across the shape, recognizing it as a sleeved arm. She slid her hand across the arm and toward the torso, felt the body jerk. It wasn't Doug; it was her mother. Good. She'd found one of them. She found her mother's hand, grasped it in her own gloved hand, and explored with her other hand again.

*Though I walk through the Valley of Shadow, I will not fear.*

Search, shift a few degrees, search.

A pant leg.

She had both of them now; her right hand was holding her mother's hand, and her left hand was on Doug's leg.

Now she just had to get them out of this tunnel. She looked around, trying to see all directions. Was the tunnel entrance behind her? She couldn't see it. She turned, tried to look behind her again. No, it wasn't there, either.

She was surrounded by darkness. She had no idea which way to go. The Shadows had blotted out the light from the tunnel entrance, and she was inside that darkness with no way out.

*Though I walk through the Valley of Shadow, I will not fear.*

That's when the moans and screams surrounding her intensified, becoming shrieks of sheer terror.

Canada still felt the Shadows surrounding her, enveloping her, but now she felt as if she were in the middle of a river current. It began gently at first, swirls and eddies, but then it intensified, getting stronger. She tried to lean into the current, but the Shadows were rippling by her so fast now that she knew she couldn't fight it. She lowered herself as far as she could on the floor of the tunnel, flat on her stomach. Down at the floor, near the trickle of water running on the granite surface, the flow was weaker, but still she could feel the current of Shadows rushing past her.

She felt something on her head slip, and she realized her hard hat and light had been swept off her head, carried away by the mass migration of Shadows.

For at least a minute, the high-pitched wails moved by them as the torrent of Shadows spilled past them. During that time, she felt Doug beginning to move. Abruptly, his hand found hers and gripped it, squeezing hard. She smiled.

*Though I walk through the Valley of Shadow, I will not fear.*

Eventually, the current slowed, and Canada raised her head. She still felt the spiders, felt them entwined in her hair, thrashing and skittering, but it didn't matter now.

She would not fear.

To the left of her, in the direction of the current, the full darkness somehow seemed to be breaking. Cracks appeared and she realized it was the light outside. The tunnel entrance. The Shadows, it seemed, were cascading out the tunnel's entrance. And their numbers in this tunnel were thinning.

She turned her head the other way and looked. Light was coming from this direction also, but it was faint, without form: a glow.

Canada smiled. Obviously, 3:45 had rolled around, and the crews had thrown the switches on the spotlights. The glow she was seeing was from one or more of those spotlights, shining into the tunnels. Most of the mines on Butte Hill had been connected by tunnels eventually, after consolidation under the Anaconda Company, so it made sense she'd see a far-off glow. When the crews had turned on the spotlights, the Shadows had obviously fled the safety of the tunnels for the outside like so many bats.

She now knew the light wouldn't stop them, wouldn't kill them. But maybe it would give her enough time to get Doug and Diane to safety.

Canada struggled and stood, and as she did, Doug stood as well. He tottered but made it. Canada found his face and when she saw him looking at her, pointed to her mom. He understood. Together, they propped her against the mine wall.

Without words, she again pointed to Diane and then herself. Doug was stronger normally but he'd been barely able to stand. It'd take all his strength to get himself out. Doug squeezed her hand, and for an instant, the Shadows weren't there. But just as quickly, Canada was back. They needed to leave. Now.

She turned to her mother. She thought of totally lifting Diane, trying to carry her, but that was probably too much. Instead, she turned her mother and let her lie on the ground. Then, she moved behind, pushed Diane into a sitting position, looped her arms around Diane's chest and began dragging her backward.

It was difficult at first, but every foot seemed to get easier, as if she were making a transition from quicksand to solid ground. She struggled, feeling the sweat pool in her goggles and rattle around inside her respirator, but the struggle was so much easier because each time she stopped to check, the light at the tunnel entrance loomed a little closer. And Doug, the entire time, was next to her, making his own painful way out of the nightmare.

In all, she guessed it took her fifteen minutes to bring her mother to the surface. It was light outside, but not as light as she'd thought it would be; indeed, it looked like dusk overhead. She should check her cell phone now, see if maybe she had spent several hours in the tunnel, but—

But it didn't matter how much time she'd spent in that tunnel.

She was on her knees, her mother's body draped across her lap, and she worked quickly, silently, wiping away the shadow spiders from her mother's skin. She pulled off the respirator, leaned close, put her ear over her mother's mouth, listened and watched. She saw the rise and fall of her mother's breathing, accelerating once again to quick spasms. Her mother's body jerked and flinched, and her mouth opened. Several shadow spiders poured out of Diane's mouth, skittering across the rock and looking for darker shadows.

Her mother was alive.

A sudden memory triggered in her mind: seeing the paramedic work on the man from the burning apartment in St. Louis. The Shadow posing as her father had told her that was a mistake, had said she could change the future by doing so.

She realized now that was true; she *could* change the future by her every action.

"*You are the kind of person who will pull people from a burning building,*" Keros had told her. Yes. She was, and would always be, that.

Convinced her mom was safe at least for the moment, she stood and moved to check on Doug. He'd made it from the mine, but she'd been so intent on her mother that now, when she turned, she saw he'd collapsed just outside the entrance, in the shadow of the shaft. She ran to him and started brushing away the shadow spiders, starting with his face.

A voice startled her. The first voice she'd heard in probably an hour. "Need help?" She turned. It was her mother, Diane, somehow, standing above her and looking no worse for the wear. Her respirator and safety goggles were gone now, and her skin was bright and pink in the pale light.

"Sure," Canada said, but realized her mother wouldn't understand her while she still wore the respirator.

Her mother, however, did seem to understand; she dropped to her knees and began helping Canada brush away the remnants of shadow.

Doug's skin was hot, flaky, ash-like.

He clawed at the respirator on his face, so Canada took it off. "I . . . I can't breathe," he whispered. "Just let me . . . just leave me here. Stupid . . . try this. I . . ." He closed his eyes again.

Canada peeled off her own respirator and goggles now, looked at her mother. She knew what was happening to Doug, what would continue to happen to him. It had happened to the woman on the street, and others; many of the men in The Mint last night had talked about people turning to ash, and she'd added her story to theirs.

A few of them felt the quarantine was about that, and Canada now thought they were right. The Shadows fed on fear, and when the fear went to a critical mass it consumed a person, inside out.

The people of Butte were being burned alive by their own fears.

But Canada, facing some of her worst fears the previous night, had also discovered how to wash away the fears. That was the other part of the scene at the service station she had missed. Light wasn't the answer, but she knew what was.

She looked at her mother. "We need water. Quick."

Her mother nodded. "Let's get him to the car. Be a lot quicker to get him to water than to try and bring some back here."

Together, they carried Doug's body toward the old green Satellite and pushed him into the back seat.

"There's houses over there," her mom said, tilting her head toward a few rooftops half a block away, down the hill and to the right of them. In Butte's heyday, the mines had been built all over the hill, making the city an odd hodgepodge; two hundred feet from a giant, smoldering head frame, you might find a row of tract houses where miners lived. One mine shaft, the Smoke House Shaft, began under the Nebraska Building in downtown Butte. "Would a hose or something—" her mother began.

"That would work."

They slid into the car and started it, then wheeled back down the small gravel spur leading to the abandoned mine. Dust boiled in through the open windows.

Canada slid to a stop at the nearest house; on the lawn, she saw a sprinkler watering a lonely patch of grass. Without hesitating, she ran to the sprinkler, twisted it free of its hose, then dragged the hose, now spewing water everywhere, as close to the car as she could get. She ran to the back door of the Satellite, opened it, then pulled Doug out onto the ground and dragged him a few feet closer so the hose could reach. His skin was hotter than ever now, and under the flakes of ash, an orange glow had begun to burn.

"Doug!" she screamed. "Wake up!" She grabbed the hose, sprayed at his clothes and skin; immediately, she heard a hissing sound rise from him, and steam coiled off his form.

He opened his eyes, looked at her; she kept the water running on his chest as he blinked a few times.

"Hey there," she said. "You had my number, and you never

THE DEAD WHISPER ON 251

called. That mean you're not interested in a second date?"

He rolled to his side, coughed, sputtered. Canada threw down the hose and tried to help, but he pushed her away. "Just go," he said. "Let me die. It's . . . it's too much, and I just want to . . ." He rolled into a ball and lay there; almost immediately, his skin began to turn to ash again. What was going on? The ash had been washed from her last night.

She looked at her mother.

Her mother.

Why wasn't Diane's skin turning to ash?

She put the water on Doug's immobile form again. "Mom, what did you do down there? In the tunnel, I mean, when they took you?"

Her mother shook her head. "I didn't do anything. What could I do? I was tied up, alone in the dark. So I thought about you; I prayed that you were safe, that you would get through all of this."

Words from her father's letter came back to her. *"Be like your mom and think of others first."* Her mother, lying in a cold tunnel and convinced she was going to die, turned her thoughts to a daughter who had ignored her for more than a decade. Could that be it? Could that be part of it? *"Whatever you do, don't make it all about you."*

That was it. The Shadows fed on fear, yes. It made them grow, it gave them power. Everybody's fears, wrapped up in one giant mass. But that wasn't what ignited them, was it? For that, the Shadows needed people to turn their focus inward. To think only of themselves.

Fear was the fuel. Self-centeredness was the spark.

"What?" her mother asked.

Canada looked at her mother, startled. She must have said something, even though she didn't remember it. "The darkness," she said. "It's us, all of us." She shook her head. "It's part of us, inside of us— our worst fears, you see? Reflected back to us as something real. But we give them that power by giving in to the fear, by shutting off everything else and looking only at our problems."

Her mother furrowed her eyebrows, shook her head.

"That's it, that's it," Canada said. "That's why you don't have the ash on you, that's why you're not burning up. Because *you* were thinking about *me*."

Canada kept the water running on Doug, grabbed his face, turned it toward her. "Look at me, Doug." For a moment, the glassy sheen stayed in his eyes, but then they focused on her. "This isn't about you, Doug. It's hard, I know it's so hard to get through this, to do all this, but the only way out now is to stop thinking of what you're going through. Because when you concentrate on the fear, you just think of yourself. And when you think of yourself, you feed the fear to that darkness inside—you make that darkness real, because it's all of us." She paused, licked her lips. "Sorry to do this, but—"

She slapped him on the cheek. Hard. His eyes dilated for a second, then focused on her.

That's what she wanted to see. She pulled away, ran water from the hose in her hand and rubbed it on his forehead. The ash fell away, revealing healthy pink skin beneath.

"What was that for?" he croaked.

She realized she was crying, and now she was laughing, too, and she felt a flood of emotions bubbling to the surface. "I had to get your attention," she said.

"You got it."

"Just don't make me do it again," she said, wiping at the tears on her cheek with the heel of her palm.

"Soylent—" Doug began, then paused to cough out a few shadow spiders. "Soylent Green is people," he said.

"What?" Canada asked, thinking maybe his time in the tunnel had scrambled him more than she'd thought.

"Old movie with Charlton Heston."

Now it clicked. "Yeah, yeah, I remember it."

"You just gave your Soylent Green speech."

She smiled. "I suppose I did."

"Candace." Her mother's voice, sounding a bit uneasy.

Canada looked up at her mother, who was standing over them with a worried look on her face.

"I don't think we're out of the dark yet," her mother said, then looked up to the sky.

Canada followed her gaze. Above them, a streetlight winked on as the entire sky boiled toward darkness.

## 35

"WHAT IS IT?" her mother asked.

"I don't know," Canada said, unable to take her eyes off the spectacle above. The darkness was a ravenous beast, swallowing the sky as they watched.

"It's the Ghosts. The Shadows," Doug said, sitting up. "Whatever is going to happen is starting. The lights didn't work."

"No. It isn't light. That slows them down. And water will wash away the ash. But the only thing that kills the Shadows . . . well, it's crawling outside yourself. Finding something else."

"Hope," Diane said.

Canada paused. "Yeah, I think that's exactly it. Focusing on fear helps it grow, helps it take root inside you. Focusing on hope kills it."

Doug got to his feet, looked at the city spread out below them. "If it's hope that kills the Ghosts," he said matter-of-factly, "Butte may be running a bit short."

Canada was about to accuse him of being a pessimist when a puff of dust appeared just to her left, followed by the long echo of a ricochet. Someone was shooting at them.

"Run!" Doug said as they scrambled toward the car.

Canada started the Satellite, punched the gas, and dropped it into gear. They left a patch of rubber on the pavement as she spun the steering wheel and took a right at the next street. Canada didn't have a chance to see what street it was, but it hardly mattered; they were going down the hill, so they would eventually reach Front Street, and then Harrison.

She looked in the rearview mirror and saw the familiar shape of a black sedan wheel onto the street behind them. "Black cars," she shouted. "What's with the black cars?"

"Bulk discount, I guess," Doug answered. "You got a gun?"

"No." It was the one thing she'd forgotten to ask Lucia about— a mistake, in hindsight.

"Hang on," she said as she took a quick left. Her mother yelped when her head hit the window next to her.

Canada took another hard left, into an alleyway. She stopped the car, put it in neutral. The other tail had fallen for the demolition derby routine; no reason to think these guys would be any different.

"What are you doing?" her mother asked.

"My thoughts exactly," Doug echoed.

"Just trust me." She waited, waited. Any moment, the car would swing around behind them and—

"Look out!" her mother screamed. Canada looked ahead and saw the black sedan barreling toward them. Their windshield spider-webbed as a bullet hit it.

"Okay," Canada said. "Time for Plan B." She threw the car in reverse, wheeled out into the street again, then hit drive, floored it, and headed downhill again.

"What's Plan B?" Doug asked.

"I'm working on it," she said.

"Okay," he said. "Take your time."

She squealed around another corner onto Arizona Street, aiming the big Satellite's hood down the hill all the way. All she could do now was run with it. They hit the next intersection, catching air when they came off the rise and bouncing hard on the pavement as they landed. Below them, something started to drag; Canada guessed it was one of the mufflers.

Behind them, the black sedan went over the same rise and caught air as well. It took the landing harder, though, and skidded across the street when it came down. The car headed for a building, and the driver overcorrected, sending it onto its side and flipping it.

Doug turned, saw the smashed, smoking hulk of the car behind them. He looked at Diane. "Hey, I guess her Plan B worked."

Canada smiled humorlessly as she slowed for the next intersection. "Actually," she said, "I'm still working on Plan B."

Ten minutes later, they piled through the doors of The Mint. Most of the other people who had worked on the day's spotlight project were there also, milling about like moths circling a flame, unsure what to do.

"Well, if it ain't Canada Mac," Joe said as she walked through the door. He did a double take. "In here with her mudder."

"Don't you ever go home, Joe?" Canada asked as she came up to the bar.

He shrugged. "You're lookin' at it. What'll yas have?"

Canada turned to Doug. "What do you want?"

"Some new underwear."

"In the meantime, what are ya gonna drink?"

"Guess I'd go for the Pepsi and bourbon. Single shot of bourbon's fine this time."

"All right," Canada said. "Gimme a Diet and hold the bourbon."

Joe grimaced and turned to Canada's mother. "And I know you, Diane, will go for a sugared gin. Might just join you."

Diane stopped him. "Actually," she said, "maybe I'll just go with a Diet Pepsi, too."

Joe rolled his eyes. "You know, you two are about eighty years late on the Prohibition bandwagon. Ain't you ever heard what happened to that anti-liquor gal Carrie Nation when she came rolling into town with her ax back in the early days?"

"The drinks, Joe."

Joe held up his hands in surrender. "Awright, awright. I'll leave you be." He retreated to the other end of the bar, poured the drinks, and brought them back.

Diane was pointedly refusing to look at her so Canada put an arm around her shoulders, pulling her in for a hug. "Thanks, Mom," she whispered. "For . . . everything." Her mother nodded, still avoiding her stare, and gave a weak smile as she sipped the Diet Pepsi.

People were milling about, pushing in tighter to see Canada. "Whaddya say, Canada?" an unfamiliar voice asked from behind her. "What do we do now?"

She kept her back turned, waited until she'd taken a big draw on her drink. The carbonation brought tears to her eyes, but it also cleared away some of the fatigue settling into her bones.

She turned to face them. "Okay," she said. "I got a thought."

A babble went up from everyone assembled. They were all willing to listen to her; no, more than that. They were willing to do whatever she told them to do. The problem was, as she saw it, she didn't know where she was going. She'd have to wing it from here.

"It's half a thought, actually," she said. "I don't have it all figured out quite yet."

More murmurs.

"The lights were a good start, but we need more," she said. "We need water. So I been thinking, there's gotta be a few of you who volunteer as firefighters." A few hands went up, and she pointed at one of the men. "You know some guys full-time Butte FD?" she asked. He nodded his head quickly. A few more guys said they knew some people in the fire department.

Behind her, Joe spoke up. "Fire chief comes in and has himself a draft most near every day."

Canada turned to him and smiled. "Okay then. You get him on the horn." She turned back to the assembled crowd. "And yous guys get in touch with the FD folks you know. We're gonna need every fire hydrant in Butte opened up."

"What's the water for, Canada?" It was Hambone asking.

She paused. "It's step one of putting out a fire."

"What's step two?" someone called from the back.

"Step two is the most important. The water washes away the ash. But that don't mean nothing without the most important thing.

"That's hope. You can't do all of it because you're scared. You can't do it because you don't wanna die. You can't do it for anything about you. You gotta do it because you love something else, someone else, more than yourself.

"And I gotta be honest with you," Canada finished. "I don't have much hope right now."

She felt her throat constricting, but she wouldn't let herself cry. "I held on to a memory of my dad that wasn't real—I remembered him being perfect. And he wasn't. A lot of you knew him, loved him like I did. But the thing is, the *real* him, the Bud MacHugh who wasn't in my memories, was actually much better. I just been figurin' that out, that what's real is so much better than what you want.

"So there you go. I can tell you you need the hope, you need to hold on to what's real, but I'm just a garbage collector who can't seem to throw away her old newspapers, so what does that mean? It means, I guess, that I don't know how to give any of you hope."

Canada expected a barrage of noise and questions, but instead, the whole bar, filled with more than a hundred people, stayed absolutely still and quiet. She opened her eyes and looked up at them.

After a few seconds, Hambone spoke up again. "I think you just did," he said.

## 36

HALF AN HOUR LATER, the bar was filled to overflowing. At least two hundred people were gathered together in The Mint, and an electrical buzz crackled among them.

Canada sat at the bar, her mother on one side and Doug on the other, working her way through another Diet Pepsi.

She turned to Doug. "I've been thinking about the other operatives in town. A couple dozen of them, you said. Why haven't we seen them here? Here at The Mint, I mean. They've tracked me, followed me other places. Why not here?"

He nodded, thinking. "Because it's real, to borrow a line from your little speech earlier."

"What do you mean?"

"Think of Keros, how the Shadows can't really do anything against him—how we, as operatives, actually ran away from him and avoided him. If there's something you can't control, something that has a power over you, you give it more power by thinking about it. You make it the center of what you're doing, without really trying to. Even if you're trying to run away from it, you're really running toward it."

"That's kind of what's happened to Butte with the Shadows."

"And what's happened to the Shadows with this place. I think this place has that same thing to it—a golem-like power. It's real, and they have no power over it; in fact, it has power over them. But they give it even more power by trying to convince themselves they can control it."

"So what about other places? I haven't seen much of the Shadows since . . . since my trailer burned."

"Because you're a closed door."

"A closed door?"

"When you thought you were talking to your Dad, you were an open door. Now that you know what the Ghosts are, though, you're a closed door. So why should they bother?"

She smiled. "You're pretty smart for a Pittsburgh fella."

He shrugged, returned the smile. "And I only charge a hundred twenty-five dollars an hour." He paused, and when he did, Diane took the opportunity to lean in.

"What are we waiting for?"

Canada closed her eyes. "What do you mean?"

She felt her mother's hand on her arm. "Look," Diane said. "You got a lot of stuff falling to you, for whatever reason. But that's fine, because you know what? You can handle it. I know you can." She picked up her Diet Pepsi and sipped it. "But I can tell, I'm sure Doug here can tell, there's something going on inside you right now. You got all these people, including the firefighters, in here and ready to go. But it's like you won't take your finger off the pause button."

Canada nodded. "I know, I know. I just have this feeling that I'm missing something. That I'm about to do something else wrong, mess the whole thing up. I already . . . I already messed up with the whole spotlight thing. I don't want to do that again."

Diane reached out and gripped her daughter's arm. "So you mess up, you go back and fix it. But doing nothing is worse; I know that too well."

The words of Keros returned to Canada's mind. *"While everyone else wanted to stand and watch the building burn, you went in and saved a man."*

Okay. Point taken. The building was burning, and she was the one who had to go in first. That was fine.

Still.

Fire department workers had been streaming into and out of the bar over the past hour, and the firefighters had broken out the big wrenches to open the valves on fire hydrants uptown.

So much of this felt right, but not . . . not *perfect*. Something big still had to fall into place; she felt this, but she couldn't force it.

That was good. All of it was good. But, as Canada had said, that left out the other part of the equation; people needed a focal point, something to draw their attention outside of themselves. She had no idea what that might be.

And, as many fire hydrants as they might open downtown, save the two hundred people in The Mint, there were about thirty thousand others in Butte who had no idea what was going on. They didn't even know they needed the water, and they would likely burn to ash as they sat, looking at the darkness above them and wondering what was happening.

"I dunno," she said, finally realizing Diane and Doug were both waiting for a response. "Something's just not right. It's like I'm missing a giant piece of the puzzle, but I don't know what it is."

She closed her eyes. Her body and her mind were tired, torn and bruised from a week of running, too much adrenaline in the system. She just wanted to sleep, forget about it all for a while, slip into a comfortable dream.

Thoughts of sleep made her think of her recurring dream of Yellowstone. She started to push the images of the dream out of her mind, but then hesitated. Yellowstone. Old Faithful.

"Canada?" It was the voice of her mother. She shook her head and held up her hand, asking her mother to wait. She was on the verge of something.

She rolled the image of Old Faithful around in her mind,

picturing its giant plume of water rising into the air more than one hundred feet. Yes, that was just what she needed. A giant water source she could use to somehow drench the city—like a huge cascade—cleanse it of the Shadows. They didn't need a trickle of water the hydrants would provide. Butte needed to be deluged, to be drenched.

But how?

She took in a deep breath and realized, with a start, she was saying a silent prayer. She hadn't started it consciously, but she latched onto it, hoping for a bit of inspiration in the midst of her desperation.

Slowly, softly, the sounds of the world around her tunneled, becoming hollow. The sounds of the bar—the conversations, the TV in the corner blaring news about Butte—all condensed and became a giant wave of warm static. And carried on that wave was a single, distinct voice she knew very well.

It was the voice of Joe, obviously saying good-bye to someone leaving the bar, repeating that well-known phrase the people of Butte had used for years.

"Tap 'er light, guys."

And then, the wave collapsed as the tunnel reversed itself; the full sounds of the bar around her crashed back over her. But it didn't matter now. She had heard what she needed.

Canada smiled and opened her eyes.

Prayer answered.

## 37

CANADA TURNED TO DOUG and her mother. "Remember I told you I was working on Plan B?"

He nodded. "Yeah."

"Remember I told you I'd let you know when I had a Plan B?"

"Yeah."

"I got a Plan B."

At that moment, all the electricity inside The Mint shut down. Everything went dark—pitch black, since the underground bar had no natural light from the outside.

"Your Plan B account for this?" she heard Doug's voice ask casually.

"No. Not so much."

The bar became filled with nervous chatter, but Canada didn't feel panic in the room. Unease, certainly, but everyone was still holding it together. Beams of two flashlights suddenly appeared behind the bar, drawing everyone's attention. One of the beams went through another doorway behind the bar; the other one, Joe held to his face.

"All right," Joe announced to everyone in the bar. "We got a generator in the back; I just sent Bobby to fire it up." He checked his watch with the flashlight, then brought it back to his face. "Thing is, I can't run all the coolers. So I suggest, you guys all want a cold beer, you best get to doin' whatever it is you need to do and get that power back on fast."

Laughter, nervous at first and then more natural, skittered around the room. *Good move, Joe,* Canada thought.

Joe continued. "I'm guessing Canada's cooking up something new, so maybe we should hear what she has to say." Joe gave her the flashlight, and she nodded to him as she took it.

She held the flashlight up to her own face so everyone could see her. "Okay," she said. "I know you've all been through some crazy stuff with me these last twenty-four hours, so thank you. But I have to tell you, it's gonna get worse. A lot worse, for anyone who stays with me. It ain't gonna be the fire hydrants—we need something a lot bigger than that. And I think I know how to do it. I think, maybe, if we pull it off, we can save Butte. Save a lot of other cities, too, because Butte's just the first. There's just one catch, as far as I can tell."

"So what's the catch?" asked a voice from the darkness in front of her. Canada recognized it as Lucia's voice. Good, he was here.

She offered a grim smile. "The catch is," she said, pausing to take a deep breath, "if you do what I ask you to, it's probably gonna kill every one of us here."

At that moment, the lights in the bar flickered, then came back on. Canada squinted her eyes against the sudden brightness, then waited for the pandemonium she was sure would come. Instead, every person in the bar was silent.

Next to her, Doug whispered out of the side of his mouth. "Boy, you sure know how to give a campaign speech."

For a few moments, the silence took on a life of its own. Then Hambone, from just a few feet away, broke the spell. "Don't sound a whole lot different from mining," he said.

Canada smiled as low murmurs spread throughout the crowd. She thought of the head frames—the gallow frames—dotting Butte's skyline, lit up in red lights. "No, I don't suppose it is a whole lot different, come to think of it."

"So what are we gonna do?" a voice asked—one Canada didn't recognize.

She realized she was still holding the flashlight, illuminated, under her chin. She turned off the beam and let her hand fall back to her side. "We're gonna blow up the Berkeley Pit."

More silence.

Again, Hambone broke the silence. "Blow it up?"

She nodded. "It's sitting at the top of the hill, a giant bowl in the mountain above the city. So even if we just bust a hole in the side of the Pit, the water will run through the city—over thirty billion gallons of it, which is a lot more than we'd ever get out of any fire hydrants. But we're not just gonna punch a hole in the Pit; we're gonna make it rain. Send that thirty billion gallons sky-high. Like a geyser."

She paused, interrupted herself. "I know Lucia's here, I just heard him a few minutes ago. Is Binkowicz here?"

Binkowicz stepped forward. "Been here all afternoon," he said.

"Okay, good. You talked about your stash of explosives yesterday, right?"

Binkowicz smiled. "Yes, ma'am."

She nodded. "I think it's time to take it out of storage."

Binkowicz shrugged. "Ain't doin' much good sitting around."

Canada looked back to the crowd. "So there you go. We blow the Pit."

Hambone spoke again. "But the Pit is poison. All those toxic chemicals, heavy metal. I mean, we blow that, and we just kill ourselves . . . along with everyone and everything in town. We're no better off."

"Yes, well. You've found the slight flaw in the plan. As I said, a lot of us—maybe most of us—will probably die. Someone's gotta set the explosives, someone's gotta detonate them. We'll likely still be out there when the big boom comes, and we'll get the toxic rain. Who knows what it will do? We all know the story about the geese that landed on the water and died—three hundred of them or whatever. So maybe we'll die quickly. Maybe we'll die slowly. Maybe we'll get cancer and die down the road several years." She pursed her lips, steadied her nerve as she thought of her father dying.

"But the town is shut off," she continued. "People are in lockdown. Most of them aren't coming out. They'll be in their homes, right? I mean, after all, Butte is under quarantine. Most folks still think there's a big outbreak here, so they're already holed up with supplies. They're already prepared for a large-scale disaster, because they think they're in the middle of one.

"So when that rain falls, they won't be in it. And most likely, they'll burn anyway. But if we do this, we save they city—the buildings and everything. We wash the Shadows away, and maybe some people will make it when they see the darkness breaking. The point is, we give Butte, and at least a few people, a shot at *surviving*. But if we do nothing, I don't think I have to tell you . . . none of us, and none of *them*, will make it through tonight. The whole city will burn. Every building. We'll all burn."

More nodding heads around the bar. "Okay, first, we're gonna need some rigs willing to haul cargo around the city—I'd say maybe ten or twelve. And we'll need volunteers to help . . . um . . . deliver that cargo. Hambone, maybe you could be in charge of pulling all that together. You're all gonna meet us at Lucia's place, one hour from now. Let's figure another hour after that until showtime.

"Oh, and one more thing. I need someone here right now, knows all the mines and shafts around uptown Butte like the back of his hand. Or her hand, as the case may be."

A voice from the middle of the crowd. "I work in the World Museum of Mining; I think I can map out the locations for you."

Canada nodded her head. "Works for me. Let's go."

Hambone and some of the other miners moved outside with most of the crowd in the bar as the man from the museum worked his way to the bar. He held out his hand. "Name's Stan Taggart. Good to meet yas." The introductions and handshakes went all around, then Canada settled down to business.

"Okay," she said. "Binkowicz, you still here?"

"Right here," Binkowicz said from behind her.

She turned around. "Get in here. We need to figure out the logistics of this," she said. "I mean, how we make the thirty billion gallons of water from the Berkeley Pit rain down on Butte."

Stan cleared his throat. "Actually," he said, "it's closer to forty billion gallons now."

"Okay, forty billion. Even better. See, I been having this dream about Old Faithful—you know how the pressure of the steam builds up in all the shafts and tunnels below the ground. I think we can do the same thing here. All the tunnels beneath Butte will act like pipes, spray water out the tunnel entrances all over the city; most of the tunnels are already loaded with groundwater. The Shadows will be swarming the town in the darkness. They'll never know what hit them."

She went silent, waited for an answer as the three of them thought. Diane was the first to speak. "Well, I don't see that it's going to ruin the place a whole lot more than it already is," she said.

Canada smiled, nodded. It made sense. It made her feel even worse, but it made sense.

"I don't know that we have a whole lot of other options," added Doug. "If we don't stop them here, another city is next. The thing is, we'll need to plan where we're going to place the charges. That's where you come in, Binkowicz. How much ANFO you got?"

"Maybe five thousand pounds. Hundred bags, at least."

"Five thousand pounds of regulated explosives?" Stan said, flabbergasted.

Binkowicz looked at Stan, obviously hurt anyone would question him. "Ain't regulated if you make it yourself."

"Okay," Canada said, interrupting. "I'm just thinking, we use it in the right tunnels and locations around Berkeley, set it off, we get a fireworks display unlike anything Butte's ever seen before."

Binkowicz's eyes lit up. "Yeah. If we had, oh, ten or so places to do it, couple hundred pounds of ANFO at each location, and if we had something to direct the blast energy—a tunnel, like you were saying, Canada—we could make a huge spray without totally collapsing the Pit. Really, we'd mostly just be blowing the water out."

Stan sighed, scratched at his face. "Gimme one of those napkins," he said, gesturing at the bar. He took the napkin and retrieved a pen from his shirt pocket, clicked it, and started drawing a rough map of Butte Hill. "Okay," he said. "Here, roughly, we got uptown Butte, right on the hill. And just above us, up the hill, is the Pit." He drew a large circle. "Lessee, I'd say maybe the Nipper, the Blue Jay and the Parrot. Those would be somewhat in the northwest corner. I'd also go for Pittsmont #4 over here, maybe the Belmont . . . no, wait, scratch the Belmont."

"Why?"

"Well, I'm still trying to stay away from mines with head frames or other things still standing. That's Butte, you see . . . we can't blow—"

"Easy, professor, you're preaching to the choir here," Canada said. "I don't wanna blow up the head frames, either. Keep going."

Binkowicz spoke up again. "Like I said, if we got tunnels to direct the blast, we shouldn't get a lot of collateral damage. Head frames would blow, of course, being right on top of the tunnels. But most of the other stuff should be safe—as long as it's out of the mouth of the tunnel."

Stan looked at his scribbles again. "Okay. Yeah, I'd stay away from the Travona, Anselmo, the Orphan Girl—that's where the museum is—and, uh, probably not the Smokehouse Shaft. That's right in the center of downtown. But I already gave you the Pittsmont #4, the Blue Jay, the Nipper and the Parrot. Let's see, we really want to surround the Pit. So here, maybe the Tuolumne, the Speculator and the Wake Up Jim. And . . . lessee . . . I guess Bell, the Colorado, and the Green Mountain. How many's that?"

"Ten on the nose," Doug said.

"Works for me," Canada said. "Let's get this list of mine shafts to Hambone and the others. They can start figuring out addresses and such."

They started to move toward the door, but Canada saw Stan hanging back. She stopped. "You okay?" she asked gently.

He nodded. "Yeah. It's just . . . here I am, telling you to go ahead and blow up part of the city. And I'm not sure what's gonna happen after that. I mean, all that water's there because of groundwater leaking in, and so when you blow it out, the groundwater's still going to leak, and . . . I don't know, I guess it'll just fill up again, won't it? But I don't know." Stan looked at Binkowicz, who was standing a few feet away and talking excitedly to Doug about something. "I don't know if we can trust that's going to happen, necessarily."

"Let's hope that's the way it works," said Canada. "But if it makes you feel any better, Butte's been blowing itself apart since the mining started."

Stan smiled. "I suppose it has."

Most of the people who were helping—already the effort had been dubbed Operation Big Bang—had already gone to meet at Lucia's place. But Hambone was waiting for them outside when they exited.

Canada walked up to Hambone and surveyed the city before them, lifting her gaze to what looked like a twilight sky. The inky blot of blackness had spread across most of the horizon now. Soon it would form a giant bubble over all of Butte. It was dark enough for most of the streetlights to be on, although all over the city, huge swaths remained unlit. Obviously, the power outage hadn't been localized.

"Well," Canada said, "I think this whole quarantine thing has gone quite well so far, don't you?"

"Seems to be working pretty well for them shadow things you been talkin' about," Hambone said.

"Hey, I don't know about that. Haven't seen you guys for years, so it was good to bring us all back together. And I've been in The Mint now, oh, four or five times in two days. Gives me a good excuse to come to the bar."

Hambone kept looking at the horizon, as if hoping to see what was coming. "Most of us, any excuse is a good excuse to come to The Mint."

"Worse places to be."

He nodded. "Yeah. I been to a lot of 'em."

They stood in silence for a few moments. Somewhere in the distance, a car alarm began, followed by a scream cut short. Canada started to speak, not wanting to hear other sounds around them, but Hambone beat her to it.

"I'm scared tonight, Canada."

Doug and Diane came out of the bar now and joined them. Canada stood, put her hand on Hambone's shoulder. It was a bit awkward to stretch and reach that high, but it seemed important. "I got you beat, Hambone. I been scared the last decade."

## 38

CANADA HAD TO HOLD BACK a gasp when she saw all the vehicles at Lucia's place. Word had obviously spread, with more people joining the effort. She stopped counting at twenty-five rigs.

Canada turned off the Satellite's engine and glanced at her mother in the passenger seat. They were alone in the car as Doug had ventured off over thirty minutes ago on an errand he saw was important. Diane looked suprisingly calm given the circumstances. "Now it gets interesting," Canada said as she opened the door.

Lucia was holding court just in front of the shed he used as a home, talking about his various collections. Canada walked up to him, breaking into his story about scoring two hundred gallons of exterior paint in various colors when a paint store in Philipsburg had shuttered its doors.

"Brought back your Satellite," Canada said, tilting her head in the direction of the car. Even from this distance, it was easy to see the new dents and scrapes, the spider-webbed windshield.

Lucia stared for a few seconds, then looked at Canada. "Looks like I might have to keep your deposit," he said.

"Yeah, well, I've had a couple people try to run me off the road; think maybe I'll give up on the driving for a while."

"Sounds like a good idea."

"Binkowicz around?"

"Sure, sure. He's in his warehouse out back. Won't hardly let me go in there. I think they've got most of the bags loaded now."

She nodded, started to walk around the shed, but stopped and turned to her mother. "You wanna come with me, or . . ."

Her mother shook her head. "You're like your dad; you need to go do your thing. I'll be here when you get back. Maybe in the meantime, I can see about what I can do to help around here."

Canada smiled. "Okay." She turned and walked around the metal building directly behind them, working her way to another warehouse.

Standing in front of the warehouse were Binkowicz and Doug, who'd completed his little plan, engaged in animated conversation. Hambone had just left the conversation; he nodded at Canada as he passed her and went back toward his truck.

Binkowicz kept nodding and smiling while he talked, a crazy glint in his eye, as Canada approached. He had a small glob of spit stuck in the scraggly beard on his chin, but no one had pointed it out to him yet. Not that it would matter.

"Hey, Canada, nice to see ya," he said.

"Nice to be seen, I guess," she answered.

Binkowicz gestured to Doug. "This guy here ya got, he's a genius. Listen what he came up with."

Canada turned and looked at Doug, smiling. "Well, let's hear it, genius."

"Genius is my middle name; call me Doug. I've been thinking how difficult it's going to be for us to detonate all these charges. I mean, we've identified how many different blast sites?"

"Ten."

Binkowicz broke in. "I been worried about that, too. I mean, when we blasted in the pits, it was always one site, you know? We didn't have to do anything across a buncha sites."

"The problem is," Doug continued, "complexity increases with each additional blast site. We're looking at something much more difficult than dropping the button on a blast to clear away a couple rocks. We need something a lot more coordinated. So, I've been thinking, we need to wire all the charges together. We need to have a coordinated blast. There are companies that will demolish sky-scrapers with controlled blasts; figure out how to do everything in sequence. Ever see them?"

"Yeah, actually," Canada said. "I think one of them did the old St. Patrick Hospital in Missoula several years ago. I mean, I wasn't there, but I saw it on TV."

"Maybe. The thing is, we need to think about this the same way. Binkowicz here has figured out the ANFO bags, and the individual triggers for them. I've been trying to figure out how to get juice to them, complete the circuit. And I think I came up with something you'll like, Canada." He pulled out her old cell phone, the phone the Shadows had given her, and smiled. Binkowicz nodded enthusi-astically again, slapped Doug on the back.

"A phone?" Canada asked, still not quite getting it.

"Well, not just a phone. *Your* phone—the old one the Ghosts gave you."

"Yeah, I figured that out."

"See, your preprogrammed number they told you to dial when-ever you needed to make a change of plan? You know, just hit 1 for help?"

"Yeah, I dialed it a couple of times. It's like the central switch-board or whatever."

"Well, when we're ready to go, you just power up this phone, hit 1, and when the connection goes through, it will ring their switch-board—along with cell phones attached to our packages." He patted a pile of three fifty-pound bags. "Like Binkowicz said, we wrap them with tubes of gelatinous dynamite—that's the booster blast we need to set off the ANFOs. And that's wired to a cell phone wrapped into each bundle. When our folks set the bundles, all they have to do is turn on the cell phones.

"So, when the time comes, you power up your phone, then dial 1 to ring the switchboard. At the same time, I've put it in relay so it hits all the cell phones tied to our bundles. You'll get a chance to say 'hello' to the switchboard, and then you'll get a nice boom." He handed her the phone.

Canada smiled as she took it. "Turning their toys against them . . . I like it. Where'd you get all the cell phones, though?"

Doug laughed. "Oh, I know a guy. Plus, we busted into every cell-phone store in Butte."

"Both of them, huh?"

"Actually, there are five."

Binkowicz jumped in. "It's brilliant, because I kept thinking, I don't have cord to tie all this together. There's no way I can pull it off; I don't have near that much gelatinous dynamite. But your friend here solved all that with the cell phone. With *their* cell phone."

Canada smiled. "Yeah, he is pretty brilliant." She took her old cell phone from him and put it in her shirt pocket. "That mean you won't be traveling with me?"

"Gotta stay here, keep the home fires burning. Also, I've been scrambling some satellite signals." He patted his computer case.

"Scrambling signals?"

"Remember? I was the tech guy—at least one of the tech guys—for the Ghosts? I can tell you they'd love to see all these cars piled together in one place on satellite images. So I thought I'd better loop back some old photos of the place. *Voilà*. No cars. Jamming their GPS, too, trying to keep them from tracking our movements if they have a lock on any of us."

"Okay, I'll see you when I get back then."

"I hope so."

She turned and ran down the incline toward the shed/house. Lucia was in the midst of a new story, telling people how he'd acquired a collection of more than two dozen hard rock picks. She scanned the others in the crowd and found Hambone.

Approaching him, she said, "Binkowicz said we're going thirty packages and not ten."

Hambone nodded. "I know. I suggested it. From what you said, I think we can expect things to get bad when this darkness totally sets in." He looked back at her. "Not sure we can count on every rig getting to where it's supposed to. So we have three for every site. As backups. All three get there, fine; we set all the packages. If not, well, maybe the odds'll work. I hope we get at least one to each place."

"Good thinking, Hambone."

"First time for everything."

"Nah, you always been a thinker." She turned toward Lucia, still holding forth a few yards away. "Let's get going, and pick an hour from now to drop the hammer." She checked her watch. "Make it 7:30 on the mark. Let Binkowicz and Doug know—and of course, everyone else here. That should be more than enough time for everyone to get there, unload their bags, turn on the cell phones, and get clear."

"Sounds good. Shouldn't take people more than half that, really. Your guy—what's his name again?"

"Doug."

"Doug really needs a nickname if he's gonna spend any time in Butte."

"I suppose he does," she said to Hambone, then she turned to Lucia, who was still chattering away. "Hey, Lucia. Think I'll need to borrow the Satellite again."

He stopped, smiled at her. "Why don't you just buy it? I'll give you a good deal."

"Hmmm, not sure about that. Look at the back of it—all those dents and stuff, the bumper's just hanging, and you can't even see through the windshield."

He threw her the keys. "Well, you take 'er for a test drive. We'll talk about a price when you get back."

She nodded and turned back to Hambone. "Let's roll."

## 39

THE TEN MINUTES BETWEEN Lucia's place and uptown Butte was a literal war zone. Everywhere she looked, she saw smoking piles of ash. In the drivers' seats of wrecked cars, along the sidewalks lining the streets, inside stores and businesses. In that same time, she saw three different people crumble into ash, a mixture of terror and disbelief on their faces.

Part of her wanted to pull the car to the side of the street, jump out and help them, but what could she do, really? How does a stranger shock a person on the brink of flame into looking anywhere outside themselves? And even if she could, that might mean she'd save four or five people—while sacrificing thirty thousand. No, she had to focus on the Pit, getting that water to the people of Butte. That was a start.

Of course, the water was poison. But there wasn't anything she could do about that now.

She passed an old tract home, its door hanging open and flopping uselessly. A pair of work boots, haphazardly surrounded by a pile of smoking ashes, kept the door from closing; wind blew the door against the boots, causing it to bounce back and forth.

She shook her head, felt tears beginning to form. It was going to be difficult to give people reason for hope in the midst of this.

A voice spoke on the seat next to her. "Where have you been, Princess?"

Her father's voice.

She looked at the seat, saw the familiar form of a Shadow throbbing on the upholstery. She opened her mouth to say something, but didn't know exactly what that should be. She closed her mouth, remained silent. No sense wasting any effort on the Shadow. *Like Doug said,* she thought, *I'm a closed door. A closed door.*

"I . . . I've been lost inside this Shadow. I came to you to help me, and you just abandoned me," the voice said.

The voice paused, and Canada did her best to ignore it. "Don't you love me? I loved you, Princess. I loved you so much. But you just left me to the Shadow, and now I'm lost forever because you won't listen."

She bit her lip, concentrating on the road ahead of her. The next block up, a car swerved and ran into a light pole. The Shadow wasn't her father, of course it wasn't her father, but it was her father's *voice*, and even now that she knew the truth, she was surprised how much power the voice had over her. She felt tears squeezing their way out of the corners of her eyes, but she still refused to talk.

"See, Princess? See how I talk with his voice, and it hits you in the gut? It makes you miss him so much, makes you want to do whatever I say?"

Canada felt a shift in the Shadow; it became heavier, and the voice deepened, changed. "I can use his voice because I ate him, Princess. Your father. You think any of your friends have a chance? What happens when I start talking to them as their dead mothers, their dead sons and daughters and wives?"

Canada shook her head and kept driving. She was passing the wrecked car now; a woman had thrown open the door of the vehicle and jumped out, but when she started to run, her legs crumbled into soot. Now her torso lay in the street, slowly disintegrating as she screamed. Canada could barely see through the flood of tears, but still she refused to speak.

The voice rose again, becoming her father's. "I'll admit I'm disappointed, Canada. But it's not too late. You can still save me if you just stop now."

"Shut up!" she screamed, feeling her vocal cords burn. "Shut up! Shut up! Shut up!"

Now the voice—the deep, throaty voice—laughed, reverberating, increasing, and eventually becoming the low steady moan she'd heard before. Somewhere inside the moan, however, the laughter stayed, echoing.

She took a right, followed the road to its end, and stopped. She was at the entry to the Parrot mine, one of ten chosen for Operation Big Bang. A huge berm of dirt blocked the road several yards from the mine entrance, and a giant bulldozer still stood on the property. For years, officials had tried to discourage people from visiting the mine tunnels, plowing giant berms across the access roads. The dozer was here, obviously, to refresh the old berm that had been beaten down by years of weather.

She sat in the car for a few moments, her breath coming in ragged gasps as she tried to clear her mind. Who was she kidding? The rest of the cars would never make it here; just as the Shadow had said to her, all the drivers would turn to mush when they heard the voices of the dead whispering to them.

Because she could do nothing else at the moment, she sat and waited. She looked at her watch; only about twenty minutes had passed since she left Lucia's place. That meant the three vehicles assigned to this mine should be showing up in the next ten minutes or so. Even if only one or two of them showed up, they could still make a go of it.

If none of them showed, it would be time for Plan C. And she had no idea what Plan C might look like.

She sighed, stepped out of the car, and sat on a rock. Looking out over the horizon, she saw that the sky was almost completely black now, the ink of the Shadows swallowing the last of the light. She turned her head to find that familiar sight, and was surprised to see it still there: Our Lady of the Rockies, illuminated by bright white lights even though it was too early for her lights to be on. How could that be? Had someone seen the gathering gloom and flipped on the lights ahead of schedule?

"What do you think, Our Lady?" Canada asked the statue aloud. "I think I'm sitting here, waiting for guys to drop off some fifty-pound bags of fertilizer so I can blow up the Berkeley Pit and wash dead Shadows out of our city. I think, as I sit here saying it out loud, it sounds incredibly stupid to even think about." She paused. "I think . . . well, I think the whole city of Butte is gonna die tonight, if you want to know the truth. I mean, they're depending on me. Me. I've been trying, you know—going on nothing but adrenaline, really, for days straight—but I'm running dry."

She looked down at her skin, saw it turning to an ash gray. She knew what that meant, but was it really so bad? Maybe it would just be easier, let herself fade to ash, wink out with a puff of smoke. Yeah, it would be a lot easier. All she had to do was turn that focus inward a little more.

She kept looking at her skin, watching it crackle and crease with gray lines now. "Answer me this Our Lady," she asked. "Is it better to burn out than fade away?"

The statue didn't answer. The statue never answered. But out of the darkness, two beams of light, headlights, swept across Canada's face. She looked up. A pickup. She couldn't quite tell what make it was, but it was definitely a pickup. Which meant it was one of the rigs carrying bags of fertilizer soaked in diesel fuel.

The lights shut off, and she could see a bit better now as she recognized the driver who slid out of the truck.

"Hey, Disco," she said, waving. "Over here."

He squinted through the gloom, then approached her.

"Canada," he said, his voice subdued. "Didn't expect you here."

She looked at his skin; gray streaks crisscrossed it, and the top layer was flaking a bit already.

"You hear someone in the Shadow?" she asked.

He stood quietly for a few seconds. "Murdock. Ten-spot. Comet."

They exchanged stares for a moment, and Canada slowly nodded. Murdock, Ten-spot, and Comet were three miners they'd lost in an accident at the Alice pit several years ago. She'd been haunted by their faces more than a few nights herself.

"Kind of ironic," she said, not taking her gaze off his face.

He shrugged. "Yeah, I guess."

"We're here, working with ANFOs, ready to blast. And the three of them . . . well, it *was* an accident, Disco. You know that, don't you? Nitro's way more unstable than this ANFO. Heck, it's hard even to get the ANFO to blow; that's why we need to use the gel instead of blasting caps."

"I know."

"But it still doesn't help."

"No, it doesn't. Especially hearing Murdock talking to me, telling me not to be stupid. He said he died in a blast, and he knew a lot more about explosives than I do. Told me I'd die trying to do this." He swallowed hard, looking past Canada now. "Will I?" There was hope in his voice, just the slightest bit. But mostly, there was resignation, a recognition that he would, indeed, be dying tonight.

"I don't know," Canada said quietly.

"You seen all the people turning to ash. Now I'm turning. You're turning, too. *You*, the one who's supposed to have it all figured out."

"I . . ." she began. But she was interrupted by another pickup pulling up to them. A few seconds later, a man she didn't know popped out of the cab and ran toward them. His skin looked fine, but he seemed manic.

"We gotta get these bags in there," he said, jabbing a thumb over his shoulder. "We gotta do it now. I think there was a third rig headed for here, but it crashed. Yeah, definitely crashed."

"Who was it?"

"The other rig? Jim Sanders from the Butte FD. Me, too. From the fire department, I mean. I'm Hank Peters. We'll save the chitchat and such for later, huh? We only got half an hour or so, so whaddya say yous guys help me stack three hundred pounds of explosives in the hole of that tunnel right now? Your bags and my bags?"

Canada and Disco both looked blankly at their new guest, and then started moving. Hank Peters bounded back to his truck in about five steps, then lugged one bag over his shoulder and headed toward the tunnel entrance.

Canada and Disco both went to Disco's truck to grab bags, stumbled to the tunnel entrance, and dropped them. By the time they returned for a second bag, Hank Peters already had all three of his unloaded and stacked in position.

"Great," Disco said. "We're working with the roadrunner."

Canada smiled as she watched Disco lug the last bag over his shoulder and head back toward the tunnel. The work helped—his skin seemed a shade lighter even now. She grabbed the belt of gel explosives out of the back of the pickup and examined it. Two thin wires ran from the middle of the gel belt, disappearing inside a silver cell phone.

She looped the belt around her shoulder and went to join Disco and Hank. By the time she got back to the tunnel, Hank had already arranged the six bags of ANFOs in a neat pyramid. "Here," he said when he saw Canada approaching. He held out his hand. She gave him the belt and watched him wrap it around the top bag in the pile. He then flipped open the cell phone and hit the power button.

He waved them away from the pile, then passed them as they all went back to their vehicles. Back at their rigs, he fished out a second cell phone and made a call. "Yeah, we're checking in from the Parrot mine. We got six bags wired and ready to go." Pause. "Sure, sure. We did that." Another pause. "Okay, will do."

He hung up his cell phone, then addressed them. "They said we should head down the hill now, try to get at least a quarter mile away from the Pit."

Now Canada's cell phone rang, making her jump.

It was Doug. "I need to warn you. I told you I've been scrambling satellite photos, tracking signals, all that, but I've been booted out of the system now. They're onto me. Which means they're onto you."

"Any more good news?"

"No, that should do for now. You helping with setup?"

"Yeah, I'm here at the Parrot mine right now, and we just got three hundred pounds ready to go."

"Good. You got your old phone, ready to make that call?"

She patted her shirt pocket. "Yup. Got it."

"All right," Doug said. "We've had five of ten locations check in now. Don't think we've had a full four hundred fifty pounds at any mine, but even a hundred fifty should make a heck of a boom. Put 'em all together . . ."

"What's our time?"

A pause. "Uh, looks like we've got just under fifteen minutes. We'll be doing a mass call for the five minute warning."

"Okay, I don't know if you're a praying man, but . . ."

"I am today. We'll see you soon."

"I hope so." She hung up her cell phone, slipped it into her back pocket. She patted her jacket pocket, making sure the black phone was still there; soon, she'd need it.

Disco and Hank were both looking at her, waiting. "Guess we should get going," she said. "I'd almost like to hit another location, but we're running out of time. Doug said five locations have checked in so—"

She was interrupted by a burst of gunfire. Canada saw a puff of dust at their feet, another just to her left. Then, a round hit Hank Peters square in the chest. He went down without making a sound.

She scrambled over the berm of dirt and slid up to the tracks of the bulldozer. Disco did the same right behind her. The only problem was, she wasn't sure exactly where the gunfire was coming from; she may have just run straight toward the shooter. Or shooters.

After a few seconds, more gunfire came, hitting the heavy iron of the dozer. Good, it sounded like the gunman was on the other side. Maybe somewhere up near the tunnel entrance.

It didn't take her long to figure out who might be shooting at her. A Shadow operative. Actually probably more than one. The Spooks, as Doug liked to call them, intent on killing her now that they'd overridden Doug's satellite scrambling. Less than forty-eight hours ago, she'd been one of those Spooks herself.

She turned to Disco. "You hurt?" she asked.

He shook his head, shaking a bit of sweat into his eyes. He wiped at his eyes with his arm, trying to clear them. Instead, a large swath of skin, nothing more than ash, sloughed off. He was teetering on the edge, she knew.

She looked at her own skin. Still a bit dusty, but it didn't seem any worse than it had been a few minutes ago.

She grabbed him, turned his face toward hers. "Stay with me, Disco. We're gonna get out of this."

"How?" It was a question, but it was also a whimper.

"I don't know, but you just gotta trust me on this. There are people out there who need us. Butte needs us. Think of saving them—"

His eyes were glassy, his voice barely a whisper. "I woulda saved you if I could, Murdock . . . What? No, no . . ."

Several more shots came, this time hitting the back of the dozer. The shooter was circling around, getting into position for a clear view of them.

Disco continued his conversation with an unseen visitor. "Yeah," he said, his voice dreamy. "Yeah, I *totally* remember that."

"Come on, Disco," Canada said. She grabbed him by the shoulders and shook him, realizing immediately it was a mistake; hot ash spilled out of the shirt and cascaded to the ground next to where she crouched. Disco moaned. He was lost to her, to the world now.

Another gunshot, this one louder and coming from behind her. The shooter had moved in closer now.

She looked around. The only option she could see was to make a break for the Satellite and try to get out of the blast's range. But it was blocked in by Disco's and Hank's vehicles. Well, maybe she could take Hank's truck; it was the last one in line.

Staying low, she sprinted to the side of the Satellite, hitting the ground and sliding to a stop as if trying to steal second base. Another shot rang out, puncturing a hole in the front quarter panel of the car.

She scrambled to her feet again, scurried around the back of the Satellite and worked her way down to Disco's truck, then Hank's. There was no gunfire as she crept to the driver's side of Hank's vehicle and tried the door. It opened, turning on the dome light and door signal, its *ding ding ding* filling her ears. Still no shots. She climbed into the seat and felt around the steering wheel.

No keys. Obviously, Hank had the keys with him. Hank's body lay about twenty yards from her, on his back and exposed. Might as well be a mile away.

She let herself fall back out of the truck again and crouched at the door. No more shots. What was going on? Was the person reloading? For all she knew, several shooters were stalking her.

She checked her arm again. Still gray, but no worse than it had been. Odd since her hopes were fading fast.

Okay, okay. *Think.* What now? She could try Disco's truck, but that might just be the same problem with no keys. Best to go for the Satellite. She might have room to negotiate a quick turn. She'd probably have to bang into Disco's truck just behind her, maybe even bounce off the front blade of the bulldozer. But she could do it.

She crept forward to the front of Hank's truck. She paused a moment, then sprinted to Disco's truck just ahead. She felt bullets whiz by behind her, chunking into the ground just to her left.

Okay, they were still on the other side of the vehicles. But they knew where she was going. They'd be ready for her to run between the gulf that separated the front bumper of Disco's pickup and the back bumper of the car. No good. She inched her way to the front of the pickup, stopped, thought for a moment. She took the black cell phone out of her shirt pocket and stripped off the shirt. She was down to a tank top now.

Canada closed her eyes, took a few breaths, gripped the black cell phone tight in her left hand. With her right hand, she threw the shirt into the open space between the vehicles; immediately, she heard shots ring out, one of them catching the shirt in midair and jerking it violently. Canada hesitated a second, then ran through the space herself.

It worked. The shooter had fallen for her decoy, responding to the flash of the shirt and being unready for her. Canada let out a deep sigh and started inching past the rear door of the car, working her way to the front. Somehow, she'd have to stay way down in the car while she turned it around.

She had no idea how she was going to accomplish this without being shot.

She made it to the front door, and was reaching up to lift the handle when her cell phone rang.

The safe cell phone, the one in her back pocket. It had to be

Doug, calling to give everyone a five-minute warning. She felt for the phone in her back pocket, her fingers searching for the power button to silence it. It rang again.

Canada felt a crack along her back and skull propelling her whole body forward. She went into the rocky dirt face-first, hard, her hands splayed out before her. The black cell phone, the trigger for the bags of ANFO, went flying.

She lay there, stunned for a few seconds. Before she had a chance to get her breath back, she heard feet sliding in the gravel behind her, along with a voice.

"I owed you that one for your little stunt in St. Louis," the woman's voice said. "I never forget a sucker punch."

Her old friend, the Goth Girl. Lisa.

## 40

CANADA ROLLED OVER, and the pieces fell into place. Lisa had been one of the shooters, but she had somehow sneaked into the back of her car and waited. That's why the shooting had stopped for a few minutes. The cell phone had rung at precisely the wrong time, letting Lisa know just where she was; Lisa had thrown open the back door of the vehicle, hitting her in the back and knocking her to the ground.

"So what do you think now, hero?" Lisa said, looking down at Canada and pointing a gun at her chest. "Gonna run into a burning apartment and save somebody this time?" Lisa shook her head, clicked her tongue. "I don't think so. Not even anybody to save your bacon."

Lisa cocked her head and shouted, "Hold up!" obviously directed at the other shooters. "The hero and I are gonna have a little chat. You guys check what she's got in the tunnel."

A muffled "Roger!" came back from the other side of the car, maybe a hundred yards away.

Canada noticed Lisa's skin was gray and glowing; she was close to disintegrating. Maybe, just maybe, she could get Lisa to crumble into dust.

Without thinking about it, Canada craned her neck to look for the black cell phone—the triggering mechanism—somewhere above her. Without that phone, everything would go down the tubes.

Lisa followed her gaze, then smiled broadly. "Wanting to call for a little help, are we? Maybe *Doug*?" Lisa moved toward the cell phone now, keeping the gun steady on Canada. "Too bad it rang at the wrong time for you, huh?" Lisa bent down to pick up the phone, and Canada felt fresh shards of panic working their way through her system. What would happen if she didn't trigger the ANFO? Would Doug? Maybe. Probably. She hoped. "How is good old *Doug*?" Lisa asked, almost spitting the words.

Lisa flipped open the phone, stared at the keypad, puzzled. "Musta knocked the battery loose," she said. She pressed the power button, staring at Canada. Her maniacal smile never left her face. Stringy, sweaty blond hair hung in her eyes, but she made no move to push it out of her vision. Yes, she was close to burning up. And Canada had a good idea why.

"You loved him, didn't you?" she asked Lisa softly.

Lisa narrowed her eyes, let her gun waver. Her movements were exaggerated, drunken. "Whaddya mean?"

"Doug. You wanted to be with him. That's why you're so upset about him right now."

Lisa shook her head, and Canada saw tears starting to form in her eyes. The gun wavered. "You ruined it all," Lisa spat. "He was . . . We were . . ." She stopped, her eyes glassy for a few moments. "No matter. You die now." The gun steadied, pointing straight at Canada's head.

"I'm sorry," Canada said. "I didn't mean to. I . . . just give me the phone, and we'll talk."

Lisa was close, oh so close to burning up. Just a little push, and she would tip over the edge. But could Canada really do that? Just condemn Lisa like that?

Canada heard a gunshot, and sand sprayed her face. Immediately, she was up on her feet, scrambling toward the back of the Satellite and behind it. A few more shots followed her.

Lisa cackled, squeezed off a few more wild shots. She swayed a bit, then steadied herself. Okay, that settled it for Canada. Kill or be killed. Good thing Lisa was so woozy right now; otherwise she probably would have been able to put that first shot between Canada's eyes. That meant she just needed to push Lisa a little more, get her to crumble, scramble out to get the phone and . . .

Wait. Could there be another way? Yes, yes. It was still a bit too early, but it was her only choice. She stood slowly, showing herself. Lisa watched, saying nothing; she was holding the handgun at her side now, swaying, stumbling. "He talked about you a lot, Lisa," Canada said softly.

"He . . . did?"

"Constantly."

"What did . . ." Lisa swayed some more, then steadied herself again. She motioned with the gun in her right hand; her left held Canada's black phone. "What did he say?"

"He said that he wished he could talk to you. He always wanted to, but . . . you know, being on the run."

"Really?" Canada saw a familiar look in Lisa's eyes. A look that said she knew she was being lied to, but wanted to believe it anyway. A look that said she wanted to listen to her heart instead of her head.

A look Canada had worn so recently when her father's voice spoke to her from the shadows.

"The heart is deceitful above all things," Canada whispered to herself.

"What?" Lisa asked, brought back from her reverie.

"Nothing, I was just thinking, maybe you could talk to him. To Doug. Right now. I . . . I know it now: he really loves you. I could never be with him, because he'd always be thinking of you."

Lisa smiled, her eyes brimming with fresh tears. She wasn't looking at Canada. Not now. She was staring into her own memory banks, examining fond scenes only she could see.

"You could call him. On my phone."

Lisa nodded, absently.

Canada crouched behind the rear bumper of the car again as she spoke. She trusted the other shooters were headed toward the tunnel. Maybe even inside it. Bad place to be, right now.

Canada was on her hands and knees now. She closed her eyes, trying to keep her focus, to keep her voice calm and soothing, not wanting to break Lisa's reverie. "He's on speed dial. Just hit 1 and hold it," she said, pushing the last bit of the puzzle into place. She peered around the car bumper to get a view of Lisa.

Lisa stiffened. "Wait! That's the speed dial for headquarters."

Canada flinched, stopping herself; she'd been ready to launch her body, and now she held back. "It *was* the speed dial for headquarters. But Doug reprogrammed it for me. I mean, come on, you know we've been off the system."

Lisa cocked her head, still unsure.

Canada kept the lie going. "He fixed it so it couldn't be tracked, couldn't be traced you know? He's good at that sort of thing."

"Yeah, he is," Lisa said, as if hypnotized.

"Well, when he did that, he reprogrammed the speed dial, put his number on the 1. I mean, if I'm on the run, I wouldn't want to accidentally call headquarters, would I?"

Lisa shook her head, smiled. She stared at the display of the cell phone for a few seconds, and Canada saw her thumb press and hold down a button.

At that exact moment, all light above them disappeared. Canada felt the darkness squeeze in around her, suddenly and irrevocably, but she didn't let the darkness stop her. She rolled across the trunk and sprinted the ten yards to where she remembered the bulldozer sat. She fell to her knees, scrambled blindly, felt her hands come in contact with the dozer's giant tread. Immediately, she pulled herself inside the tread, thinking that it was impossible for the world to be this dark, darker than a moonless midnight, darker than the tunnels that wound their way beneath the streets of Butte, darker than the heart that was deceitful above all things. She closed her eyes, squeezing them shut for a reason she couldn't quite grasp.

Somewhere behind her, she heard a single word from Lisa pierce the darkness: "Doug?"

And then, even though Canada MacHugh had her eyes closed, the world disappeared inside a blinding, all-enveloping light.

## 41

BACK AT LUCIA'S COMPOUND, Diane saw the darkness fall. Instantly. Just a few minutes to go before they were scheduled to blow the Pit, and suddenly . . . a giant blackout. But not just electricity; everything was gone—even the stars at the edge of the sky that had been slightly twinkling. Nothing.

Within a few seconds, she was shaking. She'd never been more afraid of anything in her life. Obviously, the Shadows, the things her daughter was out there trying to fight, had succeeded in blocking off the city completely. Candace had talked about this happening. But to be here, in the midst of it—

Her thoughts were cut off by a giant flash of light that strobed through the nearby windows of Lucia's tin shed, followed a few seconds later by the sound of a far-off explosion. Actually she was sure there was more than one explosion, but they all blended together in one long blast, their sonic force rattling the shed where she was taking cover. There was a sound of glass breaking. A window, probably.

The darkness returned instantly, and the concussion of the explosion continued to roll, echoing off in the distance, moving farther along the valley, rattling the other warehouses in the after-rumble.

Candace was still in that somewhere. She hoped her daughter was safe; she *needed* to be safe, because there was so much for them to talk about, so much for them to heal. They couldn't come to the brink of being together after all this time, then have it snatched away. This had to work, even though the terrifying darkness was still out there, and even though Diane felt her body beginning to shiver uncontrollably, and even though she felt tears streaming down her face as she gave in to the terror.

She felt as if the darkness were crushing her, and she couldn't breathe. Her ribs and chest felt pierced by the effort.

Then, she heard it. Just a few soft drops at first. Then a few more. Then, a shower of water, pattering on the tin roof of the shed and the surrounding warehouses.

But it wasn't just water raining down. It was . . . light. She didn't know where the broken window was, but the closest window still held its pane of glass, and Diane could see the drops of light cascading in the darkness, streaking in the night like a billion twinkling fireflies.

Almost without thinking, she found herself moving toward the door. The water was toxic, of course it was toxic, anyone who lived in Butte knew the Berkeley Pit held awful water. And if the water from the Pit's explosion was glowing, well, maybe that meant it was radioactive or something. Certainly, she shouldn't go out into the rain of light.

And yet, she felt herself needing to. The light called to something deep inside her, and she opened the front door of the shed, standing and staring in wonder for a few moments, then running out and sinking into the muddy ground. Yes, it was water. And yes, it was light. And it felt . . . indescribably warm.

Bent down in the mud, Diane MacHugh turned her face toward the heavens and let the rain of water and light cascade over her face, knowing—*knowing*—her daughter would be safe.

The rain told her so.

At The Mint, Joe's lights went out again. So much for the backup generator. Maybe it had run out of diesel. No, no. It was full, he distinctly remembered it; he should get five or six hours out of the generator, but it hadn't been more than a couple.

He grabbed the flashlight from under the bar and thumbed it on. Outside, above ground, he heard screams.

Odd. Down here, beneath the city streets of Butte, you were typically insulated from the noise above ground. This was the first time he could remember ever hearing sound coming from street level.

He swept the flashlight beam around the bar. Only four or five people in the bar—most of the regulars were out on Canada's suicide mission, and the few people in here now were stragglers. Not regular customers. When he watched everyone file out the door earlier, he felt in his gut it would be the last time many of them walked out of his place. Walked out of any place. And now . . . well, with those screams above ground, something really bad had to be happening.

He felt an earthquake rattle the whole bar for a few seconds. There was a loud rumble, and the tinkling of the glasses shaking, a couple tables and chairs skittering on the floor.

No, wait. That wasn't an earthquake, was it?

"What was that?" It was a scared voice from the corner, one of the stragglers Joe didn't know.

Joe smiled. "Probably a buncha miners blasting away some bedrock, fella."

Then, something caught his eye. Light, spilling down the stairs outside the bar entrance. And *spilling* was the right word for it. The light ran down the stairs like a river, then flooded in beneath the door. Wet light.

Joe smiled again. He wanted—no, *needed*—to touch this light. He set the flashlight down without bothering to turn it off, never taking his eyes off the puddle of light forming beneath the door and mixing with the sawdust on the floor.

He followed its glow, then bent down and put his fingers in the puddle. It was wet, like water. Okay, it *was* water. He could feel that, see that. And yet, it was unlike any water he'd ever seen. He brought his hand to his face, smelling the wet light on his fingertips. No smell, other than the dull flecks of sawdust. He opened his mouth to take a taste.

"Don't do that!" It was another voice from one of the stragglers in the bar. Maybe the same guy who had spoken before. But Joe needed to taste the water light.

It was sweet, almost as if it had a hint of honey mixed in. Joe licked his lips and looked up the stairs; at ground level, outside the second door a flight above, he could see the light coming down in a steady drizzle from the sky. Rain. At the same time, a steady stream of it was leaking beneath the street-level door and flowing down the stairs.

Without thinking about it, he moved up the stairs, moving faster as he went, and crashed through the door to the outside. He stood in the rain of light and water, watching other people in the streets, with more and more of them coming out of buildings and doorways all the time. At least a couple dozen of them were there, laughing, turning their faces toward the sky and welcoming the rain.

This had to be the poisonous rain from the Berkeley Pit. But it didn't feel like poison, and it didn't taste like poison. And so Joe, realizing he was laughing himself, turned his own face toward the sky.

———

Doug had made it to the drop point for the Blue Jay mine, and he was driving the pickup—whose pickup, he didn't know—back to Lucia's compound when the darkness hit. Complete, utter, unequivocal darkness.

He hit the brakes immediately. Most of the streetlights and homes in the neighborhoods he'd passed through were already dark; the electricity had begun to shut down while they were at The Mint a couple hours ago. But now, *all* of it was gone—along with the headlights and power in the pickup he drove.

The brakes were hard, and the steering in the car was slow, unresponsive as he brought the vehicle to a halt.

He reached for the key in the ignition, fumbling because he couldn't see, and turned it. Nothing. Not that he'd expected anything.

He opened the door, which gave way with a slight shudder and a squeak, then stepped outside. Not even the interior lights of the truck illuminated. He looked above him at . . . emptiness. No stars at all. He caught a gasp in his throat, and felt inexplicable fear paralyzing him. Surrounded by this darkness, he couldn't move, couldn't—

A flash of light pierced his vision, followed a few seconds later by a giant concussion. The truck took most of the shock wave, but it rocked on its springs as the blast threw Doug to the ground.

Light, followed by a concussive boom. Obviously, Canada had triggered the blast a few minutes before she was supposed to. He hoped she was okay; if the blast happened ahead of schedule, that most likely meant something had gone awry.

He lay on his back, trying to get his bearings. His eyes throbbed with the afterimage of the explosion he'd just seen, but in a few seconds he felt as if he could open them again.

When he did, he knew his eyes still hadn't adjusted. Maybe they'd even been injured, because he could see a million specks of light forming in the sky above him. Like the stars turning back on again, except they were *moving*.

Something hit his face. Water. And another drop. He closed his eyes, blinking to keep them open as a light rain fell on his skin.

But when he sat up and opened his eyes once more, he could see it wasn't rain. Well, yes it was. But it wasn't just rain, because the rain contained tiny prisms of light. And the rain was warm, comfortable, soothing.

This was the rain from forty billion gallons of toxic water in the Berkeley Pit, Doug knew, but somehow that didn't seem to matter. It was . . . blissful.

Doug watched the rain of water and light spilling to the ground around him for a few moments, then he reclined and rested his back on the pavement again. "Let there be light," he whispered to himself, smiling as he tasted the sweet rain on his lips.

And it was good.

## 42

ON THE HILL ABOVE BUTTE, Canada stirred. Her ears told her she was on an ocean beach; she heard the constant roar of the surf pounding, and she smiled.

She opened her eyes. No, she wasn't on a beach. She was wrapped up in some iron heap.

Her memory came flooding back. She rolled to her left, crawled slowly to her knees, and stood. She put her hand on the remains of the dozer next to her, surveying the damage. The left track of the dozer, where she had hidden, was still largely intact, as was the internal frame of iron. But the other side of the dozer, she could see now, was . . . well, it was gone, wasn't it? It looked as if it had been liquefied; the heavy iron rolled and curled back away from the blast site in monstrous patterns.

Still, she only heard the sound of the ocean in her ears.

But now she felt water falling on her. It was raining. She tilted her head back and tried to look into the sky, but the raindrops prevented it. Except it wasn't the kind of rain she was used to—this rain looked like tiny flecks of light, somehow. Obviously, the blast had rattled her. She probably wasn't seeing straight. Or, considering the heavy metals in the Berkeley Pit, the water might be an odd color.

She shielded her eyes with her left hand and saw the inky clouds in the sky breaking apart, dissipating; beneath them, a pink twilight, burnished by the setting sun, shone through. She looked to the west, saw the sun peeking out from behind the shrinking dark clouds. Hadn't it gone completely and utterly dark? Or had she imagined all that? The area surrounding her looked like some nightmare war zone.

Except.

Except a steady stream of water, coming from the tunnel on the other side of the dozer and working its way down the road; it pooled at the natural dam of the road berm, but then overflowed the berm like a miniature waterfall and cascaded down the road toward uptown Butte.

Canada turned and looked over the city. To the east she saw Our Lady of the Rockies, glowing brighter than ever, glowing larger than ever, glowing with the light of a thousand suns from her perch high above the city.

But something was different, Canada realized. Something was very different.

Our Lady of the Rockies had always stood over Butte, her hands outstretched toward the city itself, as if inviting the residents of Butte to embrace her.

But now, Canada saw, Our Lady of the Rockies had changed position.

Now the statue's arms were raised above her head, reaching toward the heavens. And even though twilight was still dancing in the late evening sky—*true* twilight—a bright moonrise was framing Our Lady of the Rockies.

A copper moon.

Canada tried to take a step, suddenly realizing her legs were weaker, much weaker, than they should be. She stumbled, fell to her knees, felt her consciousness streaming away again.

She opened her eyes once more, felt comforting wetness against her cheek, and realized she must be on the sand of an ocean beach, because the only thing she could hear was the steady roar, the steady pounding, of the ocean surf around her.

Canada awoke. Keros was there, bathed in light, smiling at her.

"Candace MacHugh," he said in greeting. She could hear him, but it was faint; an odd, static-filled sensation masked the volume in his voice.

She closed her eyes for a few moments, opened them again. "What happened?"

He smiled. "You saw a burning building, and you went inside to help."

"We saved Butte?"

"You played your part. Much was done beyond you or even I. But you played your part and it was honored."

She shifted, tried to sit up. She felt a pain in her hip, decided not to move.

"Your hip is injured," Keros said. "It will stay that way. You will recover, but you will always have a slight pain there."

"From the explosion?"

"From the wrestling. It will be a reminder."

She closed her eyes once more. "A reminder of what?" No answer. "A reminder of what?" she asked again. She opened her eyes, and Keros was gone.

The pain in her hip wasn't so bad, but she was tired, so tired. And she slept again.

## 43

SHE OPENED HER EYES to see Doug. He was staring at her, and she could tell she'd surprised him.

She smiled. "What are you looking at?"

He returned the smile. "Butte's favorite daughter, I'd say."

His voice was a bit faint, a bit tinny. Under it, she could hear a slight buzz.

"Can you hear me okay?" he asked.

"Yeah. I mean, mostly. Not a hundred percent."

Now her mom was there, too. "Docs said there might be some permanent damage, but only slight," her mother said. "Ruptured your eardrums."

Doug spoke again. "Next time you set off a couple tons of explosives and stand in the middle of it, you might want to take along earplugs."

She nodded. "Good advice."

She sat up, feeling a twinge of pain in her hip, and looked around. Obviously, she was in a hospital room. Doug and her mother were both looking at her, expectantly.

"So, how long?" she asked.

"Five days," her mother said.

She nodded. That wasn't bad. "I was worried . . . I don't know. Coma or something. You know, like five years had passed."

"Only on *Days of Our Lives*," said Doug.

She slid out of the bed, let her feet touch the floor, and stood. The pain in her hip was there, though it didn't hurt much. It felt tight more than anything. "Give me the quick rundown," she said. "Are we out of the dark?"

Doug smiled. "Out of the dark. Nice one." He cleared his throat. "Well," he said, "you're probably not going to get elected President of the Sierra Club for blowing up the world's largest Superfund site and sending the water down into the valley. But the thing is, nobody can quite figure it out. Gave the feds a good excuse to extend the quarantine, but the water . . . well, it doesn't seem like it hurt anyone. We all kinda thought we'd get fried, but I was in it, your mom was in it, heck, you were in it, and we're all standing here."

"Better than fine, Candace," her mother broke in. "When I saw that rain, I don't know, something inside me just . . . needed to go out in it. And everyone I've talked to—everyone—had the same feeling. I think we had the whole city of Butte standing out in the streets in that rain, and . . . I actually feel better than ever before. Like I'm clean, for the first time in my life. Like I was part of a miracle."

Canada smiled. "If any place could use a miracle, it's Butte."

"You look good," Doug said.

She looked down at herself, noticed the glowing freckled skin on her arms, and thought, for the first time, how beautiful those freckles were. She patted the front of the hospital gown. "Thanks," she said, responding to Doug's comment. "The gown cost me a fortune."

He laughed, and she turned to her mother. Diane held out her arms, offering an embrace, and Canada shuffled over to accept the hug.

She heard Doug speak again. "So what now?"

She turned her head toward him, still hugging her mother, and smiled. "I don't know, Doug. But I got a good feeling about it."

He returned the smile. "Me, too. But, uh . . . if you don't mind, maybe you could call me Terence. That's my real name. Doug . . . well, he's dead."

"Terence. I like that name. Call me Candace. Canada ain't dead. But she just ain't Canada anymore."

A week later, they released Candace from the hospital.

Her mother came to pick her up.

At the door to her room, a nurse met them with a wheelchair. Candace waved her off. "The hip's fine," she said. "I can walk." And it was true: the hip had a twinge in it, a faint cold numbness, but otherwise it was fine.

"Hospital regulations. I escort you to discharge in a wheelchair," the nurse said with an apologetic smile.

"And so how much does the wheelchair ride cost me?"

The nurse patted the chair. "The chair ride is free. Just don't ask me how much your breakfast was."

Candace shook her head as she took a seat. The three of them moved along in silence, first down the hallway to the elevator, then into the lobby. Diane mumbled something about pulling around the car when the discharge nurse handed Candace a clipboard of papers to sign.

Everyone was treating her like she was made of eggshells. Her ears still had a low buzz in them, and the hip wasn't a hundred percent, yet all in all she was whole.

Whole for the first time in eleven years.

The discharge nurse took the clipboard back from her, flipped through all the papers, nodded, and pushed something else toward her.

Her duffel bag.

She furrowed her eyes, looked at the bag. "Where'd this come from?" she asked.

The nurse looked up. "It's listed as your personal effects. Is there some kind of—"

"No, no. It's mine. It's just—I don't know where it came from." She filtered back through her memories. She'd pulled it from her trailer before it burned, thrown it in the back of the Jeep . . . but that was the last she remembered seeing it. She was sure she hadn't brought it along to Lucia's home, or the Pit.

"All ready?" Diane's voice, from behind her.

She tried to turn the chair around, fumbled a bit, muttered and stood as she slid the duffel off the counter. "All ready," she said.

They walked outside, and Candace stopped and smiled when she saw the car parked there.

Lucia's old Plymouth Satellite.

Its back bumper was barely attached to the frame; scrapes and dents seemed to cover every square inch of it. But surprisingly, the engine, idling, still sounded deep and throaty.

"Lucia said you talked about buying it from him," her mother explained. "I can't imagine why."

"Well, he talked about it more than I did," she said as she opened the door. "But I just might. I just might at that."

They drove in silence most of the way home, neither of them sure what to say. A few minutes later, Candace pulled the battered car to the curb in front of her mother's home. Her father's home.

Her home.

They went inside, Candace clutching the torn duffel in her hands.

That evening, after they'd eaten dinner, Diane made a pot of tea. The shrill whistle of the boiling water echoed through the home, filling the silence hanging between them. The overwhelming joy they shared in the hospital had run its course; now the two of them found themselves alone with each other. Alone with eleven years of regret. Candace didn't know how to take the first tentative steps away from their past and it was obvious her mother didn't, either.

Diane placed a hot cup of tea on the coaster in front of Candace, retreated to the other side of the room, and sat down herself.

"I put a little sugar in it for you," Diane said. "Seems like I've got lots of sugar in this house."

Candace smiled, bent to the floor next to her feet and retrieved the duffel.

"What is that?" Diane asked.

"Duffel."

"I know it's a duffel. What I don't know is why you've been hugging it like it's your best friend all afternoon."

"Good question." Candace set the duffel down on the table in front of her, careful not to spill the tea. She drew open the zipper and peered inside. A note.

> *Candace—*
>     *Thought you might want a few of these things. I'm headed back to Pittsburgh.*
>     *Terence, the Artist Formerly Known as Doug*
>     *P.S. I'm number one on the speed dial.*

She found the cell phone inside the bag and thumbed the power button. It held a full charge.

Beneath the cell phone was a box she recognized instantly. Her shoebox of photos. She brought it out of the duffel.

"What's in the box?" Diane asked.

She smiled. "Why don't you come over here and see?"

Diane brought over her cup of tea, sat down on the couch next to Candace, and waited.

Candace opened the box. On top, just as she'd imagined, was the photo of her and her mother at Yellowstone National Park, their faces caught in perpetual smiles. Genuine smiles. Behind them, the giant plume of Old Faithful pierced the sky.

But it wasn't just a loose snapshot anymore. It was now encased in a thick, shiny metal frame.

A copper frame.

Her mother picked up the framed photo and looked at it. "I remember this trip," she said, a little breathily. "I remember the exact moment your father took this photo, to tell you the truth." She turned to look at Candace, her eyes a bit misty.

Candace smiled. "Really? Why don't you tell me about it?"

As her mother began to speak, Candace lifted the cup of tea and drank. It was hot, but not scalding, as it spread its warmth down her throat.

This was her future, and she swallowed it, welcoming the sweet, comforting taste.

USA TODAY
BUTTE, MONTANA, STILL UNDER QUARANTINE
FOLLOWING TERRORIST ATTACKS

Butte, MT (AP)—After two major disasters in Butte, Montana—a deadly virus outbreak and an explosion that destroyed the city's contaminated Berkeley Pit—government officials said today they expect to keep the city under quarantine for at least another month.

At press time, city, state and federal officials were still scrambling to assess the full extent of the damages from the explosion, and to take the next steps toward rebuilding the city. Members of Montana's congressional delegation planned to ask the president to declare a state of emergency.

Unidentified sources close to the investigation hint the explosion, believed to be caused by at least 5,000 pounds of Ammonium Nitrate Fuel Oil, or ANFO, may have ties to terrorist organizations operating in the Middle East.

Federal officials cautioned that the road to recovery for Butte will be a long one. An employee with the Department of Homeland Security's office in Denver, who refused to be identified, said toxic waste was the main concern. "Butte's Berkeley Pit was the

314   T. L. HINES

largest Superfund site in the United States," the source said. "With all that toxicity now throughout the entire city, it might be several weeks before we can start letting anyone in. We have a lot to clean up first."

The official went on to say the Department of Homeland Security has uncovered potential plots to bomb several other "environmentally sensitive" sites and urged all United States residents to stock up on water and prepare their homes for unexpected disasters.

**THE END**

# AUTHOR'S NOTE

Butte is undoubtedly my favorite city in Montana. No other town comes close to Butte, America, in terms of its history, its architecture, or its people. Even though The Mint is fictional, most of the other locations and features actually exist—everything from the "Wop Chop" sandwich at the Freeway Tavern to the Berkeley Pit, from the giant head frames to Our Lady of the Rockies. The only pieces of Butte lore I knowingly changed were the closure of Columbia Gardens (it closed in 1973, which is much earlier than I suggest in the story), and the presence of spotlights on the city's headframes (red lights line those frames, but no spotlights exist). All other inconsistencies and errors are entirely accidental, but I'm sure the good folks of Butte will forgive me.

Especially if I offer to buy a round.

# ACKNOWLEDGMENTS

Thanks to Kevin Lucia, who won a role in this novel on my website (www.tlhines.com) and graciously allowed me to make him a crusty old miner. In reality, Kevin's neither crusty, nor old, nor a miner.

Music credits: Silversun Pickups, Snow Patrol, The Arcade Fire, Pivitplex, The Shins, David Crowder Band, Derek Webb, Cold War Kids, Sufjan Stevens, The Decemberists, The Pixies, Better Than Ezra.